# MINUS

## BURNING SAINTS MC BOOK #1

# JACK DAVENPORT

2nd Edition ©2020 Jack Davenport
Copyright ©2018, 2020 Trixie Publishing, Inc.
All rights reserved.
Published in the United States

Sale of this book without a front cover may be unauthorized. If this book is coverless, it may have been reported to the publisher as "unsold or destroyed" and neither the author nor the publisher may have received payment for it.

*Minus* is a work of fiction. Names, characters, places, and incidents are the products of the author's imagination and are used fictitiously. Any resemblance to actual events, locales, or persons, living or dead, is entirely coincidental.

**Cover Art**
Jack Davenport

ISBN-13: 9798611558188

Printed in the USA
All Rights Reserved

# PRAISE
## BURNING SAINTS

*Oh, good gravy, this book is good. And I'm not just saying that because he does other amazing things with his fingers!*
~ **Piper Davenport, Contemporary Romance Author**

*Holy Hot Biker Boys!!! There is an amazing advantage to an author's husband catching the writing bug. I didn't have to wait for his wife to write her next biker book to be able to visit with old loves. Jack, please don't fight the bug, go with it and give me another amazing story in the Burning Saints MC sooner, rather than later.*
~ **Trudy D**

**For My Beautiful Wife, Piper**
*Thank you for your many extended grace periods.*

**To Boston**
*The best trail mate I could ever ask for.*

# PROLOGUE

## BURNING SAINTS

*Minus*

**D**ON'T PASS OUT.
     Easier said than done, considering the crippling pain in my head. Unable to focus on anything in the room, I began to drift into darkness.
  *Don't pass out. Don't pass out. Don't… fucking pass out.*
  I forced my eyes open long enough to receive another blow. The impact from the phonebook rattling my brain like a paint can. My vision blurred, and a wave of nausea hit me. I tried to stay as lucid as possible, struggling to focus on anything around me that might aid in my escape. I was gonna have to get pretty fuckin' clever to get myself out of this before this guy bludgeoned me to death. My host had been letting his fingers do the walking upside my head for some time

now, and I wasn't going to be able to hold out much longer.
*Don't pass out. Don't pa...*

"Come on, hero, don't make me beat you to death," he said, pausing briefly from his work to slap me awake. "You know what? You really do look like some sort of hero. Like one of those comic book movie guys, or... an action figure."

"Lemme know if you want me to... autograph anything for... your kids," I replied, blood dripping from my mouth.

"Tell you what, Captain Hero Man," he said, leaning in closer. "How 'bout we wrap this up right now and you can get back to saving the universe with the rest of your tight-wearing friends?"

I said nothing.

"How about I put it another way? Tell me what I need to know or you're gonna die tied to this chair." His words swam in my head, distorted by the ringing in my ears.

It took every ounce of strength I had to form the necessary response and I almost lost my breath as I said, "All you need to know... is... you hit... like a bitch." I spit blood and bits of my fractured molar onto his boots.

For a few moments nothing happened. Then another blow to the back of my head. This time it felt like he'd taken a running start. My chin connected with my sternum and every muscle in my neck burned from the whiplash.

"He told me you'd be tough, and he was right," my torturer said. "He also said you'd be mouthy."

*I'm sure... he did.*

"And he was right about that, too," he continued, wiping sweat from his brow. "But he also said you were smart, and that I'm not buyin'."

"I'm sorry to disappoint you," I said. "They say 'never meet your heroes.'"

"If you were smart, you'd tell me where the girl and the book are," he replied.

"It seems you... have me at a disadvantage, sir," I slurred. "You seem to know so much about me, and I... don't know anything about you."

"You never stop with the jokes, do you?"

"No, really," I replied. "I'd really love...to get to know my torturer. Tell you what. Answer one question for me, then you can ask me...anything...you want."

"Fair enough. Ask away," he said.

"Does your sister know you fantasize about fucking her when you're torturing people?"

This guy must really have a sister because I felt the full impact of the phonebook, from AAA Carpet Cleaners to Zywicki's Deli. The chair I was tied to toppled over, the zip ties that bound me cutting deep into my wrists. My already pummeled head hit the floor with a thud and within seconds I was out like a light.

When I came to, I was once again sitting upright but no longer tied to the chair. In fact, I wasn't tied to anything. I'm not sure how long I remained unconscious and for a moment wondered if I was dead. Eventually I became aware that I was moving. In fact, I was in the passenger seat of a car that was hauling ass through the dead of night.

"Hang on. Stay with me."

As soon as I heard her voice, I smiled. It probably looked more like a deranged grin given the current state of my face, but I couldn't help it.

She found me, and once again she'd saved my life.

# ONE

## BURNING SAINTS

*Minus*

*One week earlier...*

"THIS IS BAD news, man."

"Well, hello to you, too," I said as I shoved my tattered duffel bag into the back of Clutch's '71 Barracuda.

"Hey, watch her interior, or I'll leave your ass on the curb," he said.

"Lucille is still the only gal for you, I see."

"You really gonna give me shit right from the jump?"

"No, really," I said. "It's inspiring to see a couple as committed as you two still making it work after all these years."

Clutch flipped me the bird. "Fuck you, Minus. What are you driving these days, a tractor? By the way, if you've got any of that cow shit tucked in your bottom lip, you'd better spit it the fuck out before you get in."

"Why? You hopin' to kiss me later?" I asked as I slid into the perfectly conditioned leather seat.

"See? You're even starting to sound like one of them good ol' boys," Clutch said. "You've changed since you left, man."

"Yeah, well I'm still smarter, taller, and better looking than you."

"You checkin' me out, Minus? You make some other big changes while you were gone, I should know about?"

I smirked. "Sorry, buddy I've told you before. You're not my type."

"Hey, man, how am I supposed to know what you're into these days? Just look at you! You're wearing fucking cowboy boots. For all I know, you're carrying pearl handled six shooters under your jacket," he said, pulling away from the curb and into the flow of airport traffic.

"From what I've heard, all of Portland is in beards and cowboy boots these days," I replied.

"Yeah, a lot has changed since you've been gone. Then again...," he paused, "... a lot of shit is *exactly* the same," he said, throwing me a sideways glance.

I said nothing, but we both knew very well what he meant. When I left town, it wasn't under the best circumstances, to say the least, and I had no reason to believe a ticker-tape parade awaited me upon my arrival.

"Don't get me wrong, brother, it's great to see you back home—"

"This isn't home," I interrupted.

"What? Savannah is?" Clutch asked.

I paused and admitted, "I can't say that either."

"Which leads me back to my original point," he replied. "It can only be bad news that the not-so-prodigal son is back in town."

"Please," I said, waiving my hands. "This warm welcome

is all just too much. You're gonna embarrass me."

"Don't get cute with me, motherfucker, you know exactly what I'm saying," he replied.

"Oh, believe me, I know all too well. Back in Savannah I'm the Yankee stranger and here I'm the long-lost redneck. I'm a man without a fuckin' country, but here I am nonetheless."

"Yeah, but *why* are you here?" Clutch asked.

"Because Cutter told me to be here."

"See? Bad fuckin' news," Clutch exclaimed.

"How is that bad news?"

"Since when is it *not* bad news when the Prez sends for you?"

I laughed. "*Sends* for you. What are we, wise guys? He called me and told me to be on the next plane to Portland, so here I am. To be honest, I thought you'd know what's going on." I paused dramatically, before sweetening my tone. "What with you being the new Sergeant—"

"I knew it." He jabbed a finger at me. "I fucking knew you'd hear about it and that you'd bust my balls."

"Sergeant Clutch. Ooooh, that does have a nice ring to it."

"I swear to God, Minus. I'll kick you right the fuck out and you can walk the rest of the way in those shit kickers," he deadpanned. "I get enough crap outta Grover and the dipshit twins."

"I can only imagine," I laughed. "Hey, man. In all seriousness, congratulations. It's a big deal you makin' Sergeant at Arms and I'm proud of you."

"Thanks, man." Clutch said. "We all miss Rusty but after he died, the club needed someone to step up and I guess Cutter thought it should be me."

"I'm sure he was right," I said.

"Bullshit. You know goddamned well if you were still in town, it'd be you wearing the Sergeant's patch."

"Well, then it's good for you I'm not still in town."

Clutch and I grew up together in Portland, back when I still went by my given name, he was called Nicky, and together we were known as nothing but trouble. We were both orphans who had been taken in and educated by the Catholic church. A handful of us kids were fortunate to receive scholarships to private schools in the Portland area and Nicky and I attended St. Mary's Academy together. That is, until he was kicked out during our sophomore year.

I loved school, especially reading. I inhaled novels, biographies, textbooks, anything I could get my hands on. I was a straight A student who tried not to hassle anyone. On the other hand, I can't recall a time in my youth, even when I was happy, when I didn't have a big-ass chip on my shoulder. Understandable if not predictable for a kid that's been abandoned by his parents, but it would begin to weigh on me heavily as I grew into manhood. Throughout my life I've a had a profound (perhaps overly sensitive) sense of justice. Seeing anyone bullied or treated unfairly threw me into fits of pure rage. This, coupled with my size (I was already pushing six feet), made me the perfect candidate to serve as the unofficial school bodyguard. Because of this, I found it easy to make friends and (more or less) fit in with whatever crowd I found myself in.

Nikolai Christakos, not so much.

Coming up in Portland in the early "noughties," Nicky had two things working against him. First, he was Greek. Second, he preferred to solve issues with his bare knuckles.

These days Portland is more of a cultural melting pot. It's got a liberal, artsy, 'college town' vibe where just about any type of person can do their thing without being hassled. This was not the case back in the days when Nicky and I were coming up. It wasn't uncommon back then to see a pickup truck flying a rebel flag or walk around for hours before seeing a face that was neither Anglo nor Saxon. Portland was still pretty dominated by a culture of white boy, blue collar types. After all, the Pacific Northwest was built on an industry of logging, shipping, and paper mills. The dot com bomb had yet to drop so the good ol' boys would readily 'come to town lookin' for trouble.' A typical conversation with a drunken local might sound something like this.

Local: "What's your name?"
Nicky: "Nicky."
Local: "That's a girl's name. You some sort of queer?"
Nicky: "It's short for Nikolai."
Local: "*Nikolai*? You a Russian?"
Nicky: "It's a Greek name."
Local: "Greek huh. That some kinda Jew?"
Nicky: Stares ahead blankly, saying nothing.
Local: Calls to his friends, "Hey, guys. We've got some sorta half-queer, half-jew thing goin' on over here. Come take a look and see what you can make of it."
Nicky: Turns and looks to me. Fight starts.

Nicky was athletic, but not into sports. Anti-social, but not a loner. Wicked funny, but never the class clown. To put it bluntly, he didn't fit in anywhere. Also, Nicky would start a fuckin' fight with anybody, and I mean anybody. Teachers, students, cops... hell, I saw him take a swing at a priest once. Fortunately for Nicky, Father Dowd was a former golden gloves boxing champ, and he easily slipped the hastily thrown punch. Unfortunately for Nicky, Father Dowd's favorite Bible passage was not the one where Jesus talked about turning the other cheek. He hauled off and hit Nicky with a stiff jab right down the middle. Blood poured from Nicky's nose as Father Dowd dragged him down the hall to the Bishop's office where he was promptly expelled from both the school and the church. To this day Clutch's nose is still a little crooked from that altercation. This kind of violence from both peers and adults was simply commonplace when we came up.

Conversely, I got along with just about everybody in the neighborhood, and always did my best to look out for Nicky. I made sure he came with me to parties and football games, the kinds of places where young people met other young people. I thought it would be good for him, but without fail some jackass would mouth off to him or he'd accidentally hit on someone's girl or make a joke someone didn't find funny and then it was on. Bloody lips, loose teeth, and black eyes seemed to follow us wherever we went.

He was a social pariah, and I was his only friend. I knew that if he was out on his own, he'd get himself arrested, beat up, or killed within weeks so I left school and we moved to downtown Portland together.

Being flat-ass-broke, we bought old, beater bikes to get around town, which led to fixing those bikes, which led to fixing bikes for other people, which eventually led us to the Burning Saints Motorcycle Club, and our current lives as Minus and Clutch.

"Hey man... ah, we've got a quick stop to make before we go to the Sanctuary," Clutch said. I could tell by the shift in his tone that I wasn't going to like where we were headed.

Turns out I was right.

\* \* \*

*Cricket*

"Don't even think about it, asshole!" I yelled at the motorist attempting to merge into our lane.

My Uber driver flinched and covered his right ear.

"Don't take your hand off the wheel, you're gonna let him in! Don't let him in!"

I was a fraction of a second away from grabbing the steering wheel and literally back-seat driving, when my long-suffering coachman shot me a look and said sternly, "Lady, if you do that again, I'm going to have to let you out at the nearest safe stopping place."

"I'm sorry," I grumbled. "I really am, I'm just very—"

"Late," he finished my sentence. "Yes, I know. You've explained this *many* times since I picked you up."

He'd clearly lost patience with me and I couldn't blame him. This poor guy was simply trying to do his job and I was sucking him into my vortex of chaos.

"I'm so sorry, it's just that I'm meeting with someone I haven't seen in a long time, and I'm a little nervous. To tell you the truth, I'm not even sure why I agreed to meet with him. I know it's going to get me into trouble with my brother, not that I really care what he thinks, because he's being a big jerk. I know he's only trying to protect me, but who asked for his protection? Not me, that's who. I don't need him or his stupid protection, or his permission for that matter" I said, sheepishly pausing to take a deep breath, now embarrassed by my outburst.

"Hey, it's okay. I've got a brother and he's an asshole, too. What can you do?"

"My brother is not an asshole," I snapped. "In fact, he's as far from an asshole as you can get."

"Sorry."

I sighed. "No, it's okay. I'm spiraling, and I must sound like a bitch... or a lunatic. Omigod, I sound like a spiraling lunatic bitch. I'm so...so sorry."

I was even more nervous than I thought. I hated being late, but more so, I hated that my oldest brother, Hatch, could still make me feel like a little girl. He was going to be furious with me and I suppose he had good reason, but I still didn't like the fact that soon he'd likely be sitting me down and scolding me for making decisions that were *mine* to make. I'm an adult and I didn't need his permission or blessing to visit a family member if I wanted to. It's true Hatch has had to act more like a father than a brother to me, and the fact he's seventeen years older makes it worse, but I wondered if there was ever going to be a time when he'd start treating me like an adult. Like his equal. In fact, I really wanted to be treated like an adult peer by all four of my brothers. They were all older than me, and every single one of them was overprotective.

*But what the hell does my uncle want?*

When I was a little girl, my dad, my uncle Cutter, and their buddy Crow used to ride with the Dogs of Fire motorcycle club in San Diego. They'd been asked by the club's president to start a new chapter in Portland, and we were all going to move, but then my mother got sick and everything changed overnight. After she died, my dad was never the same. She was his heart and soul, and once she was gone, he went off the rails, eventually ending up in prison.

My uncle and Crow went to Portland as planned, but it

seemed they had vastly different ideas of what a motorcycle club should look like. Crow stayed with the Dogs of Fire, and over time, became the club's national president, and my older brother Hatch currently serves under him. For the most part, the Dogs have always been a clean club, consisting of mostly business owners, and ex-military types. They had very few local troubles and a good relationship with law enforcement.

My uncle Cutter, however, along with a group of dirt bags and petty criminals, started the Burning Saints, and they blazed a much more violent trail. Since then, I'd seen extraordinarily little of my uncle, so why in God's name I'd been asked to meet with him is anyone's guess.

"Okay, here we are," my driver said as we reached our destination, failing to hide the relief in his voice.

"Thank you again, and sorry for the... um... backseat...driving...freak fest. I promise I'll leave you a glowing review. And a big tip," I said, slinking out of the car.

Moments later I found myself standing somewhere I never thought I'd be in a million years. I took a deep breath before pushing the grimy talkback button of the security box in front of me.

# TWO

## BURNING SAINTS

*Minus*

"IS THIS COFFEE or motor oil, Phil?"
"I'm sorry, Clutch, I would have made a fresh pot if I knew you and Minus were… stopping by. Here let me make…"

Phil Blondino tried to stand, but the barrel of Clutch's gun pointed at his head convinced him to remain seated. Phil's grease-stained office chair seemed to groan in agony from underneath his bulky frame.

"You're good right there, Phil. I'm just going to sit here and sip my *delicious* cup of Pennzoil while my good friend, Minus, looks for Cutter's money."

"Really, it's no trouble, Clutch. I'm happy to do it." Phil stammered as heavy beads of sweat formed on his stubbled upper lip, which was frozen in a nervous grin.

I shot a cold stare back at Clutch, who was now in full-on 'Sergeant at Arms Mode.' There was no question he was the right man for the job. Clutch was always calmest when smack dab in the middle of a storm of violence and chaos. Drawing or losing blood didn't seem to faze him in the least. Don't get me wrong. It's not like I'm some sort of saint. I'd never backed down from a fight and I'd even started my fair share, but Clutch looked forward to violence.

"You see, that's always been your problem, Phil, you don't listen very well. For instance, you didn't listen when I told you not to bother with the coffee. We won't be here long, and I highly doubt the next cup could possibly be any better than this swill." Clutch dumped the remainder of his cup on Phil's trash littered desk. "You also failed to hear me when I asked you where Cutter's money is, and now my associate, Minus, is probably going to get his pretty cowboy boots dirty rooting around your filthy shop looking for it."

I flipped Clutch off and began casually tossing Phil's rat hole of an office. It wasn't as if his place was some sort of secured facility. His shitty garage was on par with his persona, a low-level guy Cutter used only when needed.

"I doubt even Phil would be stupid enough to keep that much money here," I said.

"Are you, Phil?" Clutch asked.

"What?" Phil asked.

"Are you *that* stupid?"

"What?"

"You keep saying 'what.' Are you having trouble with your hearing, Phil? Maybe I can help you with that."

Clutch holstered his gun and pulled out a knife from his belt. He walked behind Phil and grabbed his head, pressing the blade to Phil's ear. Phil tried to squirm, but Clutch held firm.

"Hold still, big man."

"Please don't cut me, Clutch," Phil cried out.

Clutch smiled. "What could go wrong? This is a chop-shop, isn't it? A place where large things get cut up into small pieces."

Phil's eyes widened.

"I'm going to ask you one more time to point us in the direction of Cutter's three million dollars and if you fail to hear me this time, I'm going to be forced to improve your hearing by any means necessary."

I chuckled. "Wouldn't cutting his ear off make his hearing worse?"

"I'm not a doctor, Minus. I'm sure Phil here understands that I'm doing the best I can under the circumstances, don't you, Phil?"

Phil's bloodshot eyes bulged from their sockets, as he grunted out, "Sure, Clutch."

"I simply need my good buddy Phil to hear my question as clearly as possible. So here it goes, one more time. Where is Cutter's fucking money?"

"It's not here…"

The first drops of blood appeared as the blade pressed into the soft flesh where his earlobe connected to his head.

"I'll tell you where it is!" he screamed instantly. "I swear to God, I'll tell you where it is."

Clutch stopped, straightened, and looked at me, smiling. "See, it worked! He can hear just fine now."

"I think you missed your calling, *Doctor* Clutch," I said.

"You asshole, you almost cut my fucking ear off!" Phil snapped.

"*Come on*, Philly Cheese Steak, I barely touched you. Now, where's the money?" Clutch asked, once again leveling his pistol to Phil's head.

"A dude named Viper hired my crew to steal a car. That's it!" he squeaked. "I swear I didn't know there was money in the trunk until the car got here and they opened it up."

"But once you saw the money, you didn't think to call Cutter?"

"How was I supposed to know the money was his?"

"Don't make me shoot you for being stupid, Phil. The Burning Saints are your business partners. Three million in cash shouldn't roll through your shop without raising an alarm. You should have called Cutter as soon as you saw the money."

"You're right, Clutch. You're absolutely right." Blood ran down the rolls of pink flesh that made up his neck as his hands applied pressure to the wound.

I cocked my head. "Now tell me, who the fuck is Viper and where can I find him?"

"He's the new head of Los Psychos, the Mexican club. They hang out at the Nine Ball."

"Leo's old place?"

"That's the place! I swear that's all I know. It was supposed to be a simple job. Snatch the Caddy and bring it back here for the pickup. I didn't know anything about Cutter's money being in the trunk, or that you were involved Minus." Phil's attention turned to me. "Last I heard you moved to Texas or something."

"I'm not involved, so leave me the fuck out of this," I said.

I'd always hated Phil. He was a piece of shit, and I couldn't wait to get out of his garage. Besides being a car thief, a profession I detested, Phil was also a loan shark and a meth dealer. The exact sort of bottom feeder I'd tried to protect my club from years ago.

Phil continued, "I know Cutter and I have had our disagreements lately... and that mistakes have been made. Like I said, I didn't know it was his money and I will *personally* apologize to Cutter myself."

"Don't worry, Phil, I'll let him know how sorry you were."

The sound of Clutch's silenced .45 was still loud enough to startle me. Phil's body, now two holes greater, lie on his office floor in a heap, a pool of blood rapidly forming underneath his lumpy frame.

Clutch simply holstered his gun and shrugged.

"What the fuck, man?" I shouted

"Cutter wanted him gone," Clutch said flatly. "He's got plans for this place, and Phil was getting sloppier and sloppier."

"You didn't want to clue me in? What the fuck are we gonna do with the body?"

"You worry too much Minus, you always have. I've got a cleaning crew on standby. Cutter wants this all taken care of right away. We've got to get to the Sanctuary. Plus, now we've gotta find out who this Viper prick is."

"No, *you* need to find out more about Viper," I snapped back. "I'm here for a meeting with Cutter and that's it. Twenty-four hours and then I'm headed back to Savannah. In fact, as far as anyone else is concerned. I'm not even here."

"Yeah, well your plans may have just changed," he said, bringing his phone to his ear.

"Yes, I called earlier about a bad stain in my carpet," Clutch said. "That's correct, the one located in my hallway. I'd like to have a crew come out right away please. Thank you."

He hung up and we made our way out through the back entrance, to his Barracuda parked in the rear lot. As we got in, Clutch said, "Ya know, you still haven't told me exactly why you're back in town."

"Yes, I did. Cutter called me and asked me to meet with him, so here I am."

"I understand that, but *why*?" he asked as we peeled off into the night. "Everyone here thought you were swallowed up by some swamp, as the late great Phil so astutely pointed out."

"*Astutely?*" I choked out, surprised by his word choice.

"Hey, motherfucker, I read some of those books you sent me when I was in the joint. Anyways, don't change the subject. Why the fuck are you here?"

"I told you I have no idea, and I wouldn't lie to you. Now, slow down, will ya? The last thing we need is for your dumb ass to get pulled over for speeding while fleeing a murder scene."

Clutch, ignoring my request, continued his interrogation, "Don't get cute with me, bro. Maybe it's just me, but it seems a little odd that you're so casual about meeting with a guy you haven't spoken to directly in eight years, who exiled you to Hicksville USA, and that… Oh yeah, once tried to kill you!"

"Look, you know Cutter as well as I do," I said. "He never makes a move without good reason."

"Still doesn't make a damn bit of sense."

"Look, Cutter has his reasons for asking me here, and I have my reasons for saying yes."

"Is one of those reasons *her*?" Clutch challenged.

"Who?" I asked, knowing damn well who he meant.

Clutch laughed. "So, she *is* one of the reasons."

"Fuck you, Nicky."

"That's not a no."

"You're right, it's a fuck you, Nicky. I haven't seen or talked to her since I left, and she has no idea I'm in town," I said, the irritation in my voice rising.

"Okay, okay. Don't get all bent outta shape."

"Look, I'm just as curious as you as to why Cutter's sent for me, but I can guaran-fuckin'-tee it's got nothing to do with *her*."

"If you say so," Clutch replied.

"You're probably making a way bigger deal outta this whole thing. The old man probably has some business for me to take care of back in Savannah that he doesn't want to discuss over the phone."

"Maybe," he replied.

"I'll bet you five hundred dollars, Cutter's gonna have me on the first flight out of town tomorrow."

"After you help me with Viper," Clutch said matter-of-factly.

"I told you you're on your own with this bullshit. I don't know anything about Cutter's three million dollars, or who this Viper guy is, but this all sounds more like *your* problem, than *my* problem," I said.

Clutch finally slowed the car down. He turned to me, his expression turning deadly serious. "It's a club problem, Minus and last I checked, you still wear a Saints patch."

I nodded but said nothing.

We drove on through the ever-present Portland drizzle until we reached the Sanctuary, the Burning Saints' compound. The cluster of buildings used to belong to a paper company that went out of business years ago and were now owned outright by the club.

Clutch pulled out a remote control and punched in a code which opened a rolling security gate.

"Trust me, pal. As important as you may *think* you are to Cutter, the club's three million in cash is more important," Clutch said as he parked. "I'm gonna have to sniff around a little and see what we can find out about Viper and his crew. Los Psychos have been making a lot of noise around town, so if they really are involved it's gonna complicate things. For all we know Phil was lying through his rotten teeth but Cutter's gonna want me to make sure, and honestly, I could really use some trustworthy backup. So, are you gonna help me with this or not?"

I paused for a few moments then asked, "Who's the pile of cash from?"

"Honestly, I don't know. Cutter's been cagey lately. Super secretive and shit. He's been keeping everyone at arm's length for a while now and I don't really know what to think. Look man, I don't know what's going on, but I don't think it's a coincidence that you've been summoned here, at the same time this payment was scheduled to be delivered."

Clutch's tone shifted. "I also don't believe that you haven't thought about what you might say if you see... *her*."

"You can say her name, ya know. Regardless of what you may believe, Cutter is not omniscient," I said.

"*I* can say her name, but *you* can't, my friend. According to Cutter you can't even think about her."

"Yeah, he made that pretty clear the night he hung me over the Burnside bridge, so why the fuck do you keep bringing her up?" I asked.

We got out of the car and made our way to the entrance of the Chapel, the Sanctuary's main building, and our meeting hall.

"Just making sure you've got your head on straight

should you run into her, that's all," Clutch replied.

"Being as she and Cutter don't talk, she and I don't talk, and Cutter and I don't talk, I can't imagine why or how I could possibly run into Cricket Wallace."

As we approached the Sanctuary, I could hear what sounded like a raging party going on inside. Clutch opened the door, and it took me a few moments to register what I was seeing.

Standing amongst a sea of leather, denim, beer bottles, and beards was a stunning blonde. She had long legs which supported the sexiest body ever created and a face so beautiful, it made me forget what any other woman looked like.

Cricket Wallace was standing in the middle of the Chapel, mere feet away from me.

"Hi, Jase, it's good to see you again."

# THREE

*Minus*

"**WHAT THE FUCK** is this?" I growled to Clutch. Cricket stared back, clearly irritated by my reaction.

"*Gee, Cricket*, it's nice to see you, too. Been a long time," she said with the kind of sarcastic smile only she could pull off without looking cold. A smile that made me want to take her into one of the back rooms and chew her clothes off.

I said nothing.

"Hey there, Cricket. It's… uh, good to… see you. It's been… ah… a while. You look great." Clutch stumbled over his words, ending with, "I'm gonna… go get a beer," before disappearing into the mass of congregated Saints, leaving me alone, standing face-to-face with Cricket fucking Wallace.

I couldn't believe she was here, or that she'd gotten even hotter since I'd last seen her. I was twenty-three at the time, had just been patched in, and given my club name. Cricket was barely twenty-one and had just started hanging around the clubhouse. Her family had been estranged from Cutter and she was getting to know her long-lost uncle again. However, that reunion was short-lived when I decided to get to know Cricket myself. I'd gotten in way deeper than I'd intended, and although we tried to keep our relationship under wraps, I guess word got out.

When Cutter found out, I was sent away to the Savannah chapter and Cricket's brother, Hatch, who rode with the Dogs of Fire, forbid her to be around the Saints ever again. To say I was shocked to see her standing before me now would be the understatement of a lifetime.

"What the fuck are you doing here?" I finally blurted out.

"Okay, *that* one I'm going to take personally, Jase." She crossed her arms. "Fuck you, too."

Her reaction slapped me back to reality. For the first time, I was able to focus on the other occupants of the room. A who's who of Oregon and Washington Burning Saints were spread out within the clubhouse's great hall. Knuckle Sandwich by RatHound was playing in the background, while a group of Saints played pool in the corner. It was all bros and backslaps, like some sort of goddamned family reunion. It looked like just about every patch from the pacific northwest was present.

My attention snapped back to Cricket.

"Where's Cutter?" I asked as I pushed my way past her into the crowd. I tried to keep my head down and avoid eye contact with anyone. I had no idea I'd be walking into such a grand affair and wasn't in the mood to play catchup with everyone in the room.

"How would I know? I just got here about thirty seconds before you walked in," she said, obviously irritated.

"Well, how the fuck would I know when you got here?" I snapped back.

"Have I done something wrong to you, Jase?" she asked, staying a close step behind as I made my way through the throngs of old familiar faces.

"Minus. No one calls me Jase anymore," I ground out.

"Oh, I'm sorry I didn't refer to you by your super tough biker name. The last time I saw you, you were still Jase, at least some of the time."

"What do you want, Cricket?" I asked, still refusing to look back at her.

"Who says I *want* anything? It's been seven years since we've seen each other, and I was only trying to say—"

"Eight."

"What?"

"It's been eight years since we've seen each other and your uncle, my president, wanted it that way. In fact, so did your asshole brother, and as another point of fact, I'm not even supposed to be talking to you," I yelled over the din as I continued to scan the Sanctuary for Cutter.

"Jesus, *Minus*. Is that what this is all about? We were kids back then," Cricket said, her airy laugh cutting through the masculine clatter of the room.

I shook off the intoxicating sweetness of her voice and spun around quickly to face her, causing her to take a small step backwards in surprise.

"Wrong!" I shouted. "Maybe you were a kid, but I was a brand-new patch being dangled off a bridge, while my bags were being packed for me. It may be ancient history to you, but I wake up in Savannah every day. My shit's in a different time zone because of you."

"Because of *me*? You're saying it's my fault that you..."

Over the next few moments only fragments of what Cricket said registered in my brain. She was impossibly sexy, and I could barely focus on her words. I was also still white hot angry at the fact that she was even here. The Sanctuary of all places. I couldn't avoid her, I couldn't fuck her, and I couldn't leave.

"Jase, are you listening to me?" Cricket's elevated pitch brought me back to reality.

"Minus," I reminded her, before adding, "and no... not really." I turned around and started towards the back offices. "I'm looking for Cutter. The last thing I need is you following me around like a puppy."

"I'm not following you!" she yelled over the ever-increasing noise of *Saintfest*, or whatever the fuck was going on tonight. "Okay, maybe I *am* following you, but it's only because I was trying to take the high road and be nice. Even though you're giving me zero reason to do so. After all, you're the one who should be apologizing to me, and instead you're being an ass."

"You're right, Cricket. I'm an ass. So, before Cutter sees you, do us both a favor and go...do whatever the fuck it is you're here to do. Just make sure it's far away from me."

I stopped in front of Cutter's office door, but before I could knock, the door swung open to reveal a grinning Cutter. He smiled wide, extending his arms for an embrace before gleefully shouting, "Minus! Cricket! How perfect that you're both here at the same time. I'm so glad the two of you could make it."

*This was turning out to be one strange fucking night.*

* * *

### Cricket

I don't know what shocked me the most, seeing Jase, my first love and source of my first heartbreak after all these years, my notoriously grumpy uncle greeting me with a smile and a hug, or that his office smelled like Snoop Dog's tour bus. All of it was way too much for me to process.

"Hi, Uncle Cutter, it's nice to see you, too," I said into his barreled chest as he held me tight. I was mere inches away from Minus, who had also been entrapped in this surprise bear hug. My uncle's beard and long hair reeked of pot smoke. He finally let go and I stepped back, smoothing my hands over my hips and glancing to Minus who looked as stunned as I was.

Gorgeous, yes. Sexier than ever, yes. But definitely stunned.

He'd gotten a lot bigger...wider really, since I'd last seen him. Savannah appeared to have agreed with him. He'd grown an epic beard, and I itched to run my fingers through it. His face had the same chiseled features, and he had the same longish, dark blond hair that he'd pulled back into a band. His eyes, though, God, those blue eyes still brought me to my knees.

"Look at you two!" my uncle exclaimed. "I always thought you two made such a beautiful couple."

"Okay, what the fuck is going on here?" Minus growled out in obvious disbelief.

Uncle Cutter simply smiled even wider and said, "Come in, come in," as he ushered us into his office.

"Please sit down. Don't mind Warthog there, he's kind of like my personal assistant, but he's mostly here for the weed," Cutter said laughing. "He keeps me flush with the good shit and I'm always happy to share. Plus, I've never believed that it's good for a man to drink, or smoke, alone. Isn't that right, Warthog?"

Through the haze of smoke, I could barely make out the rather furry man seated at the end of a large leather sofa.

Warthog, who I thought looked a bit like Cheech, *or was it Chong,* simply smiled through his bushy black and grey beard. Causing his eyes to disappear behind his wire-rimmed glasses.

"We're not sitting, because we're not staying," Minus said, clearly pissed. "Actually, she can sit all she wants." He motioned to me. "What the fuck do I care, but I'm outta here," he said, turning to leave.

"Sit the fuck down, Minus," my uncle's voice boomed, his welcoming smile now completely gone.

Minus turned around slowly, but did as his president asked, sitting on the opposite end of the sofa. This of course left only the middle spot between him and Warthog open, which I reluctantly took.

"Don't be rude to my beautiful niece." Cutter turned to me and took my face in his leathery hands. "It's so wonderful to see you, my dear. Thank you so much for coming. It's certainly no surprise to see what a beautiful woman you've grown up to be. More importantly, I understand you're doing quite well at Mann Industries." His eyes were soft, and his words tender. This was not the man I remembered, or the one I expected to see, not that I quite knew what to expect. I was also shocked that he knew anything about me or my work.

I smiled. "Thank you."

"Good, we're all settled in," my uncle continued, his grin having returned. "Either of you wanna hit this?" He presented to us a large black glass bong, adorned with the Burning Saint's club logo. "Warthog here had this made special for me as a gift. Isn't it beautiful?"

"Oh, boy, Cutter, I tell ya, I'd normally join you, but I just polished off a spliff in the parking lot before coming in. How 'bout you, Cricket? It's 4:20 somewhere, right?" Minus mocked.

"I'm good, thanks," I shot back through clenched teeth.

"Alright, Minus, you don't have to be an asshole, she didn't ask you to be here, I did," Uncle Cutter said.

"And why exactly is that, Cutter?" Minus snapped.

"Hey, shithead! I may be high, but that don't make me some peace-lovin' hippie. You'd better stow that fucking attitude before I start rethinking you coming back here."

"Coming back? What the fuck are you talking about? Who said anything about coming back? In fact, who said I wanted to be here at all?" Minus stood up.

"Who said you had a fucking choice in the matter?" Cutter asked, also rising to his feet. The two men were now standing toe-to-toe, mere inches away from each other. They both stood well above six feet and were menacing in their own ways. Uncle Cutter was as 'old school' as they came and had a commanding presence. Shocks of white streaked through his jet-black hair and beard, giving him a severe, yet regal look. His arms were sleeved in blurry, aged tattoos, and rings adorned his gnarled fingers. He was clearly the kind of man who knew when to bark and when to bite. No doubt, years of leading the unleadable had gained him that skill.

Minus, on the other hand, was more like a dormant volcano that was waking up after a long sleep. He seemed calm on the outside, but I could sense a lake of molten anger bubbling deep inside him. Some of that anger began to flow out as Minus challenged my uncle and seeing the look on his face brought back a flood of memories. His beautiful features, forming into a Viking-like scowl. His fists, balled up at his sides, caused his biceps to swell. As hurt and confused as I was, I could not stop myself from feeling an instant, and overwhelming attraction to him. I had to force myself to look away.

"So, it's more of this shit again? You tellin' me where to go, where to live, who I can and can't see. Is that why you brought me here, Cutter? So that you can show me you can still fuck with my life? And why the hell is *she* here? I thought I was asked here on club business," Minus shouted.

I wanted to be pissed at the way he said "she," but at this point, I had some of the same thoughts. Why was I here? Why had my uncle asked Minus and me to be here at the same time, when he'd done everything in his power to separate us and keep us apart eight years ago?

My uncle said nothing for several seconds, but quietly motioned for Minus to re-take his seat, before finally breaking the silence. "I'm dying."

"What the fuck?" The tone in Minus's voice immediately shifted from anger to concern. I gasped, my hand reflexively covering my mouth.

"I have CRC."

"What the hell is that?" Minus asked with a slight drawl. Evidence of his time spent in Savannah.

"Jesus, Minus, you sound like a goddamned hillbilly," Cutter said with a chuckle.

"Colorectal cancer," Warthog sang out, in a mock country singer voice, to a cheery tune that did not fit the lyrics.

"Yup. Asshole cancer, stage four," Cutter said. "It's bad, I've apparently had it for a long time, it's spread… and it's gonna kill me pretty damn soon."

I sat stunned, not knowing what quite to say. My relationship with my uncle was complicated to say the least. I was at a bit of a loss as to the appropriate way to act. Plus, I wasn't quite dealing with a "normal" guy here.

"How long have you known about this?" Minus asked.

"Not long. A couple months. I've been keeping this real quiet. Hardly anybody knows," he replied before adding, "No one outside of my old lady, Big Frank, and of course, Dr. Warthog here."

"What are you doing about it?" Minus asked.

"Nothin'. Not a goddamned thing I *can* do about it. It's aggressive and it's having a fucking party all over my insides. Besides, it's not like the club has a health plan to pay for treatment. Hell, before we started getting' patched up by Doc Eldie, I hadn't seen a doctor since I was a kid. Probably why I'm in the state I am now. She was the one that spotted somethin' was wrong with me in the first place, but by then it was too late."

"Then why the fuck are you telling us?" I asked.

"Because tonight I'm announcing my retirement from the Burning Saints," he said.

"The hell you are," Minus replied.

"It's true."

Minus stared at Cutter, seemingly unable to process his words.

"It's not like it's my choice, it's the law," Cutter continued. "If you can't ride, you can't wear a patch, and I can barely walk around the block without passing out and pissing myself, let alone ride."

"You wrote the law, and you can change it."

"If I could then the law wouldn't be worth jack shit."

"You started this club."

"I remember, I was there." Cutter smiled.

"Let me get this straight," Minus said. "You're dying and no one can do anything about it, and the gathering of the tribe out there is because you're announcing your retirement."

"That's right," Cutter replied.

"So, Big Frank takes up the staff tonight?" Minus asked.

"Nope, can't do it. Big Frank's even older than me, has

two bum knees. In truth, he hasn't been able to ride for six months. We've been letting him slide, but the staff can't go to him. So, with me kickin' the fuckin' bucket, it's a good time for both of us to retire."

"And *not* ride off into the sunset," Warthog added, to an approving nod from Cutter.

"Cricket and I could've heard about all of this along with the others when you make your big speech or whatever," Minus said. "Or better yet, we could have heard about it through the grapevine and spared the travel expense, so why the private pow-wow?"

Cutter smiled wide once again, sparked his lighter, and took a huge pull from his bong. He tilted his head back and exhaled slowly, once again filling the small room with a thick, nauseating smoke. He then set his glassy eyed stare directly at us.

"How would the two of you like to run a motorcycle club?"

# FOUR

## BURNING SAINTS

### Minus

"**W**HO THE FUCK do you get your weed from, Warthog? Willie Nelson?" Cutter bellowed with laughter and smoke continued to pour from his lungs. "I forgot how funny you are when you're not being so damned serious, Minus." His laughter continued, and then turned to deep and violent coughing, causing him to stagger back a step. Warthog immediately sprang to his feet, taking Cutter by the elbow, helping to stabilize him.

"I'm fine, goddammit!" Cutter protested, waving Warthog off, sitting down on top of his large mahogany desk, before continuing. "I'm serious, Minus. I'm retiring and I want you to be the president of the club."

"You want me to be..." I couldn't form the words needed to complete the sentence. This was fucking absurd.

"And..." Cutter looked at Cricket, "I want *her* to help you."

Cricket let out a gasp as she shot me a look of pure disgust.

"Well... what do you think?" Cutter asked, his arms stretched out, ready to receive the glory for bestowing his brilliant master plan upon us.

If earlier today, you'd asked me to make a list of all the potential reasons Cutter may have asked me here tonight, him giving me his president's patch, with Cricket by my side, would not have made the top one million possibilities. By comparison, him killing me would have made the top three. After a few stunned moments I finally managed to continue.

"*What do I think*? I think you're out of your goddamned mind. I think those doctors examined the wrong fucking end. I think you must have brain cancer instead of colon cancer, and that it's rotting away your ability to form logical, rational thoughts."

"Minus!" Cricket chided.

"You stay the fuck out of this!" I snapped, causing Cricket to rise to her feet.

She jabbed her finger repeatedly into my chest like an angry woodpecker. "Don't you ever presume that you can talk to me like that or tell me what to do, Jase Vincent. I may have put up with a certain amount of your shit when we were younger, but that's not gonna happen now."

"Excuse me?" I asked, stunned. I had no idea why she was pissed at me. She was the invader here. Plus, Cutter was the one that stirred up all this fucking nonsense.

"I'm not the same person I was when you left, *Minus*. That naïve girl is far behind me. She's a distant memory, and not about to feed into your 'big swinging dick, macho, alpha asshole' routine."

I grinned, crossed my arms, and casually sat on the edge of Cutter's desk so that I was eye level with Cricket. "That girl may be a distant memory, but she clearly remembers my big swingin'—"

A slap in the face I could have handled without flinching, but she hit me with a fist. A good solid fist, and she was wearing a ring. She cut me deep across the cheek, directly under my left eye. Blood poured from my face, and I staggered back in surprise, throwing Cutter into a fit of laughter followed by another fit of coughing.

"He looks like something from a Monty Python sketch," Cutter howled to Warthog between coughs.

"What the fuck, Cricket?" I applied pressure to the wound as blood ran down my forearm.

"Don't ever talk to me like that again. In fact, don't ever talk to me again, *period.*" Her eyes were burning with rage, and I'd never felt such a mixture of shame and desire before. At that moment, I wanted her more than I'd ever wanted anyone or anything in my life. I also felt wholly unworthy of her and ashamed of the way I'd treated her all night. I had been thrown completely off balance since the moment I saw her. She'd always had that effect on me and her presence here tonight, of all nights, was even more disorienting.

"Cricket, I'm sorry—"

"Save it," she snapped, before turning to Cutter. "And *you.* I don't know what your sick game is here, or how exactly you figure I fit into all this but let me assure you that I want none of it. I have my own life and my own plans, and they most certainly do not include working for misogynistic, stoner, biker, assholes." Her face softened for a moment. "Look, I really am sorry that you're sick and I hope you get better. Now, please don't ever contact me again." With that, she walked out the door, leaving the three of us silent as I bled all over Cutter's carpet.

\* \* \*

*Cricket*

I left the Sanctuary and called a car to take me home. However, in a moment of what I was sure would end up being identified as "Jase Vincent-induced insanity," once we reached the I-5 junction, I instructed my driver to head north instead.

My hand was throbbing. It didn't feel like I'd broken anything, but it was swelling up just enough to make removing my ring an impossibility, and to remind me of what a lunatic I was. I couldn't believe I punched Jase in his big, dumb, beautiful face.

Arriving at my brother's home, I stood on the porch for a few seconds, debating whether I was going to offer my life to him on a silver platter. He was going to go ballistic, and I wasn't sure I was in the mood to suffer through a lecture.

Before I could act on any possible good sense and leave, the front door opened to reveal Hatch standing in the foyer.

"Why the fuck are you standing out here all alone?" he asked with a chuckle.

I bit my lip. "Because I don't know if I want to come in."

He cocked his head. "Christina, get the fuck in here."

I took a deep breath and walked inside. Hatch locked up and took my coat, and I hugged him. I think he was surprised, because it took a minute for him to hug me back. "Okay, what's goin' on little sister?" he asked, his arms closing around me like a vice.

"Cutter's dying."

Hatch took a deep breath. "Yeah, I know."

I met his eyes in surprise. "You do?"

He nodded. "Come on, let's talk inside."

I followed him into the family room where his wife, Maisie, was curled up on the sofa with my niece, Poppy, watching a movie.

"Aunty Cricket!" Poppy said, jumping up. "Oh my gosh, you look so cute."

I grinned. She always said that. It didn't matter what I was wearing… case in point, tonight I wore jeans and a T-shirt, with my favorite Converse Hi-Tops. Nothing special at all. "Thanks, honey. What are you watching?"

"Princess Diaries."

"Good choice."

Poppy nodded. "It's Mum's favorite."

I adored Poppy. She was, without a doubt, my favorite human being on the planet. Despite being a teenager, she didn't have that angsty bitch thing goin' on. She was genuinely sweet and had a knack for seeing the best qualities in people.

"How are you, love?" Maisie asked. "How's work?"

"I'm good. Work's great." Maisie was the former owner of Mann Industries, the company I currently worked for. She got me the job before selling it and recently I had been promoted to the position of marketing manager. As happy as I was to be finally using the degree I'd earned, I can't say I found too much satisfaction in my current day-to-day work life. Mostly, I was trying to parlay the experience gained through my current position to launch my own business. I just wasn't exactly sure what market I wanted to focus on. I was profoundly grateful for my job, but there was an itch for adventure left unscratched in my life that was becoming harder for me to ignore.

"Cricket and I are gonna talk a bit," Hatch said. "You beautiful ladies finish your movie."

"Okay, darling," Maisie said, kissing him.

"Say goodbye before you go, okay Aunty Cricket?" Poppy said.

"Of course," I said, and followed Hatch downstairs to the swanky finished basement. It was an expertly designed space, decorated with antique mid-century modern furniture and artwork.

"You want a beer?" Hatch asked.

"Maybe later."

"How did you find out about Cutter?" Hatch asked as we flopped onto the sofa.

"He summoned me."

Hatch raised an eyebrow. "Summoned you?"

"What else do you call it when you're called to see the king?"

"Called to see him? As in, at the Saints' compound?" he growled. "And you went?"

I nodded.

He scowled. "Which Dog did you take with you, so I know whose ass to chew?"

"I went alone," I said plainly.

*"Alone?"* he asked, angrily.

I raised my hand and shook my head. "Grown woman here, big brother. I can handle myself and I don't need a chaperone. Besides, none of the Saints would ever lay a finger on me, and you know it."

"Goddammit, Cricket. The compound's off-limits. I've made that perfectly fucking clear."

"You're not my boss, or my parole officer," I countered.

"Cutter knows the rules and so do you, Cricket. If Crow finds out about this, he's gonna fuckin' lose his mind."

Crow was the president of Hatch's MC, the Dogs of Fire. My brother's club treated me like family, and I loved them. The Burning Saints... not so much. There had been a long standing "bitter peace" between the two clubs, and me and Minus's young romance didn't help matters at all. Ultimately, it's why Crow and Cutter made the agreement that club and family members wouldn't darken each other's doors. If my brothers or I wanted to see Cutter, we'd meet on neutral ground. Anywhere but either of the club's compounds. Cutter broke the rules when he summoned me to the Sanctuary, and I'd broken them by going.

"In fairness to our uncle, Hatch, he *is* dying. It's harder for him to get around in his current condition."

"You should have talked to me first."

"Again, brother, grown ass woman here. I don't have to ask your permission, I'm not in your club."

He sighed. "Fair enough."

I bit back a smile. I loved Maisie. She'd tempered my brother and given him a sense of peace he'd never known before. We'd had a tough life. Our mother had died when I was little, then my father had been sent to prison after killing a man. Hatch had singlehandedly raised me and my three other brothers, despite being barely an adult himself. I owed him everything. But that didn't mean I liked it when he threw out 'maximum dad energy.'

"So, what did Cutter say?" Hatch asked.

"Well," I paused cautiously before continuing. "Cutter wants me and Minus—"

"What the fuck?" he snapped.

"Can I *please* finish?" I ground out.

"Minus was there?"

"Yes, but chill," I said.

"What could you possibly say that involves Cutter and Minus that would make me *chill*?"

"Cutter wants me and Minus to take over the Club."

"Are you fuckin' shittin' me?" he hissed.

"Well, he was as high as a kite, and obviously not in a healthy state of mind, but I figured you'd want to know what was going on."

He dragged his hands down his face. "What the fuck is he up to?"

"Who knows? A dying man attempting to pass on his legacy?"

"Maybe," Hatch said. "But why try and pass it to a guy who's on his shit list, or *you*?"

"I have no idea, but I have no intention of ever going back to the Burning Saint's Sanctuary, talking with Cutter, or Jase "Minus" Vincent again."

Hatch shook his head. "Fuck me, Cricket, I have no idea what to make of all this."

"You think I do?"

He shook his head.

"Well, I don't," I said, rising to my feet. "And rather than waste my time trying to figure it out, I'm gonna spend the rest of my evening hanging with my niece and sister, so how 'bout that beer."

He chuckled. "Comin' right up."

"And ice," I added.

"The beer's been in the fridge. It's plenty cold," Hatch replied.

"No, the ice isn't for my beer. It's for my hand."

"What did you do to your hand?" he asked.

"Nothing big, I'll tell you all about it later. Right now, I just want to unwind."

I grinned and led my brother up the stairs and back into the family room, where me, my IPA, and my ice pack settled in next to Poppy to watch the rest of the movie. Well, Hatch and Maisie snuggled close until Maisie fell asleep, but Poppy and I managed to make it until the end credits. After the day I'd had, I decided to crash on their couch.

\* \* \*

## Minus

"Well, that could've gone better," Cutter said, as he walked around his desk, opened the bottom drawer, and produced a bottle of Jim Beam and small black medical bag. The type old timey doctors took on house calls back in the day. "There should be some bandages and ointment and shit for your face in here. You can use my bathroom to clean up," he said, handing me the bag and motioning to the bathroom door.

"Cutter, what the fuck—"

"Just get cleaned up and meet me out there with the others. Just don't take too long. You and I can talk about all this later. I've got to go talk to the club, and tell them what's going on, but for now, let's just keep this little conversation between us."

*Little conversation? Was he out of his fucking gourd?*

I nodded, and Cutter exited the office with Warthog in tow. I went to the bathroom mirror and got my first good look at my latest war wound. The minute I stopped applying direct pressure to the cut, blood would pour from my face. I was most definitely in need of stiches, and Cutter's black bag had everything I needed, so I got to work.

Cricket was right to belt me, and I was happy to know that she was an even stronger person than when I'd last seen her. Acting the way I did tonight, she'd never believe how much I'd changed over the years myself. After the way she stormed out, I'd probably never get the chance to tell her how sorry I was. For now, the sting of the suture needle would have to serve as my penance.

With Cutter's whiskey serving as both antiseptic and pain killer, I got to work. When I was done, the bathroom looked like a crime scene. My shirt was soaked in blood, and after finding a Harley T-shirt in Cutter's desk drawer, I stripped it off and tossed it in the trash. I put my kutte back on, and with four crooked stiches and a whiskey buzz, I was ready for the ball.

"Holy shit, it *is* Minus!" a familiar voice called out as soon as I opened Cutter's office door. Apparently, my presence at the clubhouse had not gone unnoticed.

"Hey, Grover. Long time, brother," I said, greeting my old friend with an arm-wrestle handshake. Grover was one of the five I rode with back in the day including Clutch, Ropes, and his younger brother, Sweet Pea.

"I can't believe it's actually you, man. A bunch of guys said they saw you come in earlier… holy shit, bro! What the fuck happened to your face?"

I deflected his question with one of my own. "Hey, have you seen Cricket around anywhere?"

"Cricket Wallace? No man. Why?"

"Are you sure?" I asked. "She was here just a little while ago."

"No, I haven't seen Cricket in… no way! Did she do that to your face?" Grover was grinning like the cat that ate the canary, and then went back for the rest of its family. "You've been in town for five fuckin' minutes and you're already up causing trouble? You'd better steer fuckin' clear of Cutter, buddy."

"Me and Cutter are good, for now I guess," I replied.

"What the fuck does that mean?" Grover asked.

"Tell you what, Grover. I'll let you know when I know. Now, where's everyone else?"

"They're in the great room. Come on, man, let's go see what the fuck's going on. God damn, it's good to see you back home, brother," Grover said, one arm draped around me as we walked down the hall to the great room.

As we joined the group of already assembled Saints, the

floor shook with three loud thumps, immediately causing a hush among the rowdy crowd. Not a single Saint moved, or even dared blink. This was tradition among brothers. A sign of respect. Every Saint present knew the sound of these blows came from Red Dog's staff.

"Many years ago, our brother Red Dog laid down his life for this club." Cutter's voice boomed as he broke the silence, staff raised high. "All of you in this room have heard of him, and what he did in sacrifice for his club. Some of you rode with him. A few of you, like me, were there when he died. Red Dog's staff is a symbol of what it means to be a member of the Burning Saints Motorcycle Club. A totem which symbolizes what it means to lay down your very life in service to your club and your brothers. Red Dog's staff is also a symbol of assembly. So, with this staff I officially call this meeting to disorder!"

The staff struck the floor, three more times, causing the room to erupt in cheers, howls, and breaking bottles.

"Alright, you filthy fucking animals, calm down," Cutter said, and the room began to hush. Warthog brought Cutter a high barstool and took the staff from him.

The staff had started its life as a county hospital crutch Red Dog needed after he broke his leg in a crash. Over the years, it had been spray-painted, covered in blood, decorated, and adorned with all manner of biker paraphernalia. The crutch was eventually modified, including extending and reinforcing the base, and once he'd died, affixing Red Dog's actual skull on top. No one was sure how the club had obtained Red Dog's skull, but there were many rumors and stories on the subject.

"I know you're probably wondering why the fuck I've gathered us all here tonight. I also know that you've all been gossiping like a bunch of bitches since I called the meeting, so I won't torture you with the suspense any longer," Cutter said to laughs all around. Cutter didn't laugh, though. He kept direct eye contact with every Saint in the room. Making sure he felt a connection to each one of them before continuing. "Brothers, the time has come for me to hang up my riding gloves. I'm retiring as president of the Burning Saints."

A wave of low murmurs washed through the room. Clutch shot me a look that let me know he had no idea this was coming. Cutter wasn't bullshitting. He'd kept this information close to his kutte. I shrugged back at Clutch, unable to do anything else. I didn't understand what the hell was going on any more than he did. Hell, I was probably even more confused. Why would Cutter intentionally keep his Sergeant at Arms in the dark about his condition, and then try to give me, someone he's barely spoken to in years, the President's patch?

"That's not all," Cutter continued. "Due to some serious health issues, I may not be with you brothers for much longer. As it turns out, I don't have a whole lot of road ahead of me."

"Bullshit, Cutter! Can't nothin' kill you!" a Road Captain named Wolf shouted, with cheers from the crowd.

"I appreciate that, boys, I do, but I'm afraid it's true. I don't have long and I'm too sick to ride. We all know the code. If you can't ride, you can't hold office, so it's time for the staff to go to someone else. Normally, that person would be the club's VP, but we all know that Big Frank here is a lazy bastard and would do a horrible job," Cutter said, to laughs all around. "Plus, apparently he's worn out his knees doing… God knows what."

The crowd laughed again as Big Frank raised his hands in mock resignation. I laughed too, but my head was throbbing. Partly from Cricket's right cross, but mostly from the mental strain of trying to figure out what the fuck was going on here.

The crowd of assembled Saints murmured among themselves as they too processed the news. This was a big deal in our world. Cutter wasn't only our president, but the club's founder, and a change in leadership at this level clearly meant huge changes for the club itself. Knowing all of this made our earlier conversation even more puzzling. Cutter and I had never agreed completely about the future of the Burning Saints. I felt the club's rules and policies were archaic and going to get us all killed, and Cutter made it clear that my input on such matters was not wanted. I countered that he'd exiled me to Savannah.

Cutter fixed his gaze directly on me, causing me to sweat through my borrowed t-shirt, before saying, "I'll announce who Red Dog's staff will be going to very soon. I'll be meeting with the presidents of the Savannah and Florida chapters soon, but I wanted to tell you all face-to-face, beforehand. Please rest assured that I have this club's best interest in mind, and that I will continue to serve and protect this club until my dying day. I love every one of you brothers and it's been an honor to ride with you."

Warthog raised his beer and shouted, "To our commander and chief! Long live President Cutter!" and the place went ape shit.

The next several hours contained some of the most violent debauchery I'd ever seen at any club gathering. Ladies showed up, as did a few cases of the good stuff. The Saints were in a state of mourning, and sex, booze, drugs, and rock and roll were gonna help ease the pain, even if it killed them. I spent most of the evening catching up with old friends and matching them shot for shot…for shot. I don't normally drink in order to get obliterated, but I was bound, and fucking determined to do everything in my power to erase this nightmare of a day.

# FIVE
## BURNING SAINTS

*Minus*

THE DEMONS WHO'D cooked up last night's events had taken up residency inside my skull. They jabbed me awake with their pitchforks and set up some sort of sadistic slide show of last night's events. Strange scenes played out in my mind like fragmented flickers, and I could barely make sense of what was real, and what was imagined. The last thing I clearly remembered was a tray of shot glasses, the karaoke machine firing up, and dancing with two very handsy women. Shit, for all I knew, I was currently in bed with one…or *both of them*. I was afraid to open my eyes and look.

"Good morning, lil' cowpoke!" Clutch burst through the door.

"What the fuck Nicky? What time is it, man?" Every ray

of sunshine in the room felt like a paper cut to my corneas as I forced my eyes open.

"It's nine-thirty," he said, setting a cup of coffee, and an iPad on the nightstand next to the bed.

I pulled the covers back and checked the bed for anyone else. Thankfully, I was its only occupant. Not only was I alone, but I was still fully clothed. "Thank God for small fuckin' favors," I groaned out before sitting up, and grabbing the coffee.

"What are you looking for?" Clutch asked.

"Not what. Whom," I replied.

"Nah, man. You passed out here all alone. Not for lack of trying from a couple sexy mammas, I might add," he said with a sly smile.

"Yeah, I remember... sort of."

"Shit, man, they wanted to bring you back here together, but you were havin' none of that. They left all hot and bothered. What's up? You find Jesus down there in the Bible belt or something?" he asked.

"Where exactly is *here*?" I asked.

"My place."

"Your place? Why didn't I crash at the Sanctuary?"

"Things were getting a little wild back there," Clutch said with a chuckle. "And you were hitting the bottle pretty fuckin' hard. Harder than I can ever remember seeing you hit it."

"It was a rough night. What can I say?"

"Yeah, well that rough night left you in rough shape, so I brought you back here. Besides, I didn't want to make you stay in a bunkhouse at the Sanctuary, so welcome to Casa de Clutch."

"Thanks brother, I appreciate it. What's this?" I asked, motioning towards the iPad.

"That is all the info I could find out about Viper and his crew. Once you brighten up a little, you and I are gonna ride out and pay him a little visit," he said.

"How are we gonna ride? I don't have a bike out here anymore," I asked.

"Apparently, Cutter took care of that," Clutch replied.

"What the fuck are you talking about?"

"Come see for yourself," he said, producing a set of keys from his kutte pocket, and tossing them to me.

"What the fuck are these?"

"They're keys, shithead. Come on," he said.

I grabbed the coffee and handed the iPad back to Clutch. "I still haven't agreed to help you."

"Yeah, yeah, yeah," he said, and I followed him out to the garage. Clutch hit the lights, and I could see his old shovelhead parked next to a brand-new Harley Davidson Fat Boy.

"You get a new bike?" I asked.

"Fuck, no! I could never replace Charlene," he exclaimed. "That one's yours. Grover and Socks brought it over this morning."

"Please tell me they didn't steal this for me?"

"No, you idiot, it's a gift from Cutter. There's a card around here somewhere, too."

"A card? What is this? A fuckin' Hallmark moment?"

"I dunno, man. After all the shit Cutter said last night, all fuckin' bets are off. Maybe he's goin' soft because he's dying."

"You don't even know the half of it," I muttered.

"What?"

"Nothing," I replied.

"Well, you can ask him yourself in twenty minutes."

"Why's that?" I asked.

"Because we're going to see him."

"Seriously?" I groaned.

"Yup. Cutter told me last night before I left that he wanted us at the Sanctuary by ten o'clock this morning. I let you sleep in as long as I could, but we've gotta go. You know how the Prez gets when we're late."

"You're killin' me, brother. I'm not fully functional yet. I haven't even finished my coffee."

In truth, I was going to need a lot more than coffee to clear my head. What the fuck was up with this bike? Why was I suddenly at the top of Santa Cutter's nice list? Was the bike really a gift, or was it some sort of bribe? Either way, I was parking it on Cutter's front lawn when I left, which would be very soon I hoped.

"Slam that coffee down or put it in a to-go cup, but we gotta go," Clutch said, and got on his bike.

I had to admit, even as fuzzy as I was, the Fat Boy looked deadly as hell. It was completely murdered out. Every piece that would normally be shiny chrome, was instead finished in flat black. I slugged down the remaining contents of the cup and grabbed the helmet sitting on top of the seat.

"You gonna be able to get that brain bucket over your swollen mug?" Clutch asked.

My head was pounding so hard from last night's partying, I'd momentarily forgotten about the mouse under my eye, and who'd given it to me.

"That's strange," I said, before pausing.

"What's that?"

"I don't remember one of the books I sent you while you were locked up being a joke book," I replied.

"Here's a joke for you. Knock, knock…"

"Who's there?"

"Go fuck yourself," he said, before putting his helmet on.

I laughed. "I look forward to your first stand-up special."

"Come on, let's see if you still remember your way around town," Clutch said, and fired up Charlene.

I put the key in the ignition and started the Fat Boy. The engine came to life with a roar, and my pace quickened as I revved the throttle.

Clutch hit the garage remote on his key fob, and we sped off toward the freeway entrance. I've always said that riding is the best cure for the common cold. No matter how shitty I might feel, the minute I hit the road, my mood always improves. The fact that I was riding a brand-new Harley equipped with a 114-cubic inch big twin engine certainly didn't hurt. I didn't know why Cutter had given it to me, but right now I was more than happy to see what this baby could do.

\* \* \*

*Cricket*

*Hold this pace until you reach that tree, then sprint for one minute before stopping again.*

I did as I'd instructed myself to do and ran at full speed up the inclined path. My burning lungs gladly took in the cool morning air as I counted backwards from sixty. Once I reached zero, I slowed my pace back down to a jog, once again starting the cycle.

This was how I managed my life in all things. I'd set a short-term goal, hold myself to achieving it, no matter the pain. Once I did, I'd set another, even larger goal. This process of 'progress makes perfect' made sense to me and I saw no reason to change my methods. Why would I? Everything in my life was going great. Well, most things were going great. Some things more than others, I suppose. But the point was, I had a plan for how my life was going to go and I saw no reason to deviate from that plan. I also had a plan for how I was going to erase whatever last night was, and it included running through Cedarwood Park until my legs were jelly.

This was my favorite weekend running spot in all of Portland. I loved the way the trees could change color from one day to the next. The peaceful serenity of the winding trails and the absence of reminders of modern life made it an almost magical place. The park was *just about* perfect. I say just about, because there was one thing I absolutely did not enjoy about these trails, and as I rounded the next turn, I was face to face with one. Or should I say face to snout? Whatever you call the front part of a horse's face… was right in front of me, and believe me when I tell you, I do not like horses.

"Ho, girl!" a beautiful blonde rider said, stopping her demon steed on a dime. "Sorry about that, we didn't see you there."

My heart raced as I felt the ground shake beneath me, the giant animal standing mere inches away. Okay, maybe it wasn't that close, but it sure felt like it too me.

"No, that's okay. That was my fault, really. I was lost in thought and... the corner... I...," I said backing up quickly, hoping I wouldn't spook Horsezilla into a killing frenzy.

"Her name's Tasha. She's super friendly. Would you like to pet her?" the rider asked, unaware that I'd rather wrestle a rattlesnake away from a rabid Pitbull than come near her (or any other) horse for that matter.

"Oh, no. No thank you, I'm... I... I don't care much for horses," I sputtered, still backing up from the fiery red beast. The rider looked at me as if I'd suddenly started speaking a foreign language in the middle of our conversation. "Sorry again, enjoy your ride," I said while giving them an extra wide berth to pass me. The blonde simply smiled, and with the slightest flick on the reins, she and her two-thousand-pound terror continued down the trail.

My fear of horses is deep-seated and comes from one of my earliest childhood memories. My parents took me to a petting zoo when I was little, and I remember loving the experience at first. I remember feeding goats from ice cream cones filled with little green pellets and laughing because the goats preferred to eat the cones. This, of course, caused the feed pellets to spill all over the ground for the chickens and bunnies to eat. I did this over and over, laughing harder and harder each time. My dad bought cone after cone, just to see me happy.

This was also one of the only items of video evidence my parents captured before Mom died. So, whether it's a memory from childhood, or a continuation of the movie playing in my mind, I'm not sure. But I know I was blissfully happy.

Until...

Mom thought it would be a good idea for us to stand in the sweltering sun to have my picture taken atop Jonah the Wonder Pony. Apparently, he'd been a big deal in Atlantic City in his prime. He was in one of those high dive-horse acts who'd long been retired from the big show.

Jonah now spent his days in petting zoos, wearing a

rhinestone saddle, posing for pictures at five bucks a pop. I didn't know if I was going to pass out from the heat or the anticipation, but by the time we got to the front of the line I was near delirious with joy and/or sunstroke. My father, holding my hand, led me ever so carefully up the steps to Jonah's photo area. Looking back, he was probably a hundred years old, but he was the most beautiful thing I'd ever seen. The pony bowed his head, and I reached out my tiny hand to pet him. This was the happiest moment I'd ever known. Right up until the moment he leaned forward, and bit me on the shoulder. I cried all the way to the doctor's office, where I received *many* shots, and then I cried all the way home. From that moment on, I could do without the equine species. No more ponies, and certainly no horses. I even avoided the zebra exhibit at the zoo just to be safe.

I reached my car, my run now over, and decided I needed some sister processing time, so I dialed Maisie.

"Well, hello, favorite sister-in-law on the planet," she said.

"I'm your only sister-in-law, but I'll take it."

She chuckled. "You sound out of breath. Did you just go for a run?"

"I did. And I nearly got killed."

"What?" she asked with a gasp. "Are you okay?"

"Homicidal horse."

"Bloody hell, Cricket, I thought you were serious," she admonished. "Horses aren't homicidal."

"This one was."

"Oh, really," she deadpanned.

I sighed. "He could have been. I don't know. Whatever… they're all monsters."

She laughed again. "You can have that argument with Poppy. She'll set you straight."

Poppy was obsessed with all things horse related, she even took lessons from my dear friend and landlord, Kim, and competed in every event she could register for. I would watch her on occasion, so long as the horses stayed in a fenced area, and I could keep my distance.

"Um, so, is Hatch at church?" I asked, trying to be sly.

"Yes," she said with a tone of suspicion.

"You want some company?"

"Of course, love. You know that you're welcome here anytime. You don't even need to ring first."

I smiled. "I know... I just wasn't sure if I wanted to make the drive, but I need some advice and I'd like to see you."

"I'll put the kettle on. See you in a few."

"Awesome. Bye." I hung up and climbed into my car.

I'd left work a little early to get my run in, so I was a little concerned about traffic over the I-5 bridge, but as I pulled onto the freeway, it looked like I had a smooth drive ahead.

I loved my apartment. It was super modern and had a view of the water, not to mention, Kim gave me the deal of the century, rent-wise.

But.

It wasn't at all close to my family. Technically, it was only about twenty minutes from Vancouver, Washington, but Portland traffic had become unbearable, so it was taking longer and longer to go anywhere.

This time, luckily, it took me fifteen minutes, so I felt a little pressure leave my shoulders as I used my key and let myself into their home. "I'm here," I called out, and locked the door again.

"Kitchen," Maisie called back.

Arriving in the kitchen, I grinned. Poppy's head was bent over a textbook, while Maisie stood at the island pouring water into a teapot. "What a perfect scene of domestic bliss."

Poppy rolled her eyes, standing so she could hug me. "You can do my algebra homework, then."

"That's way out of my mental league, sweetie. Sorry." I chuckled, giving her a squeeze before planting myself at the kitchen island.

"Mummy, I'm going to take a break, okay? I only have one more section and it's not due until Friday."

"Is the rest of your homework done?" Maisie asked.

"Yep."

"Off you go, then."

Poppy cleared her mess and left the room, hugging me again before disappearing.

"So, what's up, love?" Maisie asked.

"Minus."

She pulled a stool out and sat beside me. "Hmm. Yes, I've heard all about the mysterious Mr. Minus."

I grimaced. "Ergo, you've heard Hatch's version from the filter of way overprotective and nosy brother."

Maisie giggled. "Probably. Fortunately, I'm fluent in Hatchese and have gotten surprisingly good at figuring out what he's really on about."

"Hatchese?" I couldn't help but laugh.

"It's mostly a series of primitive grunts and growls. I suppose it's a bit like learning to speak Wookie. Now, tell me, love. What's wrong?"

"Everything's a mess, Maze."

"How so?"

I filled her in on mine and Minus's altercation, as I wasn't sure how much Hatch had told her from my freak out the night before.

"So, you hit him?"

I nodded. "Drew blood. A lot, I think."

"Goodness, that's quite impressive."

I sighed. "But now I'm feeling all guilty and shit."

"Why, love?"

"How much can I tell you without it getting back to Hatch?" I challenged.

"I share everything with him, Cricket, but if it's not relevant to your protection, or something that might piss him off, I'm open to keeping that between you and me."

"Like something that happened when I was a teenager that might make my brother fly into a homicidal horse-like rage?"

Maisie laughed. "Again, horses don't willingly commit murder... but yes, that."

"Minus was my first love. He was my first... everything, and as much as I try to tell myself that I've gotten over him, I don't think I ever have. I think he's the reason I've never been able to fully drop my guard in any relationship I've been in, and why I've never been able to picture myself staying with anyone long term."

"Sounds lonely," Maisie said, sweetly.

I've always been able to use my business pursuits as an excuse for not getting overly attached to any man, but maybe Minus has always been 'the one' in my mind."

"I take it Minus is quite handsome."

"No, sis, he's fuckin' hot. And he's amazing in bed." I gasped. "Sorry, that last part was supposed to be internal."

"It's been a long time since you've been together," Maisie said. "Maybe he's not as good in that department as you remember."

"Maybe." I laughed. "God, I want to find out, though. Especially now that he's got this southern twang thing going. So, so sexy."

"You *are* an adult now, love. You can be with him if you so desire."

I shook my head. "I'm not ready to go down that rabbit hole. I mean, not that he's offering, or anything. He totally hates me, and I'd like to keep it that way, because the second that man's dick is inside of me, I know two things: I'll want more, and I'll ignore some of his glaringly bad personality flaws."

"Well, I can relate to the wanting more," she said. "But I've never seen you explain away or excuse character flaws… with anyone."

"You've never seen me with Minus," I admitted. "He's my Achilles heel. My Kryptonite"

"Wow. Your brother didn't mention all of this."

"My brother doesn't *know* all of this." I grimaced. "Minus and I were together for almost a year, but we kept the depth of our relationship secret right up until the end. No one knew the whole story."

"Him leaving must have been tough for you."

I nodded, biting back tears. "One day he was here, the next he was gone, and I never heard from him again."

"What a bastard."

"That's what I thought back then, too. But, last night… he seemed confused."

"Confused, how?"

"Like he'd kind of been bamboozled by Cutter the same way I had. It was like none of this was his choice. Of course, I knew my brother didn't want us seeing each other, and that Cutter was angry at Minus, but I figured since he never reached out after he moved away, that he simply didn't care about us." I let out a frustrated groan. "I can't go there. If I give him any leeway emotionally, I'll let him back in."

Taking the subject off my overwhelming emotions, she asked, "Hatch told me Cutter wants Minus to take over the club?"

"No, he wants *us* to take over the club."

"Bloody hell," she breathed out.

"Exactly. I think he's gone a little insane. It's the dumbest idea on the planet."

"Yes, it's a bit out there. Plus, the Burning Saints are one-percenters. They're all criminals."

"I know," I rasped. "It's a shit show. The thought of Minus going to jail is just too much to deal with."

"You mean, you don't want him to do anything criminal that would *put* him in jail?"

"No. I mean, I don't want him to get caught."

"Whoa, love," Maisie said. "That deescalated quickly. I find it interesting that you were concerned about him going to jail… not that the club or his actions might be criminal."

"You've been married to a club member long enough to know that sometimes you have to bend the law. It's not as if the Dogs are pure as the driven snow."

"I hear you, Cricket, but your brother always does the right thing and would never choose violence to resolve matters. And the club's businesses are all legal, so I don't have to worry about him going to prison. If you feel that it's okay for Minus to flat-out break the law, it seems to me you'd be able to justify any red flags that might come up in a relationship with him. And I'm sure as hell your brother'll burn the

Burning Saints down if you get dragged into anything he doesn't approve of."

"Oh, I'm aware." I sighed. "God, this is so *hard*. I just wish I knew exactly where Minus has been and what he's been up to all this time."

"You know, there's a way you can find out all the information about Minus that you need," she said.

"Booker!" I exclaimed. Booker was the Dogs of Fire resident computer guru and finder of all things. "Yes, that's perfect. I can have him hack his DMV records, utility bills, credit card statements—"

"No, silly girl. You can *ring* Minus and ask him yourself."

"I don't have his cell phone number," I said, figuring that was enough to shut that idea down.

"Perhaps, that's where you could ask Booker for assistance."

"I could," I confirmed. "But Booker will tell Hatch if I ask for information."

"Oh, sweet, darling girl," she sang. "You don't ask Booker... you ask Dani."

I let that nugget of advice sink in. "You are a devious genius, Maisie. Has anyone ever told you that?"

"Lots of times." She grinned. "My work here is done."

"Babe?" my brother called.

"Just in time," I whispered.

"Kitchen," Maisie called.

"Is Cricket here?"

"Why don't you walk your nosy ass in here and find out," I retorted.

My brother strolled in, making his way to Maisie, kissing her sweetly, before leaning over and kissing my cheek. "You good?"

"I'm great. I was in the area," I lied.

He stared at me for a second (like he did when he didn't believe me) but didn't challenge me. I let out the breath I'd been holding.

"Well, I better head out," I said, and slid off my stool.

"Early meeting tomorrow."

"Thanks for dropping by," Maisie said.

I hugged them both, then walked out to my car, but I waited until I was out of their neighborhood before dialing Booker's wife, Dani. My brother had almost omniscient ways and I didn't want to chance him hearing our conversation.

# SIX

### BURNING SAINTS

*Minus*

THE MORNING'S RIDE back to the sanctuary was shorter than I'd like. The weather was perfect, traffic was light, and as much as I hated to admit it, Cutter's gift fit me like a glove. As brief as it was, the ride helped center me, to stop my mind from racing. As to what I was going to say to Cutter once we arrived, I had no idea. I wasn't as angry for being jerked around as I was last night, but my confusion about the situation was growing.

The parking lot was populated with the rides of those still sleeping it off inside. Many of the Saints crew were getting up there in years, but still partied like they were young men. This meant longer hangovers and shorter lifespans for many of them. No doubt, last night's battle of the livers had surely left its share of casualties on the field.

The property was littered with beer cans, food wrappers, and red plastic cups. For reasons unknown to me, the chapel had been made up with Christmas decorations, complete with a giant inflatable snowman and a plastic nativity set. The three wise men had been replaced with novelty inflatable sex dolls. They were all male models, with "realistic" chest hair, and each was wearing a Santa hat over his junk. The three of them lined up with their mouths open made them look as if they were saying, "Ho, Ho, Ho."

"What the baby Jesus happened after we left last night?" Clutch asked.

"I'm not sure we really want to know."

"Let's go find Cutter," Clutch said.

"If he's not stuck in the fuckin' chimney."

The inside of the chapel looked as if a bomb had gone off during the taping of the "Burning Saints Holiday Special." A very fresh-looking fir tree was propped up in the corner and decorated liberally with beer cans, bras, and panties. The tree looked as if it hadn't been cut down, but rather pulled out of the ground. Grown ass men were passed out with Christmas ornaments hung in their beards. Tinsel was draped over every imaginable surface. Where there wasn't tinsel, there was trash. Saints were strewn about the place, asleep on any chair, sofa, or available flat surface. "Christmas with the Devil" by Spinal Tap played on repeat in the background but did little to drown out the sound of twenty or more men snoring.

"What the fuck is that smell?" Clutch held a hand over his nose and mouth, as a sickening odor wafted my way, instantly making me want to hurl. The search for the smell's source led me to the kitchen, where I'd indeed found the scene of the crime.

The murder weapon. Eggnog.

To be more specific, some sort of biker eggnog. Cartons upon cartons of eggshells were stacked by the trash, next to empty milk and Bailey's bottles. There was also at least a half-dozen bottles of Jägermeister next to a giant punchbowl, that held the remainder of this wicked holiday concoction.

"What the fuck?" Clutch asked in horror. "How much of this shit did they make?"

"How much of it did they drink?" I asked, as another wave of the foul odor hit us.

"Oh, shit. How much did they puke up? We gotta get the fuck outta here, Minus. Let's find Cutter and split."

As we made our way back to Cutter's room, I prepared myself for the worst. I tapped gently on his door and was surprised to hear him respond instantly.

"Come on in," he answered brightly.

I entered to find Cutter fully alert and dressed for the streets. His beard was trimmed, his hair was slicked back, and although he was utilizing a silver-topped cane, he looked ten years younger than the man I'd seen last night.

"Minus, good morning. You okay? You've got a goofy look on your face."

"To be honest, I expected you to be wearing a Santa suit, face down in a puddle of whatever the fuck I saw in that punchbowl," I said, motioning toward the kitchen.

"Jägenogg. It's one of Warthog's holiday traditions."

"It smells like a fucking chemical weapon," I said. "No wonder you have cancer."

Cutter laughed. "I don't drink that shit! You think I'm crazy?"

"I guess that's why you're the last man standing today."

"The boys took the news hard last night, God bless 'em, and they drank hard to soften the blow."

"What's with Santa's workshop out there?"

Cutter smiled wide. "At some point last night, one of these kindhearted idiots realized that I might not make it to Christmas, so they brought Christmas to me, presents and all."

"Hey, speaking of presents," I began my protest. "About that Fat Boy—"

Cutter cut me off. "I was about to have Warthog drive me down to my favorite coffee place. Why don't you come with me, so we can talk?" He turned to Clutch. "Do me a favor, will ya? Help get these guys up and outta here. Get some recruits to help you. Minus and I'll be back in a while."

Clutch shot me a "what the fuck" look, and I shrugged back in response.

I followed Cutter out to the back lot, where Warthog was waiting by a white Town Car.

"Still got a thing for Lincolns, I see."

"Minus, the 1996 Town Car is the greatest American sedan ever built. Why would I ever want any other automobile?"

"How can I argue with such sound logic?" I replied.

"You seem a little more agreeable this morning. That's good, because we have a lot to talk about. Ride in the back with me."

I did as Cutter asked, and Warthog headed for Front Road, toward the Pearl District.

"Minus, you're a smart young man. You figured any of *this* out yet?" Cutter asked.

"Which part exactly are you talking about? There are so many fucking crazy things going on right now I can barely keep up. I'm still not even sure what happened last night, let alone why you'd want me to wear your patch."

"I'm not asking you to wear my patch. In fact, that's the absolute *last* thing I want."

"Then, what's all this bullshit talk about me running the club?"

"It's true that I want you to be the next club's president, but I want you to wear *your* patch and leave *your* mark. Look, I get that you're pissed off about me sending you to Savannah, but I had my reasons. Some of those reasons I'm ready to share with you, but first I need to know if you're with me or not."

"Cutter, how the fuck can I be with you when you don't even trust me?"

"You think I sent you away because I didn't trust you?"

"You certainly didn't trust me with Cricket!"

"What the fuck are you talking about?"

"The minute you found out that Cricket and I were serious, I was dead meat."

"Oh, shit! You think I sent you away because of Cricket?" He and Warthog burst into laughter. "I kept the two of you apart to keep the peace with the Dogs of Fire, which is very important to me, but do you think I actually care about who you're fucking?"

"You told me to never speak her name again and dangled me over the side of a fucking bridge!" I exclaimed.

"All beneficial in getting you out of town for sure, but I would've thought that you'd have figured out by now that your exile had nothing to do with Cricket."

"Then, why send me to Savannah at all?"

"The same reason I do anything. For the good of the club. For your good, too, as a matter of fuckin' fact."

"*My* good? How the fuck do you figure you were doin' me any favors?" I snapped.

Cutter smiled. "That's a nice little drawl you've got there for a city slicker. I bet everyone around here figures you picked it up in Savannah, but I suspect it's from spending all that time with Duke."

"What the fuck do you know about Duke?"

"Who do you think sent you to him? You know he had you pegged within five minutes of meeting you. Looks like he wasn't wrong."

"What the fuck are you talking about? Zaius sent me to Duke."

"Oh, did he? Really?" Cutter raised an eyebrow.

"And, what do you mean he had me pegged? When the fuck did you talk to Duke about me?"

"Minus, as usual, what you don't know could fill a fuckin' dump truck."

I hated to admit it, but Cutter had once again thrown me a curve ball that I was wholly unprepared for. As if I hadn't already been confused enough, my two lives, the one here, and the one in Savannah had suddenly collided.

"You know why I gave you the name Minus when I patched you in?" Cutter's eyes softened.

"You told me it was because I was dependable. That I

was good at making problems go away."

"That's all true, but it's horse shit. Has nothing to do with why I gave you that handle."

"Then, why?" I asked.

"When I found you and Nicky on the streets you looked like a pair of drowned cats. The both of you were skin and bones and headed for the pound to be put down. Right away, I could tell you were both tough and loyal, and those are probably the most important qualities I look for in a soldier, but in you I saw something even more valuable."

"What's that?"

"You're teachable. I could tell that almost immediately."

"What about Clutch?"

"Clutch is the kind of man you go to in a pinch, thus *his* name, but his instinct is to fight his way out of trouble. That's why he'll be a great Sergeant at Arms. You're smart. You use your mind. You read all those big ol' books and you actually understand them."

"So why call me Minus?"

"Because for a smart guy, you're a fuckin' moron. Within moments of realizing how smart you were, I thought to myself, 'this guy is *minus* a few in the wisdom department.' For a guy that's 'off the charts' intelligent, you can be fuckin' oblivious to what's going on right in front of you. I told Zaius to send you to the old man. To see if you had in you, what I thought you might."

"What's that?"

"Leadership potential. I see a leader inside of you, Minus. I always have. But I also see a fool. You see, it's not good enough to be smart. To lead, you also must be wise. You've always been loyal, brave, and a good earner, but sending you to Duke was the beginning of your education."

About one month after I'd arrived in Georgia, Zaius, the Savannah chapter president, sent me to a horse ranch run by a man named Duke and his wife, Pearl. I lived and worked on that ranch for six months, in which I remained completely isolated from everyone and everything I'd ever known. It was the most difficult thing I'd ever done, and it changed me. Duke was my mentor, and like Cutter, had become a father figure. Over the years, I'd grown even closer with him and Pearl, and worked the ranch whenever possible.

"Duke has never once mentioned that he knew you," I said.

"That's the way I wanted it. I knew if you knew it was my idea that you were at the ranch, you'd never listen to a word Duke said."

Cutter was right, but I said nothing.

"Look, Minus, you and I were never gonna see eye-to-eye back then, and as much as I liked you and some of your ideas, you were both a thorn in my side and a pain in my ass. You know how our business works. It's all based on the balance of power and the display of strength. If we don't show a united front, the Saints will appear weak, and the moment we appear weak, we're done for."

The Burning Saints were in the protection business. The largest portion of the club's income was collected from businesses and private citizens who hired us for security purposes. Not all these businesses and individuals were exactly on the up-and-up, and/or had security needs that extended the scope of the law, so they'd call us. We were the big scary guys that chased other big scary guys away, and if they couldn't be chased, we were prepared to take things to the next level. Sometimes that meant payoffs, and sometimes that meant beat-downs. As much as I loved my club, and would lay my life down for my brothers, I was never thrilled about the way we earned, and from the day I was patched in I started making my thoughts and feelings known. Being just a pup, this was not a smart move on my part, and Cutter yanked my leash relentlessly, so I was both surprised, and intrigued at what he'd just said.

"What do you mean? Are you saying you liked some of my ideas? All you did was shoot me down back then."

"Times have changed," Cutter said. "Look, you were right when you'd spout off about our way of doing things ending, but how the fuck did you expect me to respond? C'mon man. You can't yell *meteor* to a bunch of dinosaurs and expect much of a reaction."

"I understand that now," I said.

"I bet you do. In fact, I'm betting everything on it," he replied. "I sent you to Savannah to become your own man, and I sent you to Duke because I knew he'd be able to teach you all the shit you couldn't learn from me. You've got a good heart, Minus, and I know you've always cared about this club."

"You and the Saints saved my life and I never forgot that, even when I hated you."

"Boy, I figured you'd be pissed when I sent you away, but if I'd known that a girl was involved..." He let out a low slow whistle. "Now I get why you came in white-hot last night. I'm sorry, Minus. I honestly didn't know she meant that much to you back then."

"Yeah, well, none of that matters now. She hates my guts and I've got a new scar to remind me." I pointed at my face. "Plus, her dickhead Fire Dog brother is probably gonna show up wanting to start shit with me."

"Well, I hope not, because I was kind of counting on you being able to work with him on some things," Cutter said.

"What? You want me to work with Hatch?"

"No, I want you to work with *all* the Dogs of Fire. More specifically, you and my niece. She's the key to this whole thing working."

"What's your deal with Cricket? What exactly are you envisioning here? For us to rule the land together as young king and queen? Which brings up my next point. I'm only thirty-one years old. All you do is tell me how much I don't know and point out my lack of wisdom. Why choose my young, dumb ass?"

"The truth is, I wasn't much older or smarter than you when I started this club, so I have the utmost faith in my choice. In fact, your age and differing views are strong reasons as to why I want you to wear the President's patch."

"So how does Cricket factor into all of this?"

"Not only am I hoping she can be the bridge to the Dogs of Fire, she's also a marketing and branding whiz. I've been keeping track of her career this entire time. She's got achievements and accolades up the wazoo and has been doing great work at Mann Industries."

"And you want her to help you run a motorcycle club full of criminals and leg breakers?"

"No. I want you to work with her to help the Burning Saints grow and change into something new."

"You want to re-brand a one-percenter motorcycle club."

"By Jove, Warthog, I believe he's got it," he sang out.

\* \* \*

*Cricket*

I told myself over and over that what I was doing wasn't stalking. I reminded myself that I had legitimate reasons to call Minus. I reasoned with myself that it wasn't at all creepy or wrong that I'd asked Dani, one of the sweetest women on the planet, to convince her hacker husband to commit a federal crime and keep it secret from my brother, one of his closest friends.

"This is Minus."

His voice sent a shock to my center that left me momentarily speechless.

"Hello? Who is this?"

"Uh…hi, it's…it's me…uh, Cricket…Cricket Wallace."

"As opposed to all the other Crickets I know?" he retorted.

I could hear him smiling over the phone and my face burned with embarrassment. I was glad he couldn't see me right now, as I'm sure my cheeks were bright red.

"How did you get this number?" he asked.

Ohmigod, what could I say? I couldn't possibly tell him the truth, and yet that's exactly what I did. "A hacker," I razzed.

"*You* know a hacker? Holy shit." He laughed, and my stomach dropped again.

I thought he'd be angry, but instead he seemed to enjoy this bit of information.

"Yes, I know a hacker," I replied, defensively. "For your information, he's really good at... hacking."

"Wow, you must really want to talk. You know, there were probably easier ways to get my number than violating F.C.C. laws... like through your uncle Cutter."

I felt like an idiot. I had to pull myself together. I could not let Minus get the upper hand. I was calling with questions and I wanted answers.

"Yes, I'm aware of that, but I'm not speaking to my uncle. In fact, I'm not really speaking to you, for that matter. I'm not calling for social reasons.

"No?"

"I'm calling because I want some answers. No, I *deserve* answers, and I'm not hanging up until I get them."

"Answers, huh?"

"Yes. I want to know exactly why you left, where you've been, and I don't want to hear anything about the secrecy of club business or not understanding your world." I squared my shoulders, even though he couldn't see me. "I won't stand for any bullshit answers."

"Okay," he replied.

"Okay? What do you mean, okay?"

"I mean, okay. I'll tell you everything you want to know, but not over the phone. How 'bout we meet for breakfast tomorrow morning around eleven o' clock, and we can talk face-to-face."

"That's a little late for breakfast, Jase. I can't just blow off work to meet you."

He chuckled. "Fair enough. How 'bout tonight at my hotel then?"

"A night in your hotel room isn't exactly what I had in mind," I replied, with a shudder.

The thought of spending the night with him did funny things to my girly bits.

"But you're thinkin' about it now, aren't you?" he whispered.

"Stop it."

"C'mon, you used to love it when I'd talk dirty to you

and make you blush. I bet your cheeks are already rosy."

*More like fire engine red.*

"Stop it, Jase. I mean it."

"Alright, alright. What I meant to say was Cutter booked me a suite at a nice hotel, and the word is they've got a nice restaurant inside. We could have dinner."

I paused.

"Look," he said, then sighed. "I was actually going to call you a little later. I wanted to apologize for what I said last night, but I wanted to give you some time to cool off first. I'm glad I'll have the chance to look you in the eyes when I tell you how sorry I am."

*Oh jeez, I'm gonna need new panties.*

"Okay."

"How about you swing by my hotel after work? We can eat and talk… in public. Whatever you want," he said.

"I can't tonight."

"Tomorrow night," he said. "I'll text you the address… unless, of course, you had your hacker find out where I'm staying."

"No. I didn't," I said.

"I just sent it to you, so it's on your phone now. I'll see you tomorrow night, okay?"

"See you then," was all I could manage to squeak out, then hung up.

# SEVEN

*Minus*

I HUNG UP with Cricket just as Clutch entered the shop. Perfect timing. The last thing I needed was for him to hear me talking to her. I hated that Clutch was right, but he was. I was far from over Cricket Wallace.

"Interrupting anything important?" Clutch asked as he approached.

"No, just checkin' on some things back in Savannah," I lied. "I came back here for a little peace and quiet."

"Don't blame you. The clean-up crew sounds more like a demolition crew in there," he said motioning to the main building.

"I can't believe it!" Grover shouted. "I finally fuckin' found Waldo."

He bounded into the shop, followed closely by Ropes and Sweet Pea.

"Jesus, man. Where the fuck you been?" Grover asked. "We barely laid eyes on you last night."

"Oh, I saw him," Ropes said. "He was on the dance floor with two hotties. I'll tell you what, our boy has picked up some serious moves out there in Savannah."

"No wonder you disappeared. You were buried under a pile of titties all night," Grover said.

"He crashed at my place last night. And from the looks of this place, it was a good thing we left early," Clutch said.

"Good ol' Minus. Always the responsible one," Ropes said.

"*Responsible?* What the hell are you smokin'?" I asked.

"What's not to understand? You've always been a Boy Scout."

"The fuck are you talking about?" I asked, stunned by Ropes's characterization of me. However, I could tell by their expressions, that the others agreed with him. "You're all out of your minds. How do you figure I'm a Boy Scout?"

"Are you serious?" Clutch asked. "Back in the day, you toed the line tighter than anyone."

"Cutter ran me out on a fucking rail," I protested.

"Yeah, but before that you were the golden boy of our crew," Clutch said.

"Y'all's memory is a tad bit different from mine."

"Okay, cowboy. How 'bout you tell us a campfire story," Clutch said in a mock southern drawl. "A tale from the old days. Back when the outlaw Minus the Kid would ride into town and raise hell."

"I have just as much blood on my hands as you do," I said coolly.

Sweet Pea, a man of few words, finally spoke, "But way more shit on your boots."

It felt good busting balls with my crew again, and to hear their laughter. Of course, we all kept up via text and the occasional email, but that's no substitute for hanging out face to face. Plus, bikers aren't widely known as the best pen pals.

"Seriously, though. How do you knuckleheads figure I was anywhere close to a straight arrow?" I continued my protest. "I was constantly on the club's shit list. Remember when I put that fuckin' dent in the rear fender of Elwood's bike? I had to do the repairs myself, plus work off the cost."

The four stooges looked at each other before breaking into a howling fit of laughter.

"What the fuck is so funny?" I demanded. "Elwood was mad as hell at me."

"Minus," Clutch said, catching his breath. "Do you really *not* remember?"

"Remember what?" I asked.

"Man, Grover dented Elwood's bike and you took the rap for it."

"The hell I did," I shot back. "I remember how it happened. The five of us were fuckin' off, right here in the shop. Elwood's Indian was up on the lift and we were tossing a wrench back and forth between us."

"Wrench Ball," Sweet Pea said, reminding me of the idiotic game we'd invented to pass time back in the day. As younger members, we were always assigned to the Sanctuary's grunt work. Including shit jobs like cleaning the shop at two o' clock in the morning. One of these late nights, after many beers and sleep deprivation, the idea of chucking a twelve-inch adjustable wrench at high speeds at one another sounded like the perfect cure for boredom. Thus, the invention of Wrench Ball and the cause of the dent in question.

"Right, we were playing Wrench Ball," I continued. "I threw the wrench and it hit Elwood's bike. He found out and I got busted. End of story."

"Story, my ass. That's a fuckin' fairy tale my friend," Clutch said. The others stood smiling. "Grover threw the wrench and you ducked. The wrench hit Elwood's bike and you took the blame because Grover was already rocking two strikes. If he fucked up again, he'd have been demoted back to prospect."

"Then kicked out if I screwed up again," Grover said.

"Holy shit," I said, stunned that I'd forgotten all about that.

"You saved my ass, Minus," Grover said.

"Forget it, man. Obviously, I did," I said with a chuckle.

"That's because you bleed Boy Scout khaki," Clutch said.

"I'm gonna make you bleed, motherfucker. Where's that wrench?" I asked, looking around.

"So, what's the deal? You planning on sticking around town for a while?" Ropes asked.

"Your guess is as good as mine. I'm not even sure what time zone I'm in right now," I said, hoping he wouldn't press any further. These guys were still my crew and I didn't want to lie to them. On the other hand, I truly had no idea what was going to shake out through all this and saw no reason to report on an incomplete story. I closed the topic with, "I guess we'll all have to wait and see what the Prez wants."

"Well, it's nice to have you back, brother," Ropes said.

"It's great to see you and Pea. You, too, Grover," I said.

"Hey." Clutch slugged my arm. "What about me?"

"I don't need a place to stay tonight, so I can tell you to go fuck yourself."

"You must be working on earning your dickhead badge," he replied.

"Would that make him a Chub Scout?" Sweet Pea asked to laughter all around.

* * *

*Cricket*

I walked into my home office and powered up my laptop. I had no idea what I was getting myself into with Minus and I was freaked.

And, admittedly, a little turned on.

Sighing, I faced the window and watched the boats on the Willamette. My condo was close to my office, but I loved that I had two different views of the river every day. It was cold, but the water was still, so a few brave boaters had ventured out. I kind of wished I was out there with them. Or with Jase.

"You ready?" Jase asked, picking me up from Fred Meyer. I'd been working at the supermarket since I was sixteen, and the money was helping to put me through school. I was twenty-one and ready to take on the world.

"I don't know," I admitted, gripping his jacket. "You haven't told me what we're doing."

"It's gonna involve you naked and me licking every inch of your body."

I shivered, biting my lip. "How exactly is that going to happen?"

"Come on. I'll show you."

He kissed me gently, then led me to his bike, handing me a helmet and a leather jacket. I climbed on and wrapped my arms around him, tight, wanting to stay like this forever.

Pulling up to a hotel overlooking the Columbia River, we removed our helmets and Jase took my hand, leading me inside. We didn't speak to anyone, we just made our way to the elevators and rode up to the eighth floor.

"You rented a hotel room?"

"Nothin' gets by you, baby," he retorted.

I rolled my eyes. "Why did you rent a hotel room, Jase?"

He unlocked the door and pushed me gently inside. "Because I'm gonna fuck you 'til you scream where no one will bother us."

I dropped my helmet and made a run at him so hard, he almost fell over. He didn't because he was four times my size, but he laughed as he carried me to the bed and dropped me gently on it. "Where do you want me to start?"

"Where do you think, big man?" I sassed.

He grinned, unzipping my jeans and tugging them down my legs, panties and all, and burying his face between my legs.

I let out a quiet mew as I wove my fingers into his hair. "Jase," I whispered.

"Yeah, baby."

"I want to suck you off."

"I'm not done."

I tugged on his hair. "I don't care. I need it."

He raised his head. "Need it?"

I nodded. "Need it," I pressed.

He pushed to his feet and settled his fists on his hips. "Have at it, baby. But I want you naked when you do it."

I scrambled off the bed, tearing at the rest of my clothes, then kneeling before him. He'd undressed as well, standing before me in all his naked glory.

"I don't think I'm ever going to get sick of staring at your dick, Jase," I admitted, running my tongue along the bottom, then drawing the tip into my mouth.

"Don't think I'm gonna get sick of you blowin' me, Cricket."

I smiled, hard to do when you had a giant dick in your mouth, then I took him deeper, cupping his balls with one hand while I worked his cock with my other. I licked the pre-cum from the tip, then slid him all the way to the back of my throat, moaning as he grew harder. God, I loved every delicious inch of him.

"That's good, baby," he rasped, stroking my cheek.

"I'm not—"

"Gonna fuck you hard now," he said, sliding his hands under my arms and pulling me gently to my feet. "You're not gonna give me any fuckin' grief about it, either." Turning me to face the bed, he smacked my ass. "On your knees."

I felt my pussy flood as I positioned myself on all-fours, and then he was sliding into me and I lost all ability to think. He slammed into me—

My phone pealed in the silence and I jumped slightly as I was pulled out of my erotic daydream.

"This is Cricket."

"Miss Wallace, you have a delivery. Would you like Trevor to bring it up?"

"Oh, Frank, yes, that would be great. Thank you."

"Very good."

Our security guard delivered my package and I couldn't stop a groan when the newest version of a popular vibrator sat in the box. Well, this was my life, and at least my night wouldn't be a total loss.

# EIGHT

## BURNING SAINTS

*Minus*

**F**ORCING MYSELF TO compartmentalize my emotions surrounding Cricket and my chance to be with her alone tomorrow night, I followed Clutch to our destination. We pulled up to the Nine Ball just after ten o' clock and the place was already looking pretty lively. Bikes, low riders, and vintage custom trucks filled the parking lot. The Saints, The Apex Predators, and the older clubs in town still held sway, but according to Clutch, Los Psychos, the area's newest club, had recently gained in numbers significantly, and all but taken over this, and several other spots.

"Holy shit! Look at this place," Clutch said as we approached the bar's entrance.

"I seem to recall it was in serious need of work when we

were last here," I said.

"Word on the street is, when Los Psychos bought the place, they dumped some serious cash into it," Clutch replied.

"It looks like a fucking Dave and Busters threw up on Leo's place."

We made our way inside and I noticed the beat-to-shit wooden floors had been replaced by polished, tinted concrete. The original planks had no doubt been sold as reclaimed lumber to some trendy condo builder in the Pearl district. Half of the pool tables were gone, as were all the vintage pinball machines. The sawdust and peanut shells on the floor were gone too, likely due to some city ordinance about fucking allergies. The music, geared toward teenaged girls, was pumping in synch with a blinding light show. Had most of the guys in the place not been wearing kuttes, you'd never know this was still a biker bar.

"What the fuck happened to this place?" Clutch shouted. "Leo's gotta be rolling over in his grave!"

"Leo's not dead, Clutch."

"Yeah, but still. He should dig his own grave, lie down, and fucking roll around in it," Clutch growled out. "Can you believe this shit?"

As dramatic as he was being, he wasn't wrong. 'Our kind' was running out of sacred spaces. Places where we could be ourselves. The world around us was changing rapidly, and much like the gunfighters and outlaws of the wild west, bikers would no longer be tolerated by polite society.

"Let's go grab a quieter place to sit down and scope the place out," I said.

I saw a table located in the perfect spot for our purposes. We'd have our backs to a wall, and a clear line of sight from the pool tables to the front entrance. From that table, we could casually scan the room without attracting attention.

The table was currently being occupied by two of tonight's few non-biker patrons, a beautiful young, raven haired woman, and a nervous looking young man. They looked more suited for a day of apple picking than hanging out here. Neither of them could have been a day older than twenty-two. These young folks were most certainly not in the right place.

"Wait here a sec," I said to Clutch, and walked over to their table. "Good evening, y'all," I said, smiling down at the young lovers. "I couldn't help but notice the two of you sitting here and I thought I'd come over to lend some assistance."

"Oh, okay," the young man said. "That would be great, because no one has come over to take our drink orders or anything."

I laughed. "No, man, I'm not here on behalf of the wait staff, I'm here to ask you to look around the room for a moment."

"Why...Why is that?" he asked nervously.

"Well, you see, I'm thinking no one's been by to take your order, because, despite the décor and this horrible music, this isn't quite the place for nice young people such as yourselves," I said. "Go ahead, look around this place. You notice anything all these folks have in common?"

"I... we... I just...," he sputtered.

"They're all bikers. That's right..."

"Ch... Chad."

"It's okay, don't worry, Chad, I'm not here to give you any trouble. In fact, I'm here to save your evening, and possibly your life."

Ch... Chad and his companion stared up at me in stunned silence.

"Now, I'm gonna guess you two are on a date. Am I right?"

"Yes," Chad said as the young lady nodded vigorously.

"First date?" I asked, grinning wide.

"S... second," Chad replied.

"Ahhh, that makes sense," I said. "The first date went well, but you were afraid you were a little too timid and wanted to show her your 'bad boy' side, so you brought her here to show how tough you are. Your college buddies probably told you about this pool hall where bikers hung out and serves cheap, watered-down drinks. Am I right, Chad?"

He swallowed in response.

I pulled out a hundred-dollar bill from my wallet, placed it on the table, and motioned towards Clutch. "See that guy standin' over there?"

Chad nodded.

"That ugly son of a bitch is my best friend, and this here is his favorite table. So, I'm gonna make you two a deal. I'll give you a hundred dollars for this table. You can use the cash to take your date some place nice. Go somewhere you can talk and get to know each other. Come on Chad, you can't have a nice conversation in a place like this. All you can get in here is hepatitis or stabbed."

Chad took the bill and without another word the couple, hand in hand, beat it for the door.

"Ah, young love," Clutch said smiling as he joined me at the table.

"Those two are lucky the night is still young. They would have had their bones picked clean before too long."

No sooner had the two lovebirds flown the nest than a pretty, older, heavily tattooed woman appeared to take our drink orders. She was dressed to the nines in 'pinup girl' attire, and I recognized her as a waitress from back in the day.

"You were around when Leo owned the place weren't you?" I asked.

"That's right. Sally Anne. It's been a while, Minus, nice to see you."

"Wow, you've got a good memory," I said, stunned she remembered me, let alone my name.

"It's an occupational skill I've developed after doing this for way too long. Plus, I never forget a pretty face," she said with a wink and a smile. "Although, it looks like someone recently tried to make you not-so-pretty." She motioned to the cut below my eye. "Now, what can I get you, besides an ice pack? A couple of beers, something harder perhaps"

"You can start by telling me what the fuck happened to this place," I said. "Where are the pool tables?"

"You can thank Mister Viper for all this. He's turned the

Nine Ball into his own personal Hooters," she replied. "Members from some clubs still come here to do a little business, or get shit-faced, but it's nothing like the old days."

"What's with the fuckin' disco lights and the sound system?" Clutch asked.

"All this is for the pole posse."

"The *what*?"

"Los Psychos hang out with the strippers who work the clubs they run. The girls love this bubblegum shit. This place is turning into a nightclub piece by piece. Look around fellas. The whole neighborhood has changed. All the old bars have either been revamped to attract a younger crowd or sold to build more condos. It's all beards, pork pie hats, and fuckin' micro brews everywhere you go."

"How does the old clientele feel about the hipster invasion?" I asked.

"What do you think? There are at least two fights a week in here, and that's just the strippers. I sweep up bloody clumps of hair weave every night at closing time."

"Why doesn't Viper change the place back to the way it was? Give all the MCs a place to hang and keep the peace."

"I don't think he's interested in keeping the peace, or in bikes for that matter. I think the only thing Viper is interested in is himself. He acts like he's some sort of business tycoon or something, but he's nothing but a pimp."

"Sounds like a charming guy," Clutch said.

"Don't get me wrong. It would be really easy to mistake him as some sort of joke, but the dude is scary."

"Scary, how?" I asked.

"I'm not really comfortable talking about this around here, but just be careful is all. If you'd heard or seen some of the things I have, you'd listen to what I'm saying."

"Is he around?" Clutch asked.

"I haven't seen him, but my shift just stared. He usually shows up around two in the morning with his rent-a-harem," she replied.

I turned to Clutch. "Whatta you say we take off then. We can come back later when Viper's around."

He nodded.

"Thanks for the information, Sally Anne," I said, pulling out another crisp hundred and placing it on her tray. "I think we'll come back a little later for those beers."

"I'll keep 'em cold for ya," she said with a smile.

Clutch and I turned and headed for the exit.

"Jesus, Minus, you're passing out Benjamins like they're candy. You win the lottery or something?"

"I'll be sure to put it all in my expense report. I'm guessin' Cutter will be more than happy to reimburse me once we find his money."

"You know, you still haven't told me exactly how it is you two made up. Last night you wanted to shove Red Dog's staff up Cutter's ass, and today you're ready to tear up sacred ground to get his money back. What gives?"

"I promise I'll fill you in on all the details as soon as I can. I need you to trust me for now and follow my lead."

Clutch stopped and turned to face me. "You never have to ask me to trust you. I'll always have your back."

"Thanks, man. Now, let's get the hell outta here. I'm gettin' a headache from this music."

We had almost reached the door when a giant Los Psychos member stepped in front of us, blocking our path. Neither Clutch nor I are small men, by any stretch, so believe me when I say this guy was huge. Mexican Hulk huge.

"Whoa, hey there," Clutch exclaimed, backing up a step. "Is there something we can do... for the *three* of you?"

"Viper is curious about the two Saints in his club," our living roadblock replied coolly.

"It's always flattering to know when people are thinking about you," Clutch said. "Don't you think so, Minus?"

"Indeed, it is. What was this gentleman's name again?"

"Don't get cute. You know exactly who Viper is."

"Oh, *Viiiper.*" Clutch snapped his fingers in mock remembrance. "Yeah, yeah. We heard of him. Sorry, the music is very loud in here, I couldn't hear you very well. I coulda sworn you said *douchebag.*"

Apparently Mexican Hulk doesn't turn green and smash

things when he's angry. He turns red and reaches for a gun in his waistband.

"Okay, fellas," I said, attempting to deescalate things. "No need to make a mess in such a... *charming* place. What does Viper want?"

"He wants to see both you guys right now," he grunted.

"He's *here*?" I asked.

"He's in the back, in his office. It's a private party. Let's go."

I nodded, and he escorted us down a narrow hallway which led to a room marked, "The Boss." As much as I didn't like this gorilla giving us orders, or not knowing what we were walking into, I figured if we were here to find out about Viper, meeting the man himself would be a good way to start. If we made it out of the meeting alive.

The office door was open, and as we approached, I could see the room was filled with at least a half-dozen Los Psychos members. They were standing in a circle, surrounding another man, who was down on his knees. I could hear angry, muffled voices, but couldn't make out what they were saying. What words I could make out were in Spanish, which didn't particularly help me as I barely spoke a lick of it. One word I did recognize was "no," which was now being yelled repeatedly, followed by screams of pain, then an unsettling silence.

Moments later, several men filed out carrying a wadded up, blue plastic tarp. After that, two Los Psychos members assisted the "man in the middle" past us, down the hallway. He was bound at the wrists and needed assistance from both men to stay upright. He was shirtless, and I could see club tats all over his chest and arms. One of his handlers held a bar towel to his back, which was soaked in blood. This guy had clearly been worked over and was in rough shape.

"Let's go," our oversized escort said, and he motioned us inside.

The office's decor, like the rest of the pool hall was over the top and ultra-modern. The walls were adorned with framed movie posters of Scarface and the Fast and the Furious, along with murals of Che Guevara, and Pancho Villa.

Only one person now occupied the office. A man in a purple suit, standing in front of an oversized mahogany desk. He was wiping blood off a large bowie knife. On the desk sat a brass name plate that read Viper – Chief Executive Officer.

"Gentlemen, please come in," he said, before setting the knife down and coming over to shake our hands. "I'm sorry about all the mess and the noise. We had a bit of a housekeeping problem, but it's all cleared up now."

Viper was young, handsome, and looked nothing like any MC president I'd ever seen. Hell, he didn't look like any kind of biker I'd ever seen. He looked more like a telenovela star, playing the role of a drug lord. His jet-black hair was slicked back, and he spoke with a thick Mexican accent.

"My name is Viper, and you've met my assistant, Crush," he said in a velvety smooth tone, motioning toward Mexican Hulk, which I was now fully convinced was a far better club name.

"Charmed, I'm fuckin' sure," I said.

"I wanted to welcome you both to my nightclub. It's a bit of a…work in progress, but I have big plans for the place."

"Nightclub?" I asked. "Last time I was here, this place was a pool hall… for bikers."

"Like I said, the place is in a… *transitional* phase. When it's complete, the Nine Ball will have a little something for everyone. We still hope to cater to the old clientele's needs while expanding toward the future, which is precisely why I wanted to talk with you two gentlemen tonight."

"I think you might have us confused with someone else. You keep calling us gentlemen, and that's not really our deal," Clutch said.

"Oh?"

"Yeah. You see, we came here tonight to have a few beers and shoot some pool—"

"But you two were leaving so soon?"

"I was getting a headache," I cut in.

"I'm sorry to hear that," Viper said. "Can I get anything for you?"

"Nah, I'll be alright once I get outta here. I think the combination of shitty music, bright lights, and the stench of Drakkar Noir mixed with stripper cooz doesn't agree with m—"

"You, I recognize from around town," Viper interrupted, pointing at Clutch before turning his attention back to me. "But you, I don't know."

"Well, my name is Minus, and I'm a Sagittarius. I enjoy long walks on the beach, going to the theater, and knowing what the fuck is going on around here."

"You are funny guys. You two should do a podcast or something. Don't you think so, Crush?"

Mexican Hulk nodded but remained expressionless.

Viper continued, "I have a great sense of humor, too, but I also know when to be serious. I wonder if you gentlemen know when it's time to get serious?"

Clutch puffed his chest out. "Oh, I can be serious as a fucking heart-attack, muchacho."

"What my associate Mr. Clutch means is, we can talk business, if business is the topic of discussion."

Viper smiled. "I'm glad to hear that, because I wasn't sure if what you saw earlier impressed upon you just how serious of a man I can be."

"And exactly what was it that we were meant to have seen?" I asked.

"That was a de-patching party," Viper said. "Do either of you gentlemen speak Spanish?"

"No comprendo, friend-o," Clutch replied.

I cut in. "Aw, man. That was a missed opportunity right there. You know amigo is Spanish for friend, right?" I asked Clutch.

"So?"

"So…you could have said, "No comprendo, amigo," and it still would have rhymed."

"As I was saying," Viper said, clearly irritated. "That man's name is *Loro*, which means parrot in Spanish. He's called that because of his many colorful tattoos. Little did I know, just like a fucking parrot, he had a habit of repeating things that were told to him. So, tonight I removed some of his feathers, one-by-one, and I'll continue to do so until every trace of my club is gone from his worthless body." He shrugged. "It might take days. Loro has a lot of feathers."

"So, what's your little tattoo removal service got to do with us?" I asked.

"Apparently one of the people Loro flapped his beak to on a regular basis was a garage owner named Phil Blondino."

"So?"

"So, Mr. Minus—"

"Just Minus," I said.

"And why do they call you that?"

"Because I'm good at subtraction."

"Interesting that you should say that, because shortly after Loro last spoke with Phil, two members of the Burning Saints visited him."

"So, what?"

"Well, since then no one has heard from Phil, or been able to locate him. Now two Burning Saints show up in my club. Maybe the same two Burning Saints for all I know."

"So, are we putting that information in the funny or the serious column?" I asked, remaining unfazed.

Viper's lips formed a slight smile, but his eyes burned with anger. "I have to apologize. Clearly, I didn't quite make the impression on you gentlemen that I had intended."

"Now, don't be too sure about that," I said. "If your intention was to show us that you're a psychopath that mutilates his own people due to his own personal fuckups, then let me assure you, message received. Wouldn't you say, Clutch?"

"Roger, 10-4. I read ya loud and clear, good buddy." Clutch turned to me and smiled. "Hey, remember when we were little kids and we saw Smokey and the Bandit on TV, and for like a month we were obsessed with being truckers?"

"We drove the nuns crazy practicing CB slang—"

"Clearly, you don't understand what's happening here," Viper said, raising his voice.

"I'm pretty sure it's *you* that doesn't quite get the picture here, amigo" I said. "The Nine Ball may be your place now, *not that I'd brag about that*, but the Saints will burn it down with you and all your crew inside of it, if you so much as touch us. You don't have the numbers or the muscle to start a war with us, so you're gonna wanna back the fuck off."

Viper seethed but said nothing. He knew I was right.

I continued. "As for business, the only thing we came to talk about involves two duffle bags containing three million dollars in cash. That money belongs to Cutter and the Burning Saints. We have information that tells us you may have come across this money in error. If that's the case, we want it back by noon tomorrow. We will, of course, be happy to provide you with a finder's fee once the money is retuned in full."

"And, if your information is incorrect and I don't have your club's money?"

"Then Cutter would greatly appreciate you locating it and retrieving it from those that do. If you deliver it to him by noon, the aforementioned finder's fee still applies."

"I see," Viper said, once again smiling. "And, what if I didn't come across your money in error, as you said, but instead willfully took it from the Burning Saints?"

"Then, you'd be one dumbass motherfucker," Clutch said, his fists balled at his sides.

"Perhaps," Viper hissed. "But what if I, theoretically of course, had stolen the money for a very good reason?"

I took one step toward Viper and before I could get closer Crush pulled his gun, aiming it at my chest. I casually showed him my hands and backed up. One single step.

"That's enough, Crush, put that gun away. These gentlemen and I are only talking. *Hypothetically* of course."

"You see, *Mister* Viper, that's where you're dead wrong," I said. "We're very much speaking in real terms about real money, and if you keep jerking me around, you're gonna have a *real* fucking problem."

"Then let me be perfectly clear with you, *Amigo*. I not only took Cutter's money…I've already spent it."

"Is that a fact?"
"Yes." Viper smiled wide. "Just now, in fact."
"On what, exactly?" I asked.
"Your full, undivided attention."

# NINE

*Minus*

**I** WAS THANKFUL to find the hotel gym was open twenty-four hours a day. It was just after three a.m. and I was still wired from the meeting with Viper. Having a gun pulled on you tends to cause a bit of an adrenaline spike. I was going to need to work off some of this energy if I was going to get any sleep at all. I put my earbuds in, turned the treadmill speed up, and tried to clear my head of all things club related. The treadmill faced a glass wall overlooking the Portland cityscape. I was the only hotel guest in the gym, so I'd left all the room lights off and ran in the soft glow of the city lights.

In truth, the only physical activity I wanted to be doing involved Cricket. In fact, I wanted to do just about every physical activity possible with her. Time had not lessened my desire for her. I'd been able to stow my feelings away while I was gone, but they'd never died. It's not like I sat around pining for her but living a somewhat isolated life kept me from ever having anything close to a relationship. I certainly never met anyone like her while living in Savannah.

As my pace matched the rhythm of the music, my thoughts began to drift, and focused solely on Cricket.

*"You sure, Cricket?" I asked, her soft body pressed against mine in my room at the compound.*

*"Are you?" she challenged, cupping my dick over my jeans. "You're the one who seems all squirrelly about it."*

*"Fuck," I rasped.*

*She ran her tongue over my pulse as she slid her hand under the waistband of my jeans and down my already rock-hard cock. "I want all of this."*

*I nodded, kissing her and sliding my tongue deep in her mouth. This was our third time sleeping together, and she'd begged me to go ungloved. I'd never fucked anyone without a condom, but Cricket wasn't just anyone and I wanted it more than I was willing to admit out loud.*

*"Your brother'll fuckin' kill me."*

*"My brother isn't going to know anything about it," she countered, meeting my eyes. "I love you, Jase. You said you loved me back. Were you lying?"*

*"No fuckin' way."*

*She smiled, the dimple on her right cheek sinking in and I couldn't stop myself from running my thumb over it.*

*"I've been on the pill for three months," she said. "You got tested. Why are you being such a pussy about it?"*

*I chuckled. Goddamn, I loved this woman. We might not be much more than kids, but I knew how I felt.*

*"You callin' me a pussy?"*

*She tapped my chin with her finger. "Only if you don't get your face in mine pretty damn quick-like."*

*"Strip," I demanded, and she did. Immediately.*

*I did the same and we fell in a heap of naked body parts*

on the bed. She grabbed my face and studied me. *"I'm really looking forward to you eating me out, Jase, but if you could make it quick, I'd appreciate it, because I'd really, really, super-duper, like your dick inside of me."*

I grinned, kissing her as I thumbed her clit. *"I can make that happen."*

Rolling her onto her back, I rolled her nipple between my fingers and kissed my way down her belly and between her legs. I alternated between sucking her clit and running my tongue between her slick folds as her hips arched up with every pass I took.

Her body began to shake as an orgasm flooded over her and I kissed her belly again, then settled the tip of my cock at her entrance.

*"Jase,"* she whispered, and I plunged in.

No condom, her tight heat constricting around me, I moved in and out through her climax, feeling every contraction of her orgasm. I didn't think I could get harder, but then she wrapped her legs around my hips and arched to meet my thrusts, and I lost it.

Growling, I slammed into her over and over again until I knew I couldn't prolong the inevitable.

*"Now, baby,"* she begged, and I exploded.

She wasn't far behind and I rolled us, so we were chest-to-chest on our sides.

*"Goddamn, I—"*

A shock of fluorescent light flooded my eyes, snapping me back to reality. I pulled an earbud out and turned to see a surprised janitor pushing a utility cart.

"Oh, sorry sir, I didn't realize anyone was in here."

"That's okay," I replied. "I think I'm done anyway." I stepped off the treadmill and grabbed a towel. "Take it easy," I said, as I passed him.

"You, too, sir. Thank you and enjoy your stay."

I nodded while his words rang through my head.

*Enjoy your stay.*

*My stay? Was I staying? What the fuck was I doing*

here? How had I let Cutter and Cricket, two people I'd spent the last eight years purging from my soul, back in so quickly, and deeply? Even though I'd been sent to Savannah against my will, I'd still built a life there. I got along with my crew well enough, and my work with Duke at the ranch was important to me. Not to mention, he and Pearl weren't getting any younger and depended on my help increasingly these days.

I toweled off and headed back to my room, no less relaxed or clear-headed than before I'd started my workout. Perhaps by some miracle I could squeeze a few hours of sleep in before my meeting with Cutter. I wasn't looking forward to delivering Viper's message and was hoping my evening meeting with Cricket would be better. Maybe she'd snap me back to reality and remind me of just how crazy Cutter's idea was.

* * *

*Cricket*

I had a proposal due to Jeremy Marville, the owner of the company, no later than two this afternoon and I'd been staring at a blank computer screen for the past twenty minutes.

When Maisie had sold her multi-million-dollar sex toy company, she'd made some provisions for me. Firstly, she'd promoted me from her assistant to Marketing Director, then elicited a promise from Jeremy that I'd have one year to prove myself. If I couldn't make myself indispensable to him, I was on my own.

But here I was, my third year in, and all was well; unchallenging, boring, and predictable, but well. I mean, who wouldn't want the chance to test out every new sex toy coming on the market and figure out which demographic to sell it to? And considering I hadn't dated anyone seriously in almost the same amount of time I'd been working for the company, I needed anything new that could ease my pain, so to speak.

"Christina?" my assistant knocked and peeked her head

into my office for the third time in an hour. "Jeremy's wondering if you have that proposal ready yet?"

I smiled. "*No.* I still have two hours. But you can tell him, nice try."

She chuckled. "Um, no, I don't think I will be telling the CEO of the company I work for anything other than, 'yes, sir,' or 'how high would you like me to jump'?"

"Would you mind grabbing lunch? I don't think I'm going to be able to get out today."

"Of course. What do you want?"

"Surprise me," I said, digging thirty dollars out of my purse. "Grab yourself something too, but that doesn't mean I don't want you to take your break."

She grinned and took the money from me. "I know the drill."

I'd hired Melody two years ago and I adored her. Mostly because she was awesome, but also because she loved her job. She didn't want to be anything other than an executive assistant, which meant, I would never lose her. Well, unless someone fabulous stole her from me, but that had already been tried and I won. Stupid big five tax company. I had more money at my disposal, so they could suck it.

I bit back a yawn and focused on my screen again. I had gotten next to no sleep last night because every time I closed my eyes, visions of Jase going down on me danced in my head. No sugar plums for me. Nope, just his tongue on my clit. Although, I'm pretty sure he could figure out something creative to do with sugar plums.

Damn it, I needed to be writing this proposal, not fantasizing about Jase sugaring my plums.

Forcing my focus back to the job at hand, I picked up the jar of Uncle Milton's Elbow Lube and tried not to laugh... or groan. I couldn't figure out which one was more appropriate. I could have pawned this off to one of my staff, but it was a source of pride to be able to put together a successful campaign for the most challenging products.

Jeremy and I had met with Uncle Milton (yes, his name was really Milton, and he was in fact someone's uncle), and tried to get him to change the name of the product, but he wouldn't budge.

I originally advised Jeremy to pass on Milton's lube, but the truth was, it was a great seller, even if people more than likely bought it for a novelty gift. If Uncle Milton was aware of this, he certainly never let on, he was simply happy cashing the checks.

Sitting before me was the new "Spring Meadows" scent and I cringed at what this stuff could possibly be used for or why it needed to smell like fabric softener, but tried my best to focus on coming up with a marketing plan that would get it into the hands (or onto the elbows) of every dry pervert in the tri-state area.

\* \* \*

*Minus*

The Sanctuary was a ghost town compared to how I'd seen it lately and Cutter's office was quiet.

"So, Viper's an even sneakier snake than we'd thought?" Cutter asked, before taking a pull from a portable oxygen tank.

"It would appear so. How do you want to play this?" I asked.

"It's your money, it's your show," he replied.

"*My* money? What do you mean?" I asked. "You're the one who's secretly called in every outstanding debt to the club."

"It's yours, because with this cash you and Cricket are going to lead the Burning Saints into a new era. Think of the club as a new tech startup, and this is your seed money."

"I figured this money was for cancer treatment, or for your retirement, as it very well fuckin' should be."

"Kid, I've been living my retirement out for the last 40 fuckin' years. I've been doing what I want to do and going where I want to go for most of my life. What am I gonna do now? Take up fly fishing? As for treatment. Shit, I'm not gonna spend the few days I have left on this planet tied to a poison drip, and I don't wanna hear another goddamned word about it."

I nodded.

"Aren't you forgetting something else?" I asked. "Cricket hasn't agreed to go along with any of this. Hell, I haven't even talked to her yet."

"Listen, Minus, she's smart. You explain it to her in business terms, just like I did to you, and she'll understand just fine."

"Then why don't *you* talk to her? You're the man with the plan. Why do I have to be the one to give her the pitch of the century?"

"Because she likes you, dumbass. Besides, I tried the other night and she walked out."

"Because of me," I yelled. "She walked out because of me. What makes you think she'll listen to a damned word I say?"

"She agreed to meet with you, didn't she? That's gotta mean something, right?"

"Agreed? No. She demanded," I corrected. "She called me before I even had a chance to call her."

"That's even better. See, I told you she's crazy about you. I could see it from a mile away, and from the dopey look on your face, and considering how twisted up you are about this meeting tonight, you're clearly still hung up on her."

"Alright, enough about Cricket," I said. "I'll figure out what to say to her later. Right now, we need to focus on this meeting with Los Psychos and how we're gonna play it."

"We know for sure that Viper's got the money?" Cutter asked.

"He says he does, and that he'll give it all back if you'll simply agree to meet with him," I replied.

"Alone?" He asked.

"Those were his terms, but as you can imagine, your Sergeant at Arms wasn't about to sign off on sending you alone into a potential ambush, and as much as I hate to agree with Clutch..."

Cutter smiled. "Alright, then what?"

"We agreed on a sit down in a public place, with a plus one for both parties."

"Clutch is gonna want to be the one who's there with me," Cutter said.

"I know that, but I want it to be me. I'll talk to Clutch," I said.

"Have you thought about what it'll be like with him once you're the club president?"

"*If* I agree to become president," I corrected. "But why would I have issues with Clutch? He's my best friend."

"Well, he's been here, working close with me for the past few years, and he's already an officer. There's a chance he may feel passed over. There's also a chance that he'll have trouble taking orders from someone who's been his equal for so long."

"The last person in the world I'm worried about is Clutch. In fact, the only two people I'm concerned about right now are you and Viper, so let's get back to planning this meeting."

Cutter and I worked out the details over the next half hour, and I texted Viper with the time and place of the meeting, to which he agreed. We were to meet the following day, at the Portland Saturday market. Viper would bring the money in exchange for five minutes of Cutter's time. My plan was to have Clutch waiting nearby in a van, just in case Los Psychos had anything up their sleeve. Grover volunteered to ride along, which made it feel like the old days. I was confident Viper would have hidden backup too, so I wanted to be ready in case anything popped off. Truth be told, I didn't feel good about any of it though, and I told Cutter so.

"What are you so worried about?" Cutter asked, smiling. "The whole thing sounds like a simple sit down to me. We're doing it at a public place of our choosing, so we know it's not an ambush."

"If it's simply a sit down, then why steal the cash to draw you out? Why not just ask for a meeting with you? And what the fuck was up with all the tough guy bullshit last night at his fucking wannabe nightclub?"

"I don't know Minus, but this guy sounds like a punk to me," Cutter said.

"The problem is, we still don't know much about him at all. Clutch was able to find out a little, but there are big gaps in the details."

"What *do* we know?" Cutter asked.

"He's from Jalisco, and from what we can tell, he was a low-level guy who hooked up with Los Psychos while doing a six month stretch in a Mexican prison."

"Makes sense," Cutter said. "Los Psychos started out as a group of guys from Jalisco that met while in the Oregon state pen in the early 2000s. The prison system seems to be how they vet potential members. They're a straight up street gang, who happen to ride from time-to-time. Nothing like our breed of biker."

"From what Clutch told me, they're a small club, but they're gaining in numbers, both here and back in Mexico. We need to be careful. Viper is still making his bones here state side, and he's got a lot to prove. This meeting is likely some sort of big play for him."

"Well, that's enough to know he's dangerous, so you keep your eyes open, and try your best not to get us both killed," Cutter said.

# TEN

### BURNING SAINTS

*Minus*

**I** FELT LIKE an idiot. Tomorrow I was going to have a sit down with one of the area's most violent gangsters, and I was more nervous about dinner with a woman tonight. Then again, I wasn't about to try and fool myself into thinking this was just some dinner with any ordinary woman. This was Cricket, and we had some serious shit to talk about. I knew everything I needed to tell her, but had no idea what I was gonna say, which was probably bad news for me, considering how bad I'd screwed things up last time we'd spoken.

I was so hellbent on making a good impression tonight, I'd even worn a jacket and tie. Of course, I hadn't packed any nice clothes, not that I had many in my wardrobe anyway, so I had to hit a store, with minutes left to change before we were set to meet. I felt like I was back in my Catholic school uniform. Fortunately, I didn't have to stand there squirming in my new duds for long, as Cricket's Uber car pulled up minutes after I'd walked down to the hotel's front entrance.

Cricket got out of the car, thanked her driver, and in a very business-like tone said, "Thank you for meeting with me, Jase."

Shit! She wore a tight, black pencil skirt, a silky white button-up blouse, and a pair of four-inch heeled, fuck me shoes. Her hair cascaded down her back in loose curls and I couldn't help but compare her to some eighties video vixen when the wind caught those curls as she walked toward me.

All I wanted to do at that moment was to put her back in that car and tell the driver to get as far the hell away from here as possible. I could scarcely imagine why I was about to sit this intelligent, beautiful woman down and try to convince her to go along with some crazy scheme that I barely believed in. Only loyalty to my club and my president could make to me do such a dumbass thing. And as much as I was convinced that Cricket would laugh in my face, I'd resolved myself to relay Cutter's plan as promised.

"Like I said, I really was gonna call you and apologize," I said sheepishly. "I was kind of caught off-guard by you, and Cutter and, well, everything, and I acted like an asshole."

"No, you didn't *act* like an asshole. You *were* an asshole," she corrected.

"Fair enough."

"I'm willing to give you the benefit of the doubt that you will not behave as such tonight, but you're on a short leash."

"Look, if you want to bring leashes and collars into this, we can—"

"And no dirty sex jokes!"

"I'm sorry." I smiled. "You make me nervous. You always have. Whenever you made me nervous back then, I'd always crack some stupid joke to make you blush just so you wouldn't notice how scared I was. I guess old habits are hard to break. I promise, I'll be a perfect gentleman from here on out."

I made the mistake of looking directly into her eyes for just a moment too long, which was kind of like staring straight at the sun. I saw her expression soften, before she snapped back to no-nonsense mode.

"Okay, then. Apology accepted." She extended her hand straight out, and I did my best to suppress a smile as I completed the handshake in my most business-like manner.

"So, you wanna eat here at the hotel? The food's supposed to be good. Apparently, the head chef was runner up on Chef Battle, U.S.A."

"As long as it's not served from a food truck, I'm happy," she said.

"Not down with the whole *meals on wheels* trend, huh?" I asked.

"I have no personal objection, per-se, but our office is downtown, near where the food trucks park. Unfortunately, we're down-wind from them, so at lunch-time the combined smells waft towards our building."

"And that doesn't make you hungry?" I asked.

"Far from it. Imagine the combined smells of curry, barbeque, smoked salmon, falafel, fish tacos, and smeat, all blowing at you on a hot summer day."

"What the fuck is smeat?" I asked.

"I don't know, but they've got a food truck that specializes in it."

"Well, according to Yelp, this place appears to be more of an upscale, smeat-free establishment… with proper ventilation."

"Then, by all means, lead the way inside."

"Good, because it looks like it could start raining at any second," I said, as I held the door open for her.

The restaurant at the Hotel Dufrane was as beautiful as advertised. I slipped the hostess a little something for a private table, and she instructed our server to seat us at booth number three. He led us to an intimate spot, located in the back corner, and sat us down.

"Wow, Mr. Bond, I'm impressed. A tie, a private booth. What next, a ride in your Aston Martin?" Cricket teased.

"Fat Boy."

"What?"

"Along with putting me up in this fine establishment, and paying for this dinner, Cutter has also purchased me a brand-new Harley-Davidson Fat Boy."

"Wow, he's really trying to wine and dine you, isn't he?" Cricket razzed.

"Speaking of which. Drink?" I asked.

"How can I say no, when I know my uncle is paying?" She smiled, and I swear to God it felt like my heart was being squeezed.

I turned to our server, "Champagne for the lady, something incredibly old, and awfully expensive. And I'll have—"

"A vodka martini; shaken, not stirred," she said.

I laughed and replied, "Extra olives please."

Our server left us, and for the moment we were alone. Something Cricket and I had not been for a long time.

I cleared my throat nervously.

"So, look. Here's the thing. I've got a lot to say, and to be honest with you, I'm not quite sure where to start. You said on the phone that you had some questions for me, so how about we start there?"

"You sure you don't want to wait for your drink?" she asked.

"I think I'm good, ask me anything," I replied.

"You sure?"

"I'm sure. Fire away."

"Okay, then. Why did you abandon me, disappear completely from my life, and shatter my heart into a million pieces? How do you sleep at night being such a cold, heartless monster? Why in the hell have you come back into my life, and how soon will you be leaving?"

Just then, our server appeared with Cricket's champagne and my martini, which he placed in front of me.

"Thank God," I said. "I'm gonna need this, after all. In fact, go ahead and bring me another."

"What happened to you being a perfect gentleman?" she chided.

"Would you settle for an *imperfect* gentleman?"

"Jase."

I gave our server a nod, and he replied with, "I'll give you two a little time with the menus, and come back for your dinner selections," before disappearing.

"I'm sorry, that was kind of a lot to lay on me all at once. You're gonna have to gimme a minute to make some sense of all of it."

"What part do you need clarification on?" she asked, then sipped her champagne. The tip of her tongue slipped over her upper lip briefly and I felt my zipper press against my hardening dick.

"Well, all of it. Being as the root of your feelings seems to be based on some sort of notion that I walked out on you."

Cricket's face flushed with the red I remember seeing whenever she was about to rip me a new one. "Root of my *feelings*? A *notion*?" she ground out. "What other words can I use? You *left* me, Jase. One day, you packed up and moved to Georgia, and I never heard from you again. We had been together for almost a year. You were my first love." She stopped there, as tears filled her eyes. She shook her head and stared out the window.

I reached for her hand. "Cricket, I—"

"No." She pulled her hand away. "Don't touch me. I can't handle you touching me, or being sweet, or charming. I'm angry at you, and I don't know why I'm even here. And… and… I hate you." Cricket folded her arms and slumped down in her seat, avoiding eye contact.

"I never abandoned you," I said. "Please believe me when I tell you I had no choice in moving to Savannah."

"No choice? A chance to move up in the ranks comes along and you take it, but you're telling me you had no choice?" she hissed.

I frowned. "What the hell are you talking about?"

"I know all about why you moved to Savannah. Cutter offered you a deal and you, took it, regardless of what it cost me."

"Cricket, I'm not sure what you think you know, but you're wrong. I was forced out by Cutter, mostly because of your brother."

"I know you were forbidden to see me, but if you'd really loved me, you would have told me you were leaving. You would have called me once you were there. You would have asked me to come with you," she said, tears once again forming.

"Baby, I don't think you understand how being exiled works. If I had disobeyed Cutter, he would have taken my patch. I was given direct orders to stay away from you and leave my life here behind."

"So, you just went along your merry way? How could it have been so easy for you to walk away from me?"

"Easy? You think any of this has been easy for me? You think you were the only one that was in love? It took me a year to be able to go to sleep at night without drinking myself unconscious. I would wake up in the morning and my arms would ache because you weren't in them. Every time my phone buzzed, I'd pray that it was Cutter calling to tell me I could come home and that, miraculously, you'd still be waiting for me. Every day that went by that he didn't call, it made me hate him more. And every day that went by that I couldn't have you, made me love you more."

"Then why didn't you call, contact me, anything?"

"I had to put my feelings for you aside and do what I was told."

"No, Jase you chose to put your club before me."

Her words cut into the last good remaining part of my soul.

"You're right," I replied, taking her hand. This time she allowed me, and I forced eye contact with her. "I did everything you said. I was a coward and I regret that. Cricket, I'm so sorry. Please know that I never meant to hurt you and that I had no idea what you were going through. I was so wrapped up in my own heartbreak and anger, that I figured you'd just moved on when I left."

"Well, I didn't," she said.

"I don't understand how that's possible. You're the most amazing woman in the world. There had to be a line of guys around the block waiting to date you. I figured by now, some normal, stable, responsible type would have swept you off your feet. Or, did your brother chase all the other guys away, too?"

"I'm not ready to fill you in on all of that right now," she said, and I instantly knew it had to be bad. "We'll just leave it at, you left a mark."

I grimaced.

Cricket looked at me puzzled. "You keep saying my brother had a big hand in your exile. I'm not sure you're right about that. The Dogs of Fire and The Burning Saints have nothing to do with one another."

"That's not exactly true. The clubs aren't exactly friendly, but given their shared roots, they've always respectfully steered clear of one another. According to Hatch, me dating you was a sign of our club drifting into their lane."

"I'm going to kill my brother," she said.

Although, I was happy her anger was no longer focused on me (at least for the moment), I couldn't believe it, but suddenly I found myself defending Hatch. "Don't be mad at your brother. He didn't want you dating a criminal and I can understand that. He was just trying to protect you."

"I'm so sick of everyone always saying that! I don't need protection. I'm not a child and I'm not a helpless weakling."

"I never said you were weak or thought you were helpless. You're one of the strongest women I know. Hell, I've got a permanent scar here under my eye to prove it."

Cricket cringed and looked away in embarrassment.

"Don't you dare," I said. "Take a good look at your handiwork, Cricket. It means you don't take shit from people, no matter who they are, and I'm glad you stuck up for yourself. I'm also glad you hit me, because this scar will remind me never to treat you that way again."

"I highly doubt we'll see each other after tonight, so it doesn't really matter much does it?"

I straightened my posture. "Well, besides the apology, that's the other thing I wanted to discuss tonight."

"Jase," she said in a low tone. "Please call me Minus. You have no idea what it does to me when I hear you say my name."

"Don't you dare. You promised no dirty talk," she warned.

"I'm not talking dirty, Cricket. I'm being honest. The part of me that's still Jase has deep feelings for you, but I have to be Minus right now."

"What's that supposed to mean?"

"You heard Cutter the other night. He wants me to be club president when he retires."

"You're not seriously thinking about doing that, are you?"

I shrugged but said nothing.

"Wait a minute," she said with a gasp, her eyes widening. "You're not here to try and convince me to join you and your little band of miscreants, are you?"

I studied her, but still said nothing.

"Oh, my god, you are!" Cricket slid out of the booth and stood. "I'm not hungry anymore. Thank you for a lovely evening and for your apology. I'll call myself a car."

With that, she headed straight for the exit. I stood to stop her, just as our server returned.

"Is everything alright, sir? Do you need some more time with the menus?"

"No, thank you, my date isn't feeling well, so we're going to call it a night. Sorry for any trouble, everything was great. Please, bill the drinks to my room and give yourself a ridiculously high tip."

I ran outside and found Cricket standing on the curb, in the pouring rain, violently stabbing at her phone. "Stay away from me, Jase, I mean it."

"That's all you gotta say to me?" I challenged.

"Yes."

I crossed my arms. "This isn't like you, Cricket. I was expecting more of a fight. At least a hundred words formed into several sentences that told me what an asshole I am."

She glanced up from her phone briefly. "Well, you don't know me anymore. Obviously."

"Please come back inside, it's pouring out here."

"Gee, thanks for mansplaining the weather to me, I hadn't noticed."

"C'mon, Cricket, please, just let me talk to you. I know this is all crazy, but will you at least hear me out? Just give me a little more of your time."

"More of my time?" she cried out and began pounding wildly on my chest. "How much more of my time do you want, *Minus?* You've already held me hostage for years and now you want more? I won't give it to you. You can't have any more of my time, or my heart, or me."

I pulled her close and covered her mouth with mine. Goddamn, she felt right, she felt like home. She fell into me and moaned softly. Her hands came up to my face, as she returned the kiss hungrily. She tasted even sweeter than I'd remembered, and I held her tightly as we kissed again and again.

"What are we doing?" she asked, finally breaking away.

"What we've both wanted to do for the past eight years." I stroked her face, soaked from the rain. "Come with me. We'll talk in my room."

She bit her lip but gave me a quick nod.

# ELEVEN

## Cricket

JASE GUIDED ME into his hotel room, pushing me against the wall and kissing me as he kicked the door shut. He tugged my skirt up over my hips, and his hand slid under the waistband of my panties and between my legs. "Goddammit, Cricket. You're soaked."

"That's not just from the rain. It's been a while," I rasped.

"I'm gonna make up for lost time."

Before I could respond, he tore my underwear from my body and shoved the shredded lace into his jeans pocket.

"What are you doing?" I demanded.

He grinned. "Gettin' ready to fuck you."

"No... with my panties, Jase," I clarified.

"I'm keeping those," he said and turned me, so I was facing the wall. He kicked my legs apart, and slid his hand up my right thigh, and hovered it over my pussy. "Hands on the wall, above your head, Cricket."

I flattened my palms to the wallpaper, my breath coming in pants as I anticipated his next move. His thumb slid inside me, while a finger went to my clit and I whimpered with need.

"You still like it dirty?" he whispered, his breath tickling the back of my neck.

"Ohmigod," I groaned out. "Yes."

He removed his hand and slapped it against my soaked folds. "Spread."

I spread. It wasn't easy in heels, but I made it work, knowing that whatever he planned to do to my body would be worth any discomfort I might endure.

Unzipping my skirt, he tugged my wet blouse from the waistband and slid his hand up my back to unhook my bra.

"Take these off, Cricket, or I'm gonna rip them off. Leave the skirt."

With shaky hands, I unbuttoned my blouse and let it and my bra fall to the floor.

He pushed me back against the wall, the roughness of the wallpaper stroking my nipples into tight pebbles. His chest settled against my back and I bit my lip… hard. He'd removed his shirt and the feeling of his muscular, smooth skin pressed against me almost made me come.

His hand went back between my legs, slapping me once, then twice, and I whimpered out, "Jase."

"You like this?"

I hummed in acquiescence and was rewarded with another slap. "Don't come," he ordered, sliding three fingers inside of me and stroking me deep enough to hit my G-spot.

"Oh, God."

"Not God." His fingers twisted, and my body shuddered. I didn't know how much more I could take. "Me."

He pulled out again and a finger went to my clit, then he slapped me, and I cried out as an orgasm washed over me.

"I told you not to come," he said, as he turned me to face him again.

I watched him through hooded eyes as he licked his fingers clean, then ran his thumb over my bottom lip. "Take your skirt off. Leave the shoes."

I bit my lip and shimmied out of my skirt. He took my hand and held me steady as I stepped out of the fabric. I took in his body... what I could see of it, anyway. His chest was wider, much more muscular than when we'd first been intimate, and I ached to run my tongue over every ridge. He was also much tanner than he had been back then. Gone was the paleness of the Pacific Northwest, replaced with a golden brown that made him more beautiful.

When he'd met me at the curb, I'd lost my ability to think for a moment. He'd been dressed in a black suit that appeared to be made for him, a dark grey shirt and silver tie. He was beautiful, but the first thing I thought of was how much I wanted that tie binding me to the bed.

He led me to the desk against the wall, and gently pushed me back until my bottom grazed the edge. "Brace, baby."

I nodded and gripped the edge.

"Spread."

I spread, and he slapped my pussy a few times, sliding his finger through my wet folds to my clit. "Wider."

I spread wider, and he knelt in front of me, running his tongue over my clit, then blowing gently against it. The burst of cold air gave me delicious goosebumps that raised the level of my anticipation.

His mouth pressed against my pussy, then he sucked my clit as he slid two fingers inside of me. I almost came apart right then, but Jase still knew me and my body, and backed off just enough to irritate me. "Jase," I hissed.

Keeping his hand between my legs, he rose to his feet and leaned over to kiss me. He continued to work my pussy with an expertise that always amazed me, and as my climax hit, his mouth covered mine again and he kissed me as I whimpered.

"Better?" he asked.

I nodded and ran my hand over his rock-hard cock. "Let me return the favor."

"No."

"What?" Jase Vincent *never* turned down a blow job. Ever.

"I'm not done with you yet."

I watched without breath as he removed the rest of his clothes and he stood before me with a dick that I was dying to taste.

"Love those shoes, Cricket," Jase said, sliding his hand to my neck. "But I think now would be a good time to take them off."

I held his arms and slipped them off my feet.

He lifted me, so I could wrap my legs around him, then carried me to the bed and lowered me to the mattress. Pulling my ass to the edge, he rolled on a condom and slid into me, pushing my knees back for deeper access and burying himself deeper. I took some of my power back and raised my legs, settling them against his chest. He grasped my thighs, anchoring me to his body as he moved, thrusting deeper and deeper with each pass.

I called out his name as I came, and he pushed me back down and slammed into me, over and over, until he let out a satisfied groan, whispered, "God damn, I missed you," and rolled us gently onto our sides in spoon fashion.

As he held me tight, all the emotions of his abandonment hit me, and I burst into tears.

"Fuck!" he snapped.

Pushing off the bed, I made a run for the bathroom, but Jase caught me before I could escape. "Nope," he said. "Not happenin'."

"Let me go," I demanded, trying to pull away.

"No. You're gonna talk to me, Cricket."

\* \* \*

*Minus*

"This was a mistake. I shouldn't have come up here with

you, please let go of me," Cricket protested as she wriggled.

It took every ounce of strength I had to let her out of my arms, but the last thing I wanted was for her to feel unsafe in them. I grabbed a blanket off the floor, wrapped her up, and sat down with her on the edge of the mattress.

"I can't believe I let myself do this," Cricket said. "I'm so stupid."

"What exactly was so bad about what we were just doing, baby? Personally, I was having a great time, and from where I was, you seemed to be enjoying yourself just fine."

"That!" she snapped. "All that *baby, baby, baby* crap, and romantic…shitty…shit talk."

"Shitty shit talk?" I laughed.

"I'm serious Jase," she protested. "Stop joking about this."

"I'm sorry, Cricket, but you're fuckin adorable when you get all worked up like this. I can't help it if your pouting turns me on."

"Pouting?" Her tone sharpened.

"That's not what I meant. I'm sorry, it was a poor choice of words, but you'll have to forgive me for being a little confused here. Just a second ago we were having a great time, and now you're pissed off at me for being sweet."

"I didn't want you to be sweet, I wanted you to fuck me," she snapped.

"Perhaps I'm a bit rusty, but I thought that's exactly what we were doing."

"Rusty? Yeah, right." Cricket rolled her eyes.

"What is that supposed to mean?"

"*Oh Cricket, how I've missed you so,*" she mocked.

"What the fuck are you getting at here?" I asked.

"Do you really expect me to believe that you've been pining for me for all these years? That you've been living like a monk in Savannah?"

"I never said that," I replied.

"It was implied," she said.

"Was it, now?" I challenged. "I think it should be stated that I don't imply things. If I have something to say, I say it."

"Is that so?" she hissed.

"Yes, it very well fucking is. I said I missed you because that's the truth. I missed you so bad sometimes I wanted to fucking die."

Cricket turned her head away, but I gently grabbed her chin, and guided her back to me.

"Of course, I've been with other women since I left Portland. But I've never been in love, and the relationships have never lasted long. I've never felt about anyone the way I felt about you."

"Is that supposed to make me feel better?"

"It's not supposed to make you feel any particular way. It's simply the truth, and I felt like I owed that to you."

"You owe me a hell of a lot more than that," Cricket said.

"Like what?"

"Like a full explanation of why we're here tonight. You say you want to be honest with me, but I can't help but feel like bringing me up to your room was some sort of stall tactic or diversion. Or worse, some way to try and soften me up."

"Not at all. I couldn't be away from you for one second more. That's the truth, Cricket. I think it's safe to say that neither of us planned on this happening, but I don't regret it, and I hope it's not the last time."

"I wouldn't bet on it. In fact, how much longer I remain in this room depends entirely on your honesty," she said, her tone growing colder.

"I won't ever lie to you and I promise to never keep anything from you, including my feelings."

"You're going to have to forgive me if I have a hard time believing you. The Jase I knew was more of the 'diffuse with humor and bury his feelings deep inside until they turned into a ball of rage' kind of guy."

"That's one of the reasons that it bothers me when you call me that," I said.

"What? You're telling me that criminal biker 'Minus' isn't even *harder*?"

"It's difficult to explain. I think you'd have to come to Savannah to really see who I am… or at least who I'm *trying* to become."

"I'll have to take your word for it, because that's never gonna happen," she grumbled, picking at an invisible piece of lint on the blanket. "What's the other reason?"

"Because you're the only one who's called me Jase in years, and it hurts to hear it. It reminds me of who I was when I was here, and the things that I've done that I'd rather forget about. It reminds me of leaving you, and the things about myself and my club that I hate."

"If you hate your club so much, then why are you here to convince me to work for them?"

"Cutter doesn't just want you to work for the club, he wants you to help change it from within."

"Why me?"

"For lots of reasons, and honestly, they're not all that crazy if you'd hear me out. At first, I thought Cutter was crazy just like you, but after sitting down and talking with him, his plan makes a lot of sense."

"Of course, you would like it. For you there's a brand-new Harley, the President's patch, and a roll in the hay with your ex-girlfriend. What the hell is in it for me?"

"For starters, how does a million dollars in cash sound?"

# TWELVE
## BURNING SAINTS

*Cricket*

I SAT ON the edge of the bed, wearing only a hotel blanket and what had to be the dumbest expression ever. I glanced at my reflection in the dressing table mirror. I was a tangle of post-fuck blonde hair, and yep, I had the dumbest look I'd ever had on my face. I squared my shoulders and tried to bolster my nerve.

"I'm sorry, but what the hell are you talking about?" I asked, petrified to learn (and possibly incriminate myself) more.

"Three million, actually," he said casually.

"What?" I exclaimed, not at all believing what I was hearing. Jase continued casually, as if this were a shareholder meeting for a shoe company.

"One million of that is for you personally, another portion will be your budget to rebrand the club, and the remainder is for me to use as needed during the transitional period."

"Oh, *only* a million for me? Is that all?" I mocked. "And what exactly is a 'transitional period'?"

"That's a nice way of saying potential all-out war," he replied.

"Why would there be a war?"

"Because Cutter and I want to turn the Burning Saints into a clean club."

I had to admit, of all the hairbrained schemes I'd expected to hear, this came as a complete surprise. "Jase, you can't be serious—"

"*Minus*. Trust me, Jase isn't the man for this job, but with your help, Minus can be." His eyes, and his words were soft as he spoke. "I'm starting to understand why Cutter wants you by my side for this. I'm still not sure I'm the right man to be president, but I think if you were there with me, I could do it."

"This is crazy talk. I have a life, a job, career aspirations. Am I supposed to just throw all that away to run off, and be a publicist for a biker gang?"

"Of course not. You'd be the Vice President of Marketing," he said smugly.

"Of what, Minus? Have the Burning Saints developed a new product that you need to launch at the next biker convention? Do you have something that will revolutionize the beat down industry?"

"It's exactly the opposite of that," he said taking my hands. "We want out of the protection business. In fact, we want to redirect all focus and resources on running and growing our legitimate businesses. More importantly, we wish to liquidate and/or cease all non-legal enterprises, including our security firm, and bookmaking business."

"Jesus, you weren't kidding when you said there'd be a war," I said, squeezing his hands tighter.

As confused as I was by this entire situation, his touch made me feel safe. He'd always had that effect on me. In all my life only two men had ever made me feel safe, Jase and my brother, and at this moment they were both inside my head, pulling me in two opposite directions. I couldn't believe I was even entertaining this conversation, or in bed naked with Jase, but most of all, I couldn't believe how much I wanted him to fuck me again. I had to refocus and end this absurdity.

"What you want to do is highly dangerous, if not impossible," I said. "The kind of rapid shift in the club's business model that you are proposing would create a power vacuum in Portland. Other clubs or gangs would kill each other competing to control or shake down everyone that used to be under the Saint's protection. Not to mention, the blood that would spill over all the other revenue sources the club must have its hand in. Given how long the Saints have been in the area, I'd say you've likely got a hand in just about every shady deal that goes down in this town."

"See, Cutter was right."

"What was he right about?"

"You understand club culture and how the economy of the street works. Your brother's club may be clean, but the Dogs of Fire still roll on the same dirty streets as everyone else. You understand how men like me think. It's in your blood. With your knowledge of club life, instincts about people, and head for business, you could run the Burning Saints by yourself, but I think it's safe to say that the world of outlaw bikers may not be quite that progressive yet, so perhaps a partnership isn't the old man's craziest idea."

"It *is* crazy, and so are you if you think I'm going to be your biker bitch business partner."

"I know you said that like it was a bad thing, but that would look great on your business card." He smiled wide and my stomach dropped.

"Get serious," I said, trying to push my feelings for Jase aside, and get back to something a little closer to reality. I'd worked through my heartbreak for years in therapy, and thought I was in a good place before he walked back into my world. Having him so close made me realize I hadn't worked through anything. "Does Cutter actually think waving a fantasy check for a million dollars in front of my face is the way to get me to agree to all this nonsense?"

"The money's as real as the job offer, Cricket. Cutter wants you to use it to start your own business once the club has been re-established and stabilized. Once your work with us is done, you can walk away."

"This is insane, Jase. My head is going to explode. I can't think about this anymore."

I should have been heading for the hills by now, but instead, I placed my hands on his bare chest and forced him onto his back. I straddled him, kissing his face and chest, pausing in between my greedy attacks. "I need you to stop talking about a fantasy future together that's never going to happen," I said. "I need you to help us both forget about a past we can't change. Tonight, I need Jase to go away, and for you to introduce me to Minus." I paused, kissing him deeper still, my hand moving to his rock-hard cock. "Then, I want him to fuck me."

"Fast or slow?"

"Fast," I said immediately, and he flipped me onto my back, rolled on a condom, and thrust into me. All my breath left my body with an, "Ahhh."

His mouth claimed mine as he continued to surge into me, his hand cupping my breast before sliding down to finger my clit. I cried out as my orgasm hit, but didn't have time to enjoy it, as I was flipped onto my stomach. "Cheek to the mattress, Cricket."

My heart raced as I did as he directed. He lifted my hips higher and slid into me from behind and I lost my breath. Ohmigod, I'd forgotten how good this felt.

"Make it last, Cricket."

"I... Minus," I hissed. He slapped my butt and I nearly came.

"Cricket," he warned in a whisper. "Don't come or you won't get more."

"Don't you dare stop," I growled.

He chuckled, sliding partially out and then back in.

"Control yourself."

I let out a frustrated groan and Minus gave me another three quick smacks on my bottom, making me come so hard I lost my breath for a few seconds.

"Fuck me, baby," he breathed out, sinking deeper. "You're perfect."

I closed my eyes and nodded as Minus continued to move slowly, his hands settling on my hips, and slamming deeper and deeper, building another orgasm. He shifted slightly, sliding his hand to my belly. "Spread baby."

I spread, and he lifted me, keeping his cock firmly inside of me, so I was straddling him backwards. I dropped my head back, onto his shoulder and sighed.

"You okay?"

"Definitely. Yes," I panted.

With one arm anchoring me against him, he rolled a nipple between his fingers while his other hand slid between my legs. I rose slightly, then lowered, slowing down when I feared another orgasm would hit. I wanted this one to last.

"That's right, baby," he whispered, and I raised up again, mewling as I slid back down. "Fuck," he rasped, and his finger found home.

He tapped my clit, then gently slapped at my pussy and the sting broke any control I had. "Oh, God," I groaned.

"All fours, Cricket," he demanded, lowering me again, and I pressed my pussy harder against his body.

He slid his finger around my opening, then ran it over my very, very private place, and I was both excited (and a little nervous) as to what he planned to do. But I had asked for Minus, and so far, Minus was delivering the goods, so to speak, so I went with it.

"You ready for this, Christina?" he whispered.

Shit, he called me Christina. Now I was a little more on the nervous side. "Yes," I rasped.

He pressed his finger into me slightly, stopping so I could get used to it. "Are you sure?"

I swallowed. "Yes."

That's when he moved again… and I lost my mind.

Slamming into my pussy with his cock, his finger moved in and out of me, matching the rhythm of his dick. I was sure I'd pass out from the overwhelming pleasure of it all, and I screamed his name as my body exploded around him. Unable to hold myself up on my arms made of Jell-o, I fell to the mattress and dragged in deep breaths as I tried not to hyperventilate.

Minus removed his finger, gripping my hips so he could grind into me slowly until I felt his cock pulse between my walls, and he kept our connection as he rolled us onto our sides in spoon fashion.

"God damn, baby, that was amazing."

I nodded, still trying to catch my breath. "I approve of Minus. Maybe Jase just needs to retire."

He chuckled, kissing my shoulder. "That can be arranged."

\* \* \*

*Minus*

Waking up next to Cricket this morning was at the top of my list of life's great moments. Unfortunately, the feeling was short lived as a sense of dread crept over me. We hadn't exactly finished our conversation last night. Far from it. I still had one key detail to fill her in on, and I knew she wasn't going to be happy about it.

I stared at her, studying every detail of her face while she slept. She looked peaceful and momentarily unaffected by the world, protected and safe behind the wall of sleep. I felt stabs of guilt over the idea of dragging her further into my world, but I reminded myself that Cricket was a grown woman and could make her own decisions based on the information she's given. She was strong, independent, and a hell of lot smarter than me, so if she wanted to walk away, she'd have no problem doing so, and by my calculations, her exit would not be long from now.

There was a gentle rapping on the hotel room door, and I gently rolled out of bed, careful not to wake Cricket. I'd ordered breakfast via the hotel's room service app, which had now arrived. I figured if Cricket was about to storm out of my life forever, the least I could do was make sure she didn't have to do it on an empty stomach.

"Good morning, sir. I have breakfast for two."

I raised my index finger to my lips, the porter smiled understandingly, and quietly wheeled his cart into the room. I signed for the bill, and he made his exit just as Cricket began to stir.

"Good morning, sunshine," I said. "There's some breakfast here for you. We've got eggs, bacon—"

"Coffee," she rasped.

"We do have coffee. We also have fruit, toast—"

"Coffee. Black."

"I'm sensing a need for coffee," I teased.

"Coffee. Now, biker boy."

I poured her a cup and brought it to her in bed. She was laying on her side with one leg hiked over the covers, which were gathered in between her thighs. Her ample ass was on display like the perfect apple hanging from a tree, and I could not resist the urge to take a bite.

"Hey, mister, don't even think about it. Not before I've had my coffee," she warned.

"How about a kiss?" I asked.

"That, I can do."

I set the cup on the nightstand, leaned down, and kissed her slowly and sweetly. My lips made my way down to her neck, and I felt Cricket shudder. She whimpered, slightly arching her back, before pushing me off.

"I'm serious. Do *not* get me started. You promised me coffee."

"Fair enough," I said smiling, handing her the cup as she sat up in bed. Her tits were glorious, and she made no attempt to cover herself, nor did she seem fazed at all exposing herself to me in the light of the day.

Cricket had always possessed a confidence that attracted me to her more than anything else. She was still vulnerable and sweet, but never seemed overly bothered about her appearance, or body image, not that she had a damned thing to worry about. She was perfect. Still, I knew plenty of women who were drop dead gorgeous and still hated everything about themselves... Cricket wasn't one of them. I tried not to stare, but who the fuck was I kidding?

We spent most of the next hour catching up, grazing through the bounty of our breakfast buffet, and generally avoiding any serious conversation, which I knew we couldn't do forever. We eventually got dressed, much to my dismay, and I began preparing myself mentally for bringing the flow of such beautiful morning to a grinding halt.

"Look, we never got to finish our conversation last night," I said.

"I guess I kind of derailed us there at the end, didn't I?" Cricket smiled.

"I'm not complaining by any means, it's just that I promised I wouldn't keep anything from you, and there's a very important detail that we didn't get to cover last night."

"*What* detail?" Cricket asked.

"An important one that involves the three million dollars we talked about."

"Oh, that? I'd just about forgotten all about that," she said playfully. "What about it?"

"Well... we don't exactly have it," I replied.

"Come again?" Cricket asked, no longer smiling.

"We have it, but it's not currently in our possession."

"So, then you *don't* have it?"

"No, we do. It's just that someone else currently has ownership of the money, and later today, I'm going to reacquire it from him."

"And who is this person who has taken ownership of your money?"

"Viper. The president of Los Psychos, a rival Mexican club."

In her defense, upon hearing this information, Cricket did not freak out or head for the door. However, what she did do, may have been more disconcerting. She got quiet. Really quiet. After a few tense moments, I tried unsuccessfully to soften the blow. "I know this sounds bad, but—"

Cricket cut me off. "Please allow me to get this straight. *Viper,* the Los Psychos president, has stolen your three million dollars. *So,* you're going to retrieve said money and use it for a rebranding campaign, which you want me to run. Then, with the remaining funds, you plan on greasing the gears of the criminal machine that you then wish to slip out of?" she asked in a controlled tone.

"That's about it in a nutshell," I replied, bracing myself for Cricket's exodus.

"Pour me some more coffee and tell me everything."

# THIRTEEN

*Minus*

"YOU WANNA HEAR more?" I asked in disbelief.

She raised an eyebrow. "I'm here, aren't I?"

"Flyin' baby Jesus, Cricket. I can't for the life of me figure out why?"

"Would you make up your mind please, *Minus*," Cricket ground out. "Do you want me to be a part of this, or not?"

"Actually… I don't know," I admitted.

"That's not an answer!" she snapped.

"What do you want me to say here? To be honest, no I don't want you involved in my club, because I don't want you to get hurt. I'd burn the world down if anything ever happened to you, and I'd burn myself with it if it was because I dragged you into this. I don't want you involved with guys like Viper, or guys like me, for that matter, but I think Cutter may be right. I think together we could save this club from extinction and turn it into something good."

"Then, trust me enough to let me all the way in and tell me everything. I can decide how far down the rabbit hole I go," she said.

"This isn't Alice in Bikerland. This is real fuckin' life."

"You just let me be the judge of what I can and cannot handle and spill the beans."

I filled her in on everything we knew about Los Psychos, Viper, and today's meeting. I also went into further detail about my conversation with Cutter, and his new vision for the club. She sat quietly, absorbing every word I said, taking notes on hotel stationary.

"Why Cutter's change of heart about the club?" she asked. "Is it because he's dying?"

"I think the diagnosis gave him the final push to act, but it sounds like he's been thinking about this move since before he sent me to Savannah. In fact, him sending me there was apparently all part of his masterplan."

"You're joking, right?"

"Dead serious. He told me himself that sending me to Savannah served two purposes. It got me out of your brother's hair, and that was good for our relationship with the Dogs of Fire. Cutter wants us to partner with the Dogs and learn what we can from them. His vision of the Saints' future looks a lot like the Dogs' present."

"Okay, but why the Dogs? Trust me, it's not like that club is perfect. Believe me, they have plenty of their own internal issues," she replied.

"Sure, but as far as clean clubs go, you have to admit they've done well in most respects," I countered.

"Maybe, but let's not put them up on a pedestal. I mean, honestly, what fucking idiot gave Cutter the hairbrained idea to use the Dogs of Fire as some sort of ideal template on how to build a club?"

I cleared my throat. "I did. Eight years ago."

"*What?*" Cricket's eyes were like saucers.

"It's kind of what sealed my fate and led me here right now."

"What are you talking about?" Cricket asked.

"Shortly after Clutch and I'd been patched in, I challenged Cutter publicly at Church. It was only my third or fourth meeting, and I overstepped my bounds, big time. The topic of the day, per usual, was how the old revenue streams were drying up one-by-one. Everyone was bitching about it week after week. It was all these old guys fucking talked about, day in and day out, but no one ever offered up any good solutions. Their ways of doing business were as stuck in the past as a stegosaurus in the La Brea tar pits."

"So, what did he say should be done?" Cricket asked.

"Nothing! He seemed as clueless as everyone else, as far as I could see. He'd mostly just sit in silence as his officers bitched about how tight the streets had become over the years. He'd nod and stroke his beard, and then the meeting would eventually be ended, and everyone would scatter back to the wind. It was fucking chaos, and to me the solution to surviving the game was simple."

"How's that?" Cricket asked.

"Stop playing it. Get the fuck out while we still could. As far as I could see, we had no choice. The game had become unwinnable. If it ever was in the first place. In fact, we weren't even playing the same game as everyone else on the streets anymore. The criminal world had moved into the twenty-first century, and we were still dragging our knuckles. Either way, by continuing to follow the same old rules, we'd all end up in prison or dead."

"So, your solution to him was, what? Disband the Burning Saints?"

"No, but that's how he took it when I told him what I thought our club should look like in the future."

"What exactly did you say?"

"Something to the effect of 'the club was like an old bike, with good parts, that needed to be rebuilt with newer, better parts,' etcetera."

"He didn't much care for that analogy?" she asked.

"I believe his words were, 'Boy, you ever refer to my club as an old pile of garbage again, I'll skin you alive, starting with your patch.'"

"I see," Cricket said, shifting in her seat. "The other side of my uncle that I've heard so much about."

"I'm not gonna lie. Cutter is tough. Probably the toughest guy I've ever met. He's one of the few men I both respect, and fear. I thought my days in the club were fuckin' numbered the day of that meeting. Every time I saw Cutter after that, he'd be lookin' at me with a fire in his eyes. I was convinced he hated me and wanted me gone. To be honest, it broke my heart because all I ever wanted was for the Burning Saints to have a future. I felt like we could learn something from clubs like the Dogs. I just wanted Cutter and the other officers to broaden their minds to new ways of doing things."

"So, what happened?"

"The next thing I knew, Cutter, Red Dog, and three other Saints were dangling me over the side of the Burnside bridge at four in the morning, wearing nothing but underwear and handcuffs."

"Jesus, did they really do that to you?"

"Indeed, they did. I was then told I was to drive a truck containing a load of club cargo and all my belongings, including my bike, to Savannah, Georgia. I was instructed to stay there until otherwise notified, or hell froze over, whichever came first. I was also told to, and I quote, 'Stay out of Portland, and stay out of Cricket Wallace.'"

"*Charming*," she said.

"So, that's it. That's why I was out of your life so suddenly and completely. I had no choice but to do what I was told. I was loyal to my club, and besides, it's not like I had any other options. The club was my life, my source of income, and the only family I had."

"*Was* your life. Is that not true anymore? Do you not feel the same?"

"The club is still my family and I'd die for any of my brothers, but no, I don't feel exactly the same as I did back then."

"Why the change?"

"The answer's not so much a why, but a who," I replied with a grin. "His name's Duke. He's the other reason Cutter sent me to Georgia, but that's another conversation entirely. Let's just say, that I understand Cutter a lot more now, and that he agreed with me far more than I could have ever known back then."

"Really, how so?"

"Cutter built the Saints from nothing with his bare hands. It was the wild fucking west back then, and he was able to tame a handful of misfits and make them profitable in record time. He also managed to keep his crew alive, and out of jail in a time when that took deep pockets and an iron fist. The Burning Saints were born in the wild, but the world around them was becoming civilized and he knew it."

"If he agreed with you, then why did he treat you like shit? Why did he break us up, and exile you?" Cricket demanded.

"Because, knowing the direction *not* to sail isn't enough information to take a boat into open waters. A good Captain charts a course and has the experience to know how to avoid waves when they come," I said.

"Did Cutter teach you that?" she asked.

"No, Duke did, but I now see that it applies to Cutter, and how he dealt with me."

"How so?"

"Cutter figured out most of the money had moved off the streets and onto the web, and that his way of doing things was pretty much over. He was also wise enough to know that he didn't have a viable solution to transition into the new age yet. I, on the other hand, was full of piss and vinegar but would surely go out and get myself killed trying to change the world. At least that's how Cutter saw me."

"Was he wrong?" Cricket asked.

"Of course, he wasn't. I probably would have gotten

Clutch, Grover, and our guys riled up, and embarked on some half-assed scheme that would have gotten us all shot or landed us in prison."

"Still, to hang you off a bridge, not to mention what he did to us..."

"Don't get me wrong, I'm not at all happy about the way he went about things, but knowing what I know now, he probably saved my life. Maybe even yours."

"What do you mean?" she asked.

"I was crazy about you back then, Cricket. I was more focused on you at the time than I was on the club, and that put you in a dangerous position."

"How?"

"If you're not paying attention to your enemies, you'll never know when they're coming for you, and the people you're closest to. The people you love are always the most vulnerable." Cricket's eyes met mine. "Cutter didn't send me away because of you, but I'm glad he did. I was young, angry, and too impulsive back then. I would have fucked everything up between us one way or another. At least now, maybe we have a chance."

"Slow down, tiger," she said. "Just because I'm listening, doesn't mean I'm down with the cause. And just because we fucked, doesn't mean there's a *we*."

"Is that all that was to you? A good fuck?" I asked.

"I just said it was a fuck, I never said it was good," she deadpanned.

"Ha, fucking, ha, Cricket. You know what I mean. We've both admitted how we felt about each other back then, and how hard it was to be apart. I think it's safe to say that whatever flame we held for one another back then is still burning now. I think it would be a little difficult for you to deny that at this point."

"It's not difficult for me to deny anything. My reason for talking to you last night was the same for fucking you. I had unresolved issues."

"And you don't anymore?" I asked, a little shocked by her response.

"I never said that, but let's just say that I'm good for now."

"Oh, how nice it must be for you," I said.

"What do you expect from me, Jase? Just because I have a better understanding of what you went through and why you left, doesn't mean I'm willing to forget about everything. Obviously, I still have some sort of feelings for you, but it's not like I've been sitting around pining for you all these years, or that just because we screwed, I've fallen in love with you again."

"Well, damn, Cricket. Tell me how you feel, no need to hold anything back now," I said sarcastically.

"I'm very curious to know why you think we'd have any kind of chance, romantically or otherwise. We've been down this road once before, remember? Trying to balance our love life with your club life didn't quite work out for us last time."

"I wish I could show you all the ways I've changed in the past few years. I'm aware that I've done a spotty job so far, but with a little time, and some patience on your part, I hope to prove myself to you, and show you how much I've grown as a person."

"I hope so too, because if you hurt me, you'll never hear from me again," she said, once more using her 'all business' tone. "And Hatch'll probably kill you."

"I understand," I said and leaned in for a kiss. I wanted more, but right now I needed to focus on getting our money back, and how to deal with Los Psychos. I broke our kiss and said, "I'd like to continue this conversation later tonight if you're free."

"I'll have to check my schedule, but I think I can make myself available," she said, unable to hide her smile.

"Good. I've got to go pick up Cutter and go over some last-minute details with Clutch about today's meeting."

"Be careful, Jase. You up and getting yourself shot wouldn't quite be a ringing endorsement for your proposed business venture."

"All I ask, is that you continue to keep your mind, and

legs, open to me while we figure this out." I slid my hand between her thighs and kissed her again. She moaned and pulled me closer.

Club business would have to wait.

\* \* \*

### Cricket

"You want my legs open?" I asked, pushing him onto his back and straddling his hips.

"Yeah, baby. I do." He slid his hands up the outside of my thighs, squeezing my ass once he reached it.

I ran my thumb over his bottom lip, then slid my finger into his mouth. He sucked on it and I slid it to my clit, pressing the wetness against it. I felt him shift and I shook my head. "Don't move, *Minus*."

He grinned, slipping his hands behind his head. "You want control, Cricket?"

"I already have it." I raised an eyebrow. "And I'm gonna continue to have it, hear?"

He raked his eyes over my body, his mouth turning up slightly at the corners.

"Minus."

His eyes met mine and he grinned again. "You want Minus, Cricket... or Jase?"

"Whoever's gonna behave."

"I'll surprise you, then."

I shrugged, leaning down to run my tongue between his pecs. God, I loved the taste of him. I kissed my way down his body, stopping at his cock, already hard and waiting for me. I wrapped my hand around the thickness and licked the precum off the top, before wrapping my mouth around the tip then taking him deeper.

I slid my hand up and down, cupping his balls with the other, and drawing him in so deep I nearly choked. I couldn't get enough. I wanted him as much as I did before... if not more. I might not be willing to admit it out loud right now, but I loved this man. More than life. The feelings had never gone away, and I realized pretty fucking quickly that the reason none of my relationships had worked after Jase was because none of them *were* Jase.

I gave a gentle suck and without warning, found myself hauled up and flipped onto my back. "I was in the middle of something!" I snapped.

"Minus doesn't give a shit," he growled. "On your knees, Cricket."

I wanted to argue. I wanted to smack the smirk off his face, but I also wanted Minus to fuck me... hard. That desire won out and I scrambled onto my knees, ass high and ready.

I heard foil rip and then his dick was blissfully buried so deep in me, it pressed against my womb. I cried out, pressing back against him.

"You okay?"

"God, yes," I breathed out.

He grabbed my hips and squeezed, moving slowly at first, then slamming into me until I knew I couldn't wait another second. "Minus!"

"Hold it," he growled.

"I can't!"

His palm landed on my ass and I came... *hard*.

"Minus," I whimpered out, falling to the mattress.

He fell with me, rolling us so we were on our sides, and continuing to move inside of me. One hand slid between my legs and he cupped my pussy, palming my clit as he buried himself deeper inside of me. Even though my orgasm wasn't fully over, he built me up again and he bit my shoulder gently.

"I'm gonna come," I warned.

"I can feel it, baby."

"You slap me again, it's gonna be all over... just F.Y.I."

"But you love it."

"I do." I closed my eyes. "So, so much."

His hand left my clit and he gripped my hip as he slammed into me twice more, landing another slap on my ass, and we came together.

He kissed my shoulder, whispering, "Come to Savannah

with me."

"When?"

"Monday."

"That's in two days."

"I'm aware," he said, as he slipped out of me and headed to the bathroom.

"I can't just run off to Savannah, Jase. I have a job."

I heard the toilet flush, then he walked back into the room. "It'll only be for three or four days. In fact, why not take the whole week off, we can spend some time getting to know each other while I take care of wrapping up some loose ends back home."

I watched him walk toward me, my body wanting him all over again. "I *do* have a shit ton of vacation and no critical meetings next week."

He climbed back onto the bed, hovering over me, running his tongue over a nipple, before kissing the sensitive spot just above my collarbone. I reached up to run my hands over his beard.

"So?" he prompted.

"Yes, Jase, I'll go to Savannah with you."

He grinned, kissing me deeply. "I'll make all the arrangements."

"I like that."

He chuckled and kissed me again, then he showed me just how much he appreciated my answer.

# FOURTEEN
## BURNING SAINTS

*Minus*

THE PORTLAND SATURDAY Market was started in the seventies, right around the time many of the area's biggest clubs were just beginning to get organized. The Burning Saints were among these "early settlers," and still put a high value on the people and places that continue to make Portland what it is.

The market was a maze of vendors and artisans that was set up and torn down every Saturday during the spring and summer months. Families could easily mix in with the hippies and freaks of Portland and enjoy live music, as well as demonstrations about *organic, free-range, non-GMO, artisanal Christmas tree farming*, or whatever the local college kids were currently fired up about. All the area clubs viewed the market as neutral territory. A safe public place where parties could meet openly without hassle.

Cutter and I arrived at Ankeny Square ten minutes early to find Viper and Crush waiting.

"Well, at least he showed up," I said as we approached the designated meeting spot. More importantly, I noticed two black canvas duffle bags at Crush's feet. I hoped this meant the money was here, and the meeting would be smooth sailing. However, if the bags didn't contain our money, I wasn't sure if the market was going to remain a blood-free zone for much longer.

Viper smiled wide and extended his arms as we approached. "Mr. Cutter, it's so nice to finally meet you. My name is—"

"I know who the fuck you are," Cutter snapped. "Now give me my money and tell me why we're here."

"You are a man who gets straight to the point. I like that," Viper said.

"And, from what I've seen, *you* aren't, so let's cut the shit," I said.

He focused on me. "Mr. Minus, it's so nice to see you again. I was hoping it would be you that accompanied Mr. Cutter today. I found you so… *amusing* last time we spoke."

"Yeah. I'm a real laugh fuckin' riot." I raised an eyebrow. "You said you wanted five minutes of Cutter's time, so how 'bout you hand over those bags and we can start the clock."

"Right down to business it is, then." Viper motioned to Crush, who picked up the bags and dropped them clumsily at my feet. His eyes remained locked on me the entire time.

"You keep those eyeballs pinned on me like that, and I'll roll 'em to the back of your head for you," I said.

"Try me," Crush ground out, before rejoining Viper.

"You'll find that all your money is there," Viper said. "As promised, I didn't touch a single dollar. You can look it's all there."

Cutter carefully unzipped one of the bags.

"It's alright, there are no tricks or tracking devices." Viper held his hands up in surrender. "I'm returning your money, just as I found it."

"'Found it' is a funny way to put it. Personally, I think *steal's* a bit more accurate, don't you? So, tell me why you stole my money, only to give it back?" Cutter asked.

"To show you that I could, Mr. Cutter. To prove to you that whatever you possess, can be mine if I so desire."

"You hired a crew to steal a fucking Cadillac that had my money in the trunk. That doesn't make you a criminal mastermind," Cutter replied.

"Yes, but how did I know your money would be in the trunk and when it would be coming in? And as you yourself asked, why give the money back?" Viper was clearly impressed with himself, but for the life of me, I couldn't figure out why. I imagined picking him up by his silk tie and shaking him until his neck snapped.

Viper continued, "I'm giving your money back to you, because three million dollars is pocket change to Los Psychos. We don't need it, and we don't want it."

"Then what exactly *do* you want? I've got shit to do, and the constant pan flute music around this place is getting on my fucking nerves," Cutter said.

"One thing, Mr. Cutter. I want only one thing, and then we can conclude our meeting."

"And what would that be?"

"I want your ledger."

Cutter laughed, struggling to stifle a cough. "What the fuck are you talking about?"

"Your black book. The ledger you keep locked away. The one that contains your club's contacts, business associates, bank codes. You know the one I'm talking about."

Cutter's face turned to stone. "Whatever the fuck you think you *may* know about my club—"

"Oh, I know a great deal about you and the Burning Saints. Much more than you could possibly imagine. It's partly because of the knowledge I have of such things, that I don't care about your three million. I know, for instance, that your book contains a vast array of information regarding the various *sources* of that money, and that is what I'm interested in. Why go after three million, when there are hundreds of millions out there for the taking?"

"So, lemme get this straight," Cutter said. "I'm supposed to hand you some fictitious book in exchange for money that you stole from me. And with the information in said fictitious book, you plan on taking over all my businesses. That sound ''bout right?"

"More or less. Yes. I believe you get the basic idea," Viper said coolly.

Cutter's teeth clenched. "Do you know who I am? I am the president of the Burning Saints. Hell, I *am* the Burning Saints. This is my town. Do you have any idea of how much hellfire I can bring down on your ass at a moment's notice?"

"I thought perhaps this would be your reaction, so I made sure to bring more than just a financial incentive with me today," Viper said. Crush pulled out a tablet, tapped the screen, and handed it to Cutter.

Cutter's eyes filled with rage, and his hand began to shake. "You motherfucker, I'll tear your fucking heart out and feed it to your children," he growled.

Crush straightened, ready to step in should Cutter advance further.

"It's okay, Crush," Viper said, smoothing his suit jacket. "Mr. Cutter knows this is sacred ground. He won't spill blood here. Besides, he wouldn't want his friend to get hurt… any further… would he?"

Cutter handed me the tablet, which was playing a video stream of a dark, dirty room. Inside that room, Warthog was gagged and tied to a metal chair. From the looks of it, he was beat to shit. Some fucker with horrible acne scars was holding Warthogs bloodied head up by his hair, shaking it back and forth for the camera.

"You've made a big mistake," Cutter said.

"I don't think so. In fact, I believe that it's you that's underestimated me. While it is true that, historically, the Burning Saints have always run the security game here in Portland, times are about to change… starting right now."

"I suppose you think Los Psychos is going to take over?" Cutter asked.

"Who better? Look how easily we got to you!" Viper exclaimed. "I know everything about you and your operation. I even know that you've already got one foot in the grave."

Cutter looked at him with an unfiltered rage. If Warthog's life wasn't currently in Viper's hands, I think he would have gone for his throat right then and there. I was afraid the fine folks who'd come to the market for a churro and a reasonably priced alpaca wool-knit cap were about to witness a murder.

"If you kill Warthog, I'll come at you with everything I have," Cutter said. "I won't care where we are."

"Maybe so, but that won't really change anything, will it? Your time is over, Mr. Cutter. Your club is vulnerable, and soon to be without its leader and founder. Take this money and retire someplace warm. Get away from all this rain and bloodshed before it's too late."

"The day I start taking orders from little piss ants like you, is the day they put me in the fucking ground."

"That day may be closer than the doctors have told you. Not just you, but Warthog, Mr. Minus here, and your whole club," Viper said.

"Don't bet on it," I replied.

"I find it funny that the two of you talk so tough when you are in no position to do so. If I do not get word to the man on the other side of that screen by the designated time, he will begin removing pieces of your friend. He'll start by taking his toes, one by one, before moving his way upward."

"I don't know anything about a book," Cutter said defiantly.

"And I say you're lying. You have twenty-four hours to bring it to me or Warthog is dead, and you can look forward to finding pieces of him in your mailbox throughout the year."

"It's the gift that keeps on giving," Crush said, smirking.

I went to hand him back the tablet but dropped it on the ground just before it reached his oversized hand.

"Sorry," I said flatly.

Just as Crush bent to pick up the device, I delivered a headbutt directly to the bridge of his nose. He staggered back a few steps stunned, as blood erupted from his face, spraying the both of us.

"Oh, buddy, I'm so sorry!" I lied. "I guess we both bent down at the same time. Are you okay?"

I moved towards him in mock concern, pretending to lend assistance, trying to avoid the attention of the crowd. I moved in closer, pulled the gun I'd hidden in my waistband, and pressed it against his ribs.

"Don't you make a fucking move, or I'll drop you right here, big boy," I whispered to Crush. "Hey, *Roger*," I called out to Viper. "How about we get *Irving* here to the medical tent? I think he may have hurt himself real bad."

I motioned for everyone to move away from the crowd, towards a small grove of trees behind the bandstand. I stuck with Crush and ordered Viper to grab the bags. Once secluded by a grove of trees, I told Viper to drop the bags, and put some distance between us.

"Call your guy and tell him to let Warthog go, or I swear to God, I'll put a bullet in each of you. Hell, I'm feeling generous. Let's make it two apiece."

"You're not going to execute us in a public place, with all these witnesses and security around."

"You're holding one of my brothers hostage, you threatened my president, and you stole from my club. Believe me when I tell you that I'd cut your throat in front of a judge and a priest for a lot less."

"You'll regret spilling blood here today," Viper said.

"I've regretted just about every moment of my life since hearing your fucking name. Why should right now be any different? I'd go to the gas chamber with a smile on my face for the privilege of shooting you in yours."

"And I'm a dead man anyway, so what the fuck do I have to lose?" Cutter asked with a smile.

"Make the call. Now," I said.

Viper began to reach into his inside jacket pocket.

"Move slowly and keep your hands where I can see them," I instructed, and he produced a cell phone and dialed.

"This is Viper. Let the old man go. Yes, I'm fucking sure," he bellowed into the phone.

"Tell your guy to drop Warthog off at the Corner of Capitol and Virginia, and give his phone to him, so we know he actually gets out safe," I ordered, and Viper did as he was told.

"Good, now this is how this is gonna go down," I said. "You're going to give me your phone, turn around, and exit via the far end of the market. You're going to make sure Warthog is delivered safely, and you're going to walk the fuck away from the Burning Saints. You made your move and you failed. You underestimated us, and you won't get a second shot. If you make one more move in our direction, we'll know about it and we'll end you and your fucking club. Do you understand me?"

"Once again, it's you who doesn't understand. I'll walk away for now, and I'll let your man go, but if you think this is over between us, you're crazy." He shifted his gaze to Cutter. "I gave you the three million, and I want your book in return. If it's not delivered to me, you're going to be praying the cancer kills you before I do."

With that, he and a bloodied Crush turned and walked towards the south entrance.

"Let's get the fuck outta here," I said to Cutter. Tucking the gun and Viper's cell phone back into my jeans, we grabbed the bags and briskly walked back to the van where Clutch and Grover were waiting.

"Any problems?" Clutch asked as we entered the van.

"Easy as pie," I said.

"Glad to hear it. You, took a little longer than—" Clutch did a doubletake. "Is that blood all over you?"

# FIFTEEN
## BURNING SAINTS

*Minus*

I HIT THE last number dialed on Viper's phone and Warthog answered.

"Where are you?" I asked.

"He dropped me off near Shelly's old place," he replied.

"Stay there. We're on our way. Find someplace out of sight—" That was as far as I got before the phone call cut off.

"Fuckers must have killed the phone remotely," I said, tossing it aside.

"What the holy hell is going on, Minus? What happened back there?"

"Viper and his goon tried to get cute, so I had to improvise a little. They were holding Warthog hostage, but I *con-*

*vinced* them to let him go."

"Jesus, Minus, when I told you to start using your head more, that was not what I meant," Cutter said laughing. "Shit, that felt like the old days."

"Does Eldie still work in the E.R.?" I asked.

"No, she has her own clinic now," Cutter replied.

"We still good with her?" I asked.

"Solid as a rock as far as I know."

"Perfect. We can drop Warthog off there on our way back to the Sanctuary. We need to figure some shit out, pronto."

"Starting with how the hell Viper knows so much about our club's business," Cutter said.

"Cuz, if we've got a mole, we're gonna need to find him fast, and deal with him even faster. Not to mention all that bullshit about a secret *black* book," I said with a laugh. "What the hell was that all about?"

Clutch glanced back at Cutter, who sat in silence. A silence that lasted a little too long.

"Are you fucking kidding me? That shit is real?" I asked in disbelief.

"As real as the moon landing," he replied.

"You're lucky Warthog isn't here. He'd have some strong feelings about that statement," Grover said.

"You actually keep a fucking ledger of all your criminal activity? A master file, on paper, of the club's business?" I asked, in stunned disbelief.

"How the fuck else am I gonna keep track of everything?" Cutter bellowed.

"For starters, most clubs have a treasurer to take care of this stuff," I said.

"I don't trust 'em. I take care of the club's books. Always have, always will. I believe it's the President's responsibility."

"Fine, but why a fucking ledger? They have these things called computers you know. They were invented during the last century, and can be used to compile, and safely store data," I said. "You know, with passwords and encryption and shit."

"Oh, sure, those things are fucking secure. Have you watched the news lately? *Hackers* this, and *security breach* that. I keep my information on paper, locked up tight, where only I have access to it," Cutter said.

"Well, your top fucking secret isn't a secret anymore. We need to get that book as far away from here, and you, as possible. We also need more able-bodied guys around here. No offence, but some of your top guys are getting up there and might not be up for the fight we just picked."

"You got a plan?" Cutter asked.

"I'm thinking it's time for Clutch to round up a posse, and for me to get the fuck outta Dodge."

We reached Warthog's pickup location and scanned the spot for any sign of him. After one pass around the block, I spotted him in an alley, next to a bike shop. He was slumped on the ground, leaning against the building. Clutch pulled over, we jumped out, and helped the badly battered Warthog into the van. He could barely stand and looked far worse in person than he did on the video. Both of his eyes were almost swollen shut, his right arm appeared to be broken, and he reeked of gasoline. Someone had spent some time on him. I saw brand marks and bruises and his hair was matted with blood.

"Easy now, careful," Cutter said, his voice trembling with concern, as we lay Warthog down in the back of the van. "What happened, man?"

"I took the Lincoln in to get detailed," Warthog rasped.

"Sure, it's Saturday," Cutter said. "You went to Dashmasters?"

"Yeah. I was on the bench outside, waiting for the car, and they grabbed me. They knew I was gonna be there."

"Los Psychos?"

"They were all patched except the guy that worked me over. It sounded like they'd hired him. He was gonna torch me. He kept saying he was gonna burn me alive, man," Warthog rasped as Cutter held his head.

"It's okay, man, we're gonna get you to Eldie's and

she'll take care of you. We'll get you out of these clothes and get some good ol' morphine into you. That sounds good, doesn't it?" Cutter smiled, trying his best to comfort his friend, before turning to me. "When we find the guy that did this, he's going to pay double for this."

"I'll find him for you, I promise," I said.

"You promise him," Cutter said, motioning to Warthog.

"On my patch," I said.

We reached the medical office of Dr. Gina Gardner, or as she was known to our club, "Eldie," which was a derivative of L.D., which stood for Lady Doctor. This was unfortunately what Red Dog called her when he was brought into the E.R. after getting a bottle busted over his head in a bar fight. Rather than take offence, Dr. Gardner wore the moniker with pride, and became a trusted friend of the club over the years. We always knew that Eldie would take care of you when needed. Apparently, she'd since moved up from her days in the E.R. and had her own small practice. I was wondering if she'd be as welcoming to the Burning Saints as she once was. As it turns out, I wouldn't have to wait long. Clutch and I were on opposite sides of Warthog, carrying him up the walkway, and had only made it halfway there when Eldie bound through the front door with a very large Samoan man in nurse's scrubs, pushing a wheelchair.

"What happened to him?" she asked, as the nurse gently placed Warthog into the chair and wheeled him through the front entrance.

"He was kidnapped and beaten, that's all I know. I'm not even sure how long they had him, or what they did to him. Just help him the best you can okay, Doc?"

"You know I will," she said sweetly. "It's good to see you again, Cutter, even if it's for the same old reasons."

"You, too, sweetie," he said, leaning in. "Be okay if we stash him here for a few days while he heals up?"

"I've got a place in back. He'll be comfortable and out of sight," she replied.

"Thanks, babe. I owe you," Cutter said.

"You know my price," she said with a wink, and exited

the waiting area.

"What was that all about? What's her price?" I asked as we made our way out.

"None of your damned business. That's between me and the Doc," he said sternly.

"Damn, Cutter! You got somethin' goin' on with Eldie?" Clutch razzed.

"You fuckin' idiot, she's damn near young enough to be my granddaughter," he barked. "Besides, you jealous or somethin'? Now, get in the fuckin' van and let's get out of here."

We piled in and Clutch started the engine. "Where are we headed?" he asked.

"Take me back to my hotel," I said. "I'll grab my stuff, and car to the airport from there."

"Airport?" Clutch asked. "Why are you going to the airport?"

"Because I'm going back to Savannah. I'm going to take Cutter's book there to keep it safe, and while I'm there I'm going to talk to Zaius about bringing a couple of guys back with me."

Zaius, the Savannah chapter president, was named due to his striking resemblance to Dr. Zaius from the 1969 film The Planet of the Apes. Like his orangutan film counterpart, he was a pear-shaped man with a fiery red beard and hair. Also like the character, he was very smart, but pretty much a complete prick.

"Good luck with that," Cutter said with a chuckle.

I smirked and nodded.

Clutch killed the van's engine.

"What the fuck?" I asked.

"What the fuck *me*? What the fuck is up with you two guys?" Clutch asked, throwing his hands in the air. "The last time I checked, you two were oil and vinegar, and now suddenly you're chocolate and fucking peanut butter. So, as the Sergeant at Arms of this fucking club, I'd like to know what's up, peanut butter cup?"

Cutter pulled a flask from his inside pocket and handed it

to Clutch. "You're gonna need a pull from this."

*  *  *

"This is a joke, right? You're fucking with me. You have to be fucking with me."

"I'm dead serious, Clutch. I've asked Minus to take up the staff. I want him to be the next president of the Burning Saints."

"*Him*?" Clutch asked, pointing violently at me.

I shot him a look but said nothing. He had the right to be pissed.

"With Cricket Wallace?" he continued.

"No, not *with* Cricket. She wouldn't be Co-President; she'd be more like a business advisor. A sub-contractor to help us with our transition," Cutter replied.

"A sub-contractor?"

"That's right."

"What the fuck are you talking about, Cutter? We're a motorcycle club! Did I miss a memo? Did we take a vote at the last shareholder's meeting? When did we decide to liquidate our portfolio, and diversify our tax shelters?"

I laughed.

"This funny to you, motherfucker? I haven't heard anything to laugh about tonight, that's for damn sure."

"Calm down, Clutch I—"

"Don't tell me to calm the fuck down. In fact, don't ever tell me what the fuck to do," Clutch snapped at me. "You're not my president. Actually…I outrank your ass."

"And I outrank both of you, so shut the fuck up," Cutter growled.

"This is bullshit, and you know it, Cutter. Minus hasn't been around for years. How the fuck is he supposed to know how to run this chapter, let alone the club?"

"Just because he hasn't been in Portland doesn't mean he was working at some Bed Bath and Beyond. He's been doin' club business in Savannah. Right where I wanted him. Besides, I have faith in Minus. I trust that he's the right one for the job, and I would think that, as his best friend, you'd have no problem serving under him, and helping him become the best president he can be."

"Some fuckin' best friend," he said without looking at me. "Didn't even talk to me about any of this shit."

"I'm sorry, Clutch. Everything happened so quickly, and I hadn't even decided what I was gonna do yet," I said.

"So, you've decided now?" Cutter asked.

"After what happened today, all I know for sure, is we've got to tighten shit up around here. We need to find out where our security leaks are, get some more muscle, firepower, and prepare for war." I turned to Clutch. "The Saints need a Sergeant that's focused on the good of the club and protecting the President. I'm just a soldier, and maybe that's all I'll ever be. Cutter's asked me step in and deal with Viper, so that's what I'm gonna do. We'll figure out everything else later, but right now we've got work to do. You with me or what?"

"Fine, but this conversation is far from fuckin' over," Clutch said, pointing a finger in my face.

"Fair enough. Alright, let's get to the hotel. I've gotta call Cricket on the way there."

## SIXTEEN

*Cricket*

I HIT THE button on my electric kettle, then grabbed a mug and teabag. I had a lot on my mind (for obvious reasons), so even though I wanted wine, tea would keep me clear.

The kettle finished boiling just as my doorbell rang. I poured water into my cup, then walked to the foyer. Since my building had a doorman and a security guard, whoever was ringing could only be one of a dozen people. I looked through the peephole and sighed. *Shit!*

Pulling open the door, I forced a smile. "Well, hi there, big brother. What do I owe the pleasure?"

"You, took a leave of absence," he said, pushing through the door. "You sick or something?"

"Please, come in. Make yourself at home," I mumbled under my breath as I closed and locked the door again.

My brother faced me, his eyes soft with concern, as he studied me. "You sick, Cricket?"

I shook my head. "Fit as a fiddle."

He crossed his arms and cocked his head. "Are you being purposely obtuse?"

"Yes."

"You gonna fill me in?"

I shook my head. "Isn't that the whole point of being obtuse?"

He closed his eyes briefly and dragged a hand over his beard. I chose to wait until he was ready to rip me a new one before throwing him out of my apartment.

"Worried about you, baby sister. I'd really appreciate it if you'd fill me in on what's goin' on."

"While I appreciate your attempt at communication without the normal intimidation tactics, this isn't something I can talk to you about."

"You can talk to me about anything."

I scoffed. "That's not true, and you know it."

He shrugged off his leather jacket and slung it over the back of my sofa.

"Oh, so you're staying," I deduced as he walked into my kitchen.

"We're gonna talk, Cricket," he said grabbing a beer. Flopping onto the sofa, he twisted off the bottle top and took a swig.

I rolled my eyes, but without the spine to kick my brother out (and, admittedly, craving his advice), I grabbed my tea and sat in my oversized cuddle chair, tucking my feet under my butt. He watched me. Waiting. My brother was a pro at the stare down. So much so, I was never good at evading his questions and would always tell him way too much as a kid.

"I took a leave of absence because I've been feeling a little restless in my job. I mean, how many times can I come up with a new tagline for a dildo? It's marketing for a dildo… it's not rocket science, or *pocket-rocket* science." I sipped my tea and Hatch said nothing. Just waited. "So, I was presented with an opportunity to change that. I don't know if I'm going to take it, but it's intriguing enough that I'd like to explore it a bit."

"What kind of opportunity?"

"Nope."

"Cricket—"

"No. You'll freak the fuck out, and I'm too tired to deal with that."

"What the fuck have you gotten yourself into?" he demanded.

"Well, this has been nice," I said, setting my mug on the side table, and rising to my feet. "Please ride safely back to your beautiful home. Kiss the family for me."

He raised an eyebrow. "Sit down, sissy."

"I swear to God, Connor. I don't want to have this conversation with you."

He sighed. "You really thinkin' about takin' the job with the Saints?"

I groaned.

"Have a seat, Cricket."

I flopped back into the chair and glared at him. "I really can't handle a lecture right now, Con."

"Look, I see you're at a critical pivot point in your life right now. I get that you've got some serious shit to figure out, and I think you're smart enough to make the right decision. You know how I feel about the Saints… and Minus."

"Don't," I snapped.

"Crick—"

"No, Hatch. You are a big reason this whole shit show is happening in the first place, so I don't want your platitudes or negative opinions." I slapped my hand against my chest. "I loved him. With all my heart. You forced him out of my life, and I have suffered because of it. Minus has suffered because of it."

"Don't be so dramatic."

"Fuck you!" I let out a frustrated squeal and jumped to my feet again. "I *loved* him. I get that I was young, and I also get that our connection was quick, but that doesn't change the fact that what we had was real. Your heart might be calcified to the point of stone, but mine was broken, Con. Shattered. It's the reason every man I've ever been with has been compared to him." I jabbed a finger toward him. "You broke my heart, but now I have a chance to see where this takes me and I'm going to do it. With or without your blessing."

"By getting involved with a one-percenter?"

"He doesn't *want* to be a one-percenter, Hatch. He wants to clean up the club and go legit."

He leaned forward, settling his forearms on his knees. "Do you know how hard that is to do? The danger of trying to pull off something like that without the whole club backin' you? You didn't see what we went through in San Diego, Cricket. I shielded you from all of it."

"And I appreciate that," I said. "But I was a child. Like, a baby child. It was appropriate that you shielded me from that. But exiling Jase was way beyond your protective authorization."

"The hell it was. You're my sister, and I'll do whatever I have to if it means you're out of harm's way."

Just then my phone rang, and I silently thanked whoever was interrupting this conversation. However, once I looked down and saw who was calling, I wasn't so sure. The look on my face must have said it all, not to mention Hatch could read me like a book, and not one of those big thick, complicated Russian novels that took forever to get through. My brother could read me like a pop-up book.

"Is that him calling?" he asked in an *irritatingly bright* tone.

"No," I lied.

He simply raised an eyebrow.

"Yes, so?" I retorted.

"Well... are you going to answer it?"

"Not with you here!"

"Suit yourself, he's your business partner," he replied glibly.

"Hatch, I swear to God, if this wasn't a brand-new

phone, I would throw it so hard at your stupid head."

The phone pealed one more time, and I answered with a flustered, "Hello!"

"Cricket, thank God, I was starting to worry." Minus' voice made my insides feel like they were filled with bubbles coated in butter.

I cleared my throat. "Worry? Why? What is there to worry about?"

"Nothing, don't worry about it."

"So, there *is* something to worry about?"

"I said forget it," Minus said, his tone shifting from concern to impatience.

"No. You said don't worry about it. Which implies there is an 'it' and that there is a reason to fear said 'it.'"

"Goddammit, Cricket, would you please listen to me for a second," he hissed. "I'm not sure what Viper knows or what kind of surveillance he might have on us."

"Did things not go as planned?" I asked, and my brother perked up, his interest in my conversation clearly piqued.

"Not so much. Can you meet me at the last place we were together in fifteen minutes?"

"Fifteen minutes? No. I can make it in maybe twenty-five if I leave now," I said.

"Leave now then," he replied matter-of-factly.

"I'm kind of in the middle of something," I said.

"Cricket, unless you're hiding a dead body, I need you to meet me there as soon as possible, and be ready to fly out tonight."

"Very funny, but my brother is here, and I haven't even finished packing." In truth, I hadn't yet started. "Besides, I thought we weren't leaving until tomorrow,"

Hatch's face turned red, and he stood up. "Christina, hang up the phone."

"Plans have changed," Minus said.

"Excuse me?" I replied to my brother.

"I said hang up the phone now, you're not going anywhere with him," Hatch said.

"I said plans have changed," Minus repeated.

"No, not you baby, I was talking to my brother."

The word *baby* slipped out of my mouth so naturally that it startled me. I was mortified. The moment it left my lips, I felt the heat creep up the back of my neck, and my ears start to burn.

"Baby?" Hatch growled.

"What was that, Cricket? Something about your brother? Sorry, I'm in the back of a van."

At least Minus hadn't heard me.

"I'll meet you at the place, ready to go, as soon as possible. Um, over and out," I said, and hung up.

Ohmigod, I felt like the biggest idiot in the world. *Baby*? *Over and out*? What was wrong with me? Why was I letting Minus rattle me like this? And in front of my brother, no less!

"Christina," my brother continued, in his best chastising tone.

"I don't want to hear it. Not a word." I raised my index finger in the air and headed to my bedroom to begin packing.

"This is what you took an unscheduled leave of absence for? To take an out of town trip with your *baby*?"

"I didn't mean that. It just came out. Honestly, I don't know why," I protested.

"Don't know why? Don't know why? Let me clear it up for you. You still have feelings for Minus!"

"I told you I didn't want to hear it, and *you* have no idea how *I* feel," I said pulling an empty roller bag down from the top shelf of my closet, and throwing it onto the bed.

"You know that's not true. I just about raised you, and I can—"

"Read me like a pop-up book, yeah, whatever," I sassed, and frantically began to rummage through drawers, throwing clothes into the bag.

"I was gonna say I can tell when you're spinning out," my brother countered. "Christina, stop packing, and look at me, goddammit."

I turned to face my brother, my arms folded, wearing what I hoped was a badass warrior scowl, but feared I looked more like Bubbles from the Powerpuff Girls.

"I'm worried about you," he said. "You've been a mess since Minus got back to town."

"A mess?" I protested. "How am I a mess?"

"You're all over the map! The last time we spoke, you'd just decked Minus and now you're ready to run off with him, pissed at me for chasing him off years ago."

"I'm not *running off with him*. It's not like that."

"Then what is it like, Cricket?" he challenged, leaning against the doorframe. "Tell me, because I'm very confused. I'd honestly love to hear what the hell you're thinking directly from you, instead of second-hand through my wife."

"Do you *really*? Do you want to know all about my life, and how I'm bored out of my mind at work? How the thought of coming up with the next tagline for some porn star's latex vagina makes me want to scream? I will forever be grateful for Maisie for hooking me up with this job, but I'm seriously over the sex business and all its so-called glory. I just want a regular life."

"Running a one-percenter club in the heart of Portland," he ground out.

"It won't be one-percenter once we're done with it." I grabbed shoes and dropped what I hoped were matching pairs into the bag.

Hatch dragged his hands down his face and took several deep breaths. "I don't like this."

"Noted," I said, then faced him. "Don't make me choose between you and him, Connor. Please. I love you, but this is my life."

"You don't know him!"

"I know him enough," I said. "And I know myself. I'm not an idiot. If he does anything out of line, I'm out. He knows this. Give yourself credit, big brother, you raised me right, but now your job is done."

"What am I supposed to do if this all goes to shit?"

"You open up your arms and hold me while I cry. Think you can manage that, Con?"

He sighed. "I have no fuckin' idea."

I closed the distance between us and laid my hand over one of the patches on his kutte. "I have faith in you, and I know the Dogs have both of our backs. I need you to trust me, okay? If I need you, I promise I'll tell you. I won't do anything reckless."

He frowned. "Why doesn't that make me feel better?"

"Because it's hardwired in you to protect," I explained. "My brothers are the same way. I was the only girl and the baby of the family. I was at the top of every one of their 'protect at all costs' list."

"So, you understand."

"Of course I do, but right now, though, I don't need you to protect me, okay?"

He studied me for a few seconds before giving me a slight nod.

"Hallelujah. Lock up on your way out, please."

Before I could escape, he pulled me in for a hug… one of his signature bear hugs that made you feel safe and gooey. "Love you, Cricket."

I wrapped my arms around his waist and squeezed. "Love you, too, Connor."

"Text me when you get to wherever you're going. I want to know you're safe."

"I will," I promised.

Hatch left me to my packing, which I finished in record time. Then I locked up and rushed to meet my man.

## SEVENTEEN

*Cricket*

"CRICKET. WAKE UP, baby. We're here."

I forced myself away from the comfort of dreamland and sat up. Apparently, I'd fallen asleep on Jase, and he grinned as I reached my hands above my head and stretched. He waved a finger toward my mouth. "You got a little drool right there."

"I don't drool," I snapped, even as I wiped at my face.

He chuckled, leaning over to kiss me gently. "Don't worry you're still cute as a fuckin' button."

I wrinkled my nose. "Whatever."

"Gonna make you wet in a different way when I get you home," he whispered, and I closed my eyes with a shiver. I couldn't wait.

Because it was so late, and we hadn't checked any luggage, we were able to leave the airport relatively quickly, grab a taxi, and head to his condo which was in an old tobacco warehouse. It had been converted into three huge loft/condos, and Jase's was on the top floor.

"Wow," I whispered as I took in the space. "This place is amazing."

Exposed brick, hardwood floors, everything was open. Except for the two bedrooms and three bathrooms. There was also an office off the great room with French doors letting light in.

"I like it," he said, dropping our bags on the floor. "Close to the barn and the club… close to restaurants. Everything I need within walking distance."

"I love it."

He grinned, closing the distance between us, and kissing me quickly. "Gonna fuck you now."

"I'd love a shower first," I admitted. "Get the plane funk off me."

"Okay then, we can fuck in the shower."

I nodded, then his mouth was on mine and I was in his arms, my legs wrapped around his waist, and we were headed to his bedroom. He set me on my feet, tore my clothes off, continuing to kiss me while he turned the water on.

Once he was naked, he walked me under the water and he hissed out, "Shit."

"What's wrong?"

"Forgot to grab condoms."

"Like, from the store?" I asked, my stomach falling.

He smiled. "They're in the nightstand."

I sighed. "Oh, thank God."

He chuckled, and we took the quickest shower on earth, then after toweling off, he carried me back into the bedroom, dropping me onto the bed. He settled his mouth between my legs and sucked my clit, his tongue swirling as he added pressure with each pass he made.

Pushing his fingers inside of me, my body shuddered with need, and when I lost his mouth, I whimpered.

"I'm coming back, baby," Jase promised, and grabbed a condom, rolling it on before he climbed up my body, linking his fingers with mine and holding them over my head. As he slowly slid his cock into me, I sighed and wrapped my legs around him, arching up. He slammed into me repeatedly. This time sex was rawer and more animalistic than it ever had been, and I didn't think I could love him more.

"Jase," I rasped. "I…" I came undone and Jase kissed me, releasing one of my hands to stroke my neck as we climaxed, and anchored me to him as he rolled us to the side.

His hand cupped my bottom and he kissed my temple. "So much wasted time."

I stroked his beard. "Shh, baby, we're making up for it."

"Not fast enough," he complained.

"Well, that's on you, bub."

"You wanna keep bustin' my balls, Cricket?" he asked, slapping my bottom.

"Yes." I shifted so I was straddling him and cupped his face. "If it means I get more of that."

"I love that you like it dirty, baby." He slid his hand between us and thumbed my clit.

"Hell, yes, I do." I dropped my head back and rocked against him.

"Grab the headboard, Cricket."

I did as I was told, and he slid down, so his face was between my legs, lifting his head up so his mouth covered my core. I pressed my body down, but he gripped my hips and anchored me where he wanted me. I tried to move, but he was stronger than me, and he held firm, his tongue sliding in deeper and deeper.

"So fuckin' wet, baby," he rasped, and sucked my clit.

"Again, that's on you, bub," I retorted.

He chuckled and slid out from under me, shifting me so I was on all fours. "Cheek to the mattress, Cricket."

I obliged immediately, and he lifted my hips, running his finger around the tight ring. "One day, baby, I'm gonna take this." He slid his finger over my wetness and moved it to my very forbidden area.

"I bet I can find a toy for that at the warehouse," I panted out. "Remind me to check when I go back."

"You're never goin' back. Regardless, you won't need me to remind you," he said, kissing the rise of my bottom. "You're never gonna forget this."

He wasn't wrong, and I groaned with need.

"Finger your clit, baby," he ordered, and I reached back.

His cock slid inside me, slowly at first, and I worked my clit while he tortured my pussy. "Minus," I breathed out.

"No," he growled. "You use Jase when I'm makin' love to you."

"Jase," I corrected.

"Brace, baby."

I grabbed the edge of the mattress and he slammed into me, harder and harder. "I'm—"

"Don't come," he ordered.

"I have—"

He slapped my bottom, which *really* didn't help. "Hold it, Christina."

I bit my lip and tried to keep my orgasm at bay, but then his finger slid into the tightness of my ass and I exploded, screaming his name into the pillow as I collapsed onto the mattress. Jase rolled us to our sides again, staying connected as he continued to move, his hand sliding between my legs and cupping my pussy as he worked my clit. "More?"

I just nodded. I didn't have enough breath to speak.

While one hand worked my clit, his other rolled my nipple into a tight bud and he slammed into me, building yet another orgasm. He slapped my pussy, once... then again... and my body shook.

"Come, baby," he whispered, and I let go.

Jase held me tight as we caught our breath and I closed my eyes unable to focus. "Holy... oh, my... I'm..."

He kissed my shoulder. "Fuckin' beautiful, baby."

I rolled to face him and stroked his cheek. "I'm liking your definition of making things up to me."

Jase laughed, kissing me gently. "Good. There's plenty more where that came from."

"I'm counting on it."

He climbed off the bed and headed to the bathroom, returning with a warm washcloth and cleaning me up.

Slipping back under the covers, he pulled me onto his chest. "You need to sleep?"

I shook my head. "I'm actually really wired. Want to watch a movie?"

"Yeah, baby, we can do that."

\* \* \*

The next morning, we drove about forty-five minutes out of town, to the Double H Ranch. This was the home of Duke and Pearl, whom I knew little about, other than they knew my uncle, and that Minus had lived with them for a while. The scenery along the way was breathtaking, becoming more beautiful with every mile closer to the ranch.

"This is gorgeous," I said as we pulled off the main highway, and onto a long private road.

"Wait 'til you see the property itself," Minus said. "Not to mention the house. Pearl's always got the place decked out like she's getting it ready for the cover of 'Fancy Ranch Monthly' or something."

"Really? That's not what I'd pictured for a couple of ranchers," I said.

"Why's that?" Minus asked.

"I don't know, I guess I've just never spent any time around people that live out in rural areas. I'm a city girl. All I have to base my expectations on is what I've seen in movies and on TV. Even Kim and Knight who own property in Portland... it's still close to the city, so it just doesn't register with me, I guess."

He grinned. "I suppose those stereotypes exist for a reason, but most of the ranchers I've met are educated, run high-tech operations, and have serious money. These aren't guys that ride tractors, or sit on rickety porches, holding shotguns with straw hangin' outta their mouths."

"What are Duke and Pearl like?"

Minus grinned. "Well, Duke is kinda the guy with the

tractor and the shotgun, but he's also brilliant. They're the best. The most loving people I know, and they are going to adore you."

We continued down the road, passing underneath a large HH Ranch sign.

"What does the HH stand for?" I asked.

"I've never been able to get Duke to tell me."

"Oooh, a mystery."

"Probably not. I think Duke just likes fuckin' with me. Pearl says is stands for, 'Healing Hugs.'" Minus chuckled. "But I somehow doubt it."

"She sounds sweet," I said, as Minus parked.

"You should be prepared before we get out. They're probably gonna make a big deal out of you being here."

"I'll prepare myself," I said smiling, as we exited the car.

No sooner had I closed my door when I heard a loud crack echo through the forest walls.

"Get down!" Minus yelled, as he dopped. After what felt like an eternity to process what he was saying, a second shot rang out, whizzing directly over our heads.

"Cricket! Get the fuck down!"

I dropped to the ground, tearing my jeans and skinning my left knee on a rock as I did. I flattened my body and wriggled under the car as best I could.

"Whoever you are, you'd better get the fuck off my property, because the next one will be more than a warnin' shot!" a voice called out.

*This is some warm welcome.*

"It's Minus, you crazy old bastard! Hold your fire!"

The shooting stopped, and after a few moments of silence, a voice called out.

"Minus? Is that really you?"

"That's what I just said, Duke!" Minus replied. "Now, will you please put the rifle away before you shoot someone. And by someone, I mean me or my guest, *Cricket Wallace*?"

"Cricket's with you? Where? I can't see anybody," Duke called back.

"That's because we're on the ground, Duke. You know,

on account of all the shooting. I'm gonna stand up now and I'd kindly appreciate it if you didn't put any unnecessary holes in me." Minus said, before rising and coming over to my side of the car.

"Lemme help you up. Are you okay?" he asked, while looking me over.

"I just hurt my knee a little. I'll live."

I heard footsteps crunching rapidly down the gravel driveway and looked up to see a man in a white beard and overalls, trotting towards us, carrying a hunting rifle.

"Sorry, Minus. I didn't recognize the car, and wasn't expecting you," he said, out of breath.

"Jesus, Duke. What's with the display of firepower?"

"We've got guys growing pot on our land. I've been finding plants in the heavily wooded areas for a while now."

"Since when?"

"I guess it's been around five months. It must be harvest time, because I've seen more people around lately. I chase 'em off whenever I do, but it ain't helpin'. Every time I find a plant, I pull it up, but I can't keep up with 'em. Strange cars and trucks have been pullin' up day and night."

"Why didn't you tell me?" Minus asked.

"Because it's my goddamned ranch and I'll chase those punks off myself. Plus, I didn't want to bother you. I know you've got plenty of club business in town to tend to."

"Bullshit. You, Pearl, and the ranch come first. You call me next time you have a problem. In the meantime, I'm gonna make sure this little unsanctioned grow operation is taken care of, and that you're compensated for your trouble by these assholes."

Duke nodded at Minus, then smiled wide at me. "Well, ain't you the prettiest little thing! Sorry if I gave you a fright."

"That's okay," I said extending my hand. "Hi, I'm Cricket."

"Oh, we know all about you 'round here," Duke said grinning at Minus.

"Is that so?" I asked.

"Golden boy here moped all around the ranch for six months when he first got here on account'a you." He leaned close to me. "There's only one kinda sick that can make a man act like that. *Woman sick*," he said dramatically.

"Woman sick, huh?" I asked.

Minus grinned sheepishly. "Alright, I think that's about enough of that," he said.

"Yes, ma'am, and Minus here had it bad," he continued, ignoring Minus. "All we heard about was Cricket this and Cricket that, that is when he wasn't bitching about how much of a prick Cutter is." He turned to Minus. "How is Cutter, by the way?"

"Yeah, about that," Minus said sternly.

"My sweet Lord look at your knee," Duke said, ignoring Minus.

"It's nothing. Just a scrape. I'll be okay," I said, trying my best not to think about the bits of gravel that I'd have to pick out of my stinging flesh.

"We'd better get you inside so we can have Pearl take a look at that. She'll get you patched up proper. I'll tell you, Pearly's gonna read me the riot act for this one."

"I can keep a secret if you can," I said, as we walked up the front steps.

"I can, but not from Pearl. The woman's got a gift for sniffing out my bullshit from a mile away," he said, smiling.

An elderly woman with rosy cheeks, and perfectly styled hair met us at the front door as soon as we reached it. She wore a beautifully tailored lemon-yellow dress, and her ensemble was complete with high heels and a string of pearls.

"I heard gunshots. Is everything okay?" she asked.

"Everything's fine, I thought it was those damned squatters come for their wacky tobacky, but it's worse."

"Minus! What a surprise, it's so nice to see you," she sang out in delight before hugging him. "And who is this stunning young woman you've brought with you?"

"Pearl, I'd like to introduce you to Miss Cricket Wallace."

Before I could react, I found myself in Pearl's arms. She

smelled like a freshly baked apple pie, and her hug was as warm and sweet as one.

"I'm so glad y'all are here," she said before finally breaking the embrace, taking a step back to face me. "You are even more beautiful than Minus described you."

Before I could react to that bit of information, Pearl squeaked, "Oh, my! You're bleeding, dear."

"Oh, it's nothing. I tripped outside, it's no big deal. I just need a wet paper towel and a bandage, and I'll be fine," I said.

"Nonsense, you come with me to the first-aid room and I'll take care of everything."

"First-aid room?" I asked.

"It's better if you don't argue with her or put up any kind of fight," Duke said. "She looks sweet... but she's a mean woman and she always gets her way."

"Randal Urias Hill, if I find out you had something to do with this, you're gonna find out just how mean I can be..."

"Promises, Promises," Duke said.

"Don't you sass me."

"Yes ma'am," Duke replied, sheepishly.

I smiled at their adorable exchange before Pearl gently took me by the elbow and led us out of the room.

"Come on, dear, we'll stop off in the kitchen and put on a pot of coffee," she said.

"Can I help with anything?" I asked.

"Well, aren't you just the sweetest thing? I can't wait to get to know each other and talk all about these horrible men."

# EIGHTEEN

*Minus*

THE MOMENT THE ladies left the room, Duke turned to me. "Buy you a drink?"

"It's a little early, isn't it?" I replied.

"Yup. That's what the coffee's for, but that ain't ready yet, so we'll just have to make do 'till then," he said smiling.

"Well, when you put it that way. Two fingers over ice, please."

We walked to Duke's den and I took a seat on the sofa as he poured us two bourbons.

"I take it from the fact that you and Cricket were smiling, despite the gunplay, that you two are on good terms again?" he asked.

"For now, I guess," I replied, still unsure of where we

stood.

"Well, son, the way I see it, us men are always floatin' around in some sort of state of grace when it comes to women. The trick is to extend the periods in between the times they're hoppin' mad at us."

"To extended grace periods," I said, and raised my glass.

"And may the whiskey flow when the grace don't," Duke said, clinking my glass.

I took a sip and allowed myself a moment of peace and pleasure before digging back in with Duke. "Let me ask you a question," I said.

Duke nodded. "Fire away."

"In all the time I've been here, you never thought to mention that you knew Cutter?"

"You never asked," Duke said plainly.

"We've had a hundred conversations about the man, and you never once brought up a story from your past, or said, "Ya know, the thing about Cutter is..." You never said a word. You'd just tell me some old story about a Greek fisherman, or quote Beckett."

"Well, I don't know what *you'd* call that, son, but where I come from, that right there is a conversation."

"So, the fact that you're affiliated with the Saints goes beyond Savannah, not to mention leads all the way back to Cutter, simply never came up during one of those *conversations*?"

"Why never mention you *knew* him?"

"I suppose it never seemed relevant," he replied. "Your relationship with Cutter is quite different than mine. He sent you here for *you* to work on *you*, not for *me* to talk about *him*. You get me?"

"Not entirely, being as I never recall enrolling in a self-help ranch program. You'll have to forgive me, if the fact that y'all have been playing with me like some goddamned chess piece is still a bit unsettling to me."

"Aw, grow the fuck up, boy. Cutter saw something in you, so he sent you to me so's I could see if he was right. It's as plain as that. I may never have patched in with the Saints, but I rode with them for years back in the day. I've always been an ally to the club and this place has always served as a safe haven for any Saint that needed a place to lay low or get patched up. Cutter would always make sure we got help when we needed it, and from time-to-time, he'd call on me for help with one of his brood. If he saw potential in someone, he'd sometimes send 'em my way. I'd work 'em hard, try to knock a few lessons into their heads, and send 'em back home when I felt it was time."

"Act two: *Our hero is sent to Dagobah to receive further training*," I muttered softly.

"My ears are old, but I ain't deaf. Besides, Cutter's no Obi-Wan, and I sure as shit ain't fuckin' Yoda," Duke snapped back.

I looked at him, shocked.

"What? You think you're the only one with a fuckin' VCR?" Duke asked.

"I think you're the only one *left* with a VCR," I replied.

"Look, Minus, you've got to understand something. Just because we're old dogs, don't mean we're completely out of touch, and I ain't just talkin' about movies, ya understand?" Duke looked at me with a softness in his eyes.

"Yes, sir."

"Cutter may be a tough bastard, but he loves his club. He probably loves it more than anything, so if he's askin' you to run it, you can bet he's given it plenty of thought."

"So, you know about what's goin' on?" I asked.

"Cutter filled me in. I didn't know you'd be comin' back so soon, though," he replied.

"We've run into some trouble with a local club, and I had to get outta town as quickly, and silently, as possible."

"If you're having local trouble, what are you doing here, and why all the cloak and dagger?"

"We appear to have some holes in our security. These pricks have been a step ahead of us everywhere we go lately."

"Your leaks tech or personnel related?" Duke asked.

"I'm not sure yet, so I didn't want to take any chances

with this." I pulled Cutter's ledger from my duffel and set in on the coffee table in front of us.

Duke glanced at the leather-bound book and then looked back at me blankly. "Thanks, Minus, but I've already got a Bible, and I can't say I spend much time readin' that one."

"You know it's never too late to pursue that dream of being a standup comic."

He grinned. "Duke the Cable Guy's gotta a nice ring to it, doesn't it?"

"Sure, your catch phrase could be "I'll get 'r done... tomorrow."

"How ''bout this for a catch phrase? "Hey, Minus. Shut your yankee mouth or I'll put a boot in your fuckin' ass.'"

"Perfect, we'll call Carnegie Hall fir a booking as soon as we're done here," he said picking up the ledger. "Now, what the hell am I lookin' at?"

"A ledger containing current club financials, business contacts, and laundering sources."

"Jesus, Minus. There a specific reason such a hot item is currently in my home?"

"I had to get it as far away from home as possible and I couldn't think of a better place than here in your safe. I'm gonna talk to Zaius about posting a couple of patches here until all of this blows over, and I'm going to need you to get some more of the younger guys around here up to speed. I'll need all the allies on my side I can get both in Savannah and Portland."

"So, does that mean you're gonna do it? You're taking over when Cutter retires?"

"I was hoping to get your advice on that too," I admitted.

"What the hell could I say at this point? You either think it's the right thing to do, and you take the position, or you don't, and Cutter finds someone else to become President."

"What do you mean, someone else?" I asked.

Oddly enough, the thought had never occurred to me, as to who might become President should I turn Cutter down.

"The club has to have a president, and if it's not you, it'll be someone else."

"What if it *was* me?" I asked.
"Then we'd have our work cut out for us, wouldn't we?"

\* \* \*

## Cricket

After putting a pot of coffee on to brew, Pearl led me to the back of the gigantic ranch house, where she pushed on a wall panel and a door popped open.

"Oh, my word, you have a Scooby Doo door?" I breathed out.

Pearl chuckled. "I've never heard them called that, but that's what I'm calling them from now on."

"Them? There are more than just this one?"

"I have six *Scooby Doo* doors. Never know when we gotta hide a Saint from a sinner."

I followed Pearl into the 'first-aid' room and tried to keep my mouth from dropping open. This was a glorified hospital room, complete with lights, a rolling IV bag stand, and an official hospital bed. Pearl patted the mattress and smiled. "Hop on up, honey."

I sat up on the end of the bed and Pearl leaned down and frowned. "I'm gonna need you to get those jeans off, so I can dress it," she said. "You feel comfortable with that?"

"Is the door locked?"

"Yeah, honey, it's locked."

I nodded and pushed my jeans down past my knee. "I love your dress, Pearl."

She grinned. "Thank you. Duke loves me in dresses, so I've worn one every day since we started going steady."

"Really?"

She nodded while she tended to my knee. "Yep. I've pretty much worn the same thing, since our first date. A pretty dress, heels… and no panties."

I choked on a laugh, so surprised she'd offered up that unnecessary piece of information.

"It's important you please your man," she continued.

"Isn't it important he please you, too?" I asked.

"Of course, honey. If you're with a good man, he will. And, if you're with the *right* man, he'll please you without you asking." She washed her hands and pulled on gloves. "They risk their lives, you know."

"I know," I said quietly.

"Some men'll go to hell and back for their woman. You find a man like that; you don't let him go."

"Did Duke go to hell and back for you?"

"On more than a couple of occasions." She met my eyes. "Minus has done the same for you."

"I'm not sure—"

"Honey child, that boy has loved you for as long as I've known him. He ain't never looked at another woman like he looks at you, and since I love him like a son, I hope you won't take that for granted."

I bit my lip. "I won't... I don't."

I wasn't prepared to go into detail about my insecurities when it came to Jase, but I liked hearing that this lovely woman saw his love for me even though I'd never met her before. It solidified several things for me, and I knew my future included Jase... and Minus... and whatever other side of his personality might appear.

"Glad to hear it, honey," Pearl said, then took a few minutes to flush my wound, making sure any gravel that burrowed into my skin was gone. Then she put some antibiotic cream on it and bandaged me good and tight.

I pulled my (now stylishly torn) jeans back up while Pearl cleaned up, then she led me through another door (a regular one this time) and into a bunk room of sorts. I mean, it was most certainly a bunk room, but it was kind of... well... fancy.

"This is where we stash bikers who need to stay hidden for a while," she said.

"It's really nice, especially considering your usual guests." I glanced around the room. "I've always figured anyone who needed to disappear would be relegated to some remote cave somewhere. This is way better."

Pearl nodded. "We take care of our boys."

"I can see that." I smiled at her. "Thank you for doing that."

"My pleasure, honey." She patted my arm. "Let's go find the boys. I'd imagine yours is already pining for you."

I giggled. "I doubt it, but that's sweet to imagine."

Pearl led me back the way we came, and we ended up in the kitchen where Duke and Jase were making coffee.

Minus handed me a cup and then wrapped his arm around me and kissed my temple. "How's your knee?"

"It's all good," I said, giving him a squeeze.

"Well, Pearl and I got some shit to do," Duke said. "You comin' back for dinner?"

"We'd love to come back for dinner," Jase said.

"Right. We'll see you at six," Duke said. "Sharp."

"Sounds good. I'm gonna give Cricket the fifty-cent tour of the property. Then we'll get cleaned up and meet you back here."

"It was lovely to meet you both," I said.

Pearl grinned, taking Duke's hand. "You, too, honey."

We finished up our coffee, then headed back to the car.

# NINETEEN

## BURNING SAINTS

*Cricket*

**J**ASE DROVE US over to what he referred to as the 'main barn' and I couldn't stop my mouth from dropping open as we walked inside. It was nicer than any barn I'd ever seen. Not that I'd seen many, but I'd seen a few from watching Poppy's competitions and visiting Kim and Knight's home. None of them were as clean as Duke's. From the first-aid room, to the bunk room, and now the barn, I wondered just how much money Duke had stashed away.

Jase pushed open a door marked with "Tack Room" above it and guided me inside. It was huge. Against the wall directly in front of me was a row of saddles (small ones, like the one Poppy rode with), and the things that go over their face on hooks next to them. To my right were the big bulky saddles with horns, and to my left there was a wall of armoires with trunks in-between.

"Fancy," I said. I shook my head. I seemed to be using this word to describe all manner of things today.

Jase chuckled, closing the door. "Yeah, I suppose so."

Jase took my hand and pulled me up against him, leaning down to kiss me. I slid my arms around his neck and wove my fingers into his hair. "What are you doing?" I asked in suspicion.

He grinned, reaching behind him to lock the door. "I'm planning on giving you a positive memory about horses to take with you."

"How ya gonna do that?" I challenged.

"Gonna fuck you hard enough you won't forget."

"You or Minus?"

"Who do you want?" he asked.

I bit my lip. "I had Jase earlier... so.... Minus, please."

His eyes darkened with desire and he slid his hands to my neck. My heart raced, and I licked my lips in anticipation as he kissed me again, before helping me remove my boots and socks. He kicked his off, then removed his shirt and I ran my hands over his chest, his rock-hard abs heady to the touch.

He kissed me again, then his lips moved to my neck, while a hand went to the hem of my shirt and pulled it off in one quick swoop. He pulled one bra cup down, scraping a nail across my nipple before leaning down to draw my nipple into his mouth. I gasped as he blew gently where he'd sucked, feeling the bud tighten as he sucked again.

I felt the clasp of my bra give and then Jase slid it down my arms. "Gorgeous, baby," he whispered as he cupped each breast and kissed me again.

My hand went to the waistband of his jeans and I unbuttoned the top and slid the zipper down, feeling his hard length against my hand. I slipped my hand under his boxer briefs to cup him, wrapping my hand around him and squeezing gently.

"Fuck, that feels incredible."

I smiled, running my hand up and down his length until he pulled my hand away.

"Want this to last, baby."

He kissed me quickly as he pushed my jeans and panties from my hips. I lost all coherent thought after that as he slid his hand between my legs and grinned. "Already wet."

I nodded and then gasped as he dragged my wetness to my clit with his finger. In the middle of the room was a circular bench, and he led me to it, sitting and pulling me onto his lap. I straddled him, and he fisted his cock, then guided it inside of me.

Slowly.

Gently.

I took his face in my hands. "What are you doing... *Minus?*"

He grinned. "Fucking you."

"This isn't fucking, Jase," I argued.

"I beg to differ. My dick's hard, it's inside your warm, wet pussy... usually, there's a hell of a lot less chatter, but I'm pretty sure we're doin' it right," he retorted.

I leaned in closer. "You're being... *nice*. In case you didn't get the memo, I'd like Jase to go away for a bit."

He glanced at something over my head, then met my eyes again. "You want Minus, Cricket?"

"Yes, please." Lifting me off his lap, I almost cried to lose his cock. "Minus."

"Stay there. Don't turn around," he ordered.

I stayed, my pussy contracting with need. "Jase," I hissed.

"Jase isn't here, remember?" His breath whispered over my skin and I shivered. "Hands on the back of the bench, Cricket. Legs spread."

I didn't ask why; I just did as I was told. Something soft and cool slid down my back and I arched into it.

"I said, spread," Minus growled and a sting hit my ass.

I cried out as I spread my legs wider.

His front hit my back and he gripped my hip. "What I

have here, baby, is a riding crop. English riders use them to make their horses obey."

I bit my lip as he slid it up one thigh, then the other, before running it between my slick folds. "Oh, God," I rasped.

The crop hit my ass again and I squeaked quietly.

"Not God, Cricket. Who?"

The crop moved between my legs again and I groaned.

"*Who*, Christina?"

"Mi… Minus," I whispered.

"That's right." He slapped my pussy gently with the soft leather end, then pressed it against my clit. "You want me to fuck you, Cricket?"

"God, yes."

"Uh, uh, uh." He slapped my ass again. "Who?"

"Sorry," I hissed out, even though I wasn't exactly sorry. Maybe if I made a few more mistakes, I'd get more of the crop. I closed my eyes and whispered, "Minus."

He grabbed my hips and slid into me. Harder than before and I almost came. My head dropped back of its own accord and I sighed with relief.

"You gonna control yourself?" he asked.

"Will I get more of the crop?"

"Do you *want* more of the crop?"

"Holy shit, yes, I do."

"Then, don't come."

I bobbed my head up and down and was rewarded with the crop sliding up the outside of my leg before slapping my ass again. "Good girl."

"Maybe do that at the end," I rasped.

"Okay, baby." He chuckled and dropped the crop on the bench beside me. "Brace yourself."

I braced, and Minus slammed into me. Flesh slapped against flesh as our bodies connected, and an orgasm threatened to hit. I wanted to come… wanted it more than anything, but I needed this to last. Goosebumps whispered across my skin and I knew I wouldn't be able to wait much longer. "Minus," I begged.

"Wait."

"Mi... oh, God."

"Not. God," he panted out as he thrust into me. "Say it."

"Minus!" I screamed as I came, my pussy contracting around his cock.

He thrust again, then once more, his hand connecting with my bare flesh with a smack, and I cried out as another orgasm hit.

Sliding out of me, he ordered, "Stand up."

I did, and he slid his hand between my legs, cupping my pussy. "This is mine. Understand?"

I nodded as I worked to catch my breath.

He turned me to face him and I moved to grab my discarded clothes. "Don't," he said. "I want you to feel my cum dripping down your legs. Remember who your pussy belongs to."

It was in that moment, I realized he hadn't used a condom. Fuck, that was hot. I licked my lips, my body primed and ready for more as the proof of his ownership created a coolness on my inner thighs.

He slid his arm around my waist and kissed me. "The clean bill of health was waitin' for me in my mailbox," he whispered. "Figured you'd like me ungloved."

"Yes," I whispered. "Always."

He patted my hip. "You ready to ride?"

"I'm ready to ride *you* again."

He grinned. "There's a bathroom right there." He nodded his head toward a door at the back of the room. "We'll clean up, then you're gonna meet Boston."

I gripped his arm. "I really don't want to."

"I hear you, Cricket. But you're gonna have to get over that."

"Jase—"

"Do you trust me?"

"I don't think you want me to answer that," I grumbled.

"Gonna let that one slide, baby." He smiled slowly, stroking my cheek. "You trust me."

I leaned into his hand and nodded. Of course, I trusted him. I probably *shouldn't* trust him as deeply as I did, but I did. "Please don't let me die by horse."

"Fuck me, you're adorable, Cricket." He dropped his head back and laughed. "I got your back. You won't die." He kissed me one more time, then we cleaned up and stepped out of the tack room. Jase let out a quiet whistle, then the sound of a horse whinnying echoed through the space.

For the first time since we'd reconnected, I watched Jase's face completely change. His eyes lit up like a kid on Christmas morning and his nostrils flared slightly, like he was drawing in the scent of his surroundings. He grabbed my hand and led me around the corner to where the prettiest horse I'd ever seen had his head peeking out of a stall, whinnying up a storm, as we approached.

"Hey, Bossy Boy," Minus crooned, and the horse threw his head up and down. Minus stroked his nose and grimaced. "I know, buddy, it's been too fuckin' long, huh?"

Standing across from them, I smiled… until someone shoved me from behind. I turned to give them a piece of my mind when I discovered it wasn't a someone at all. It was another horse. I let out a frightened squeak and stepped back, only to find Jase's arm snake around my waist and walk me back toward the horse. I planted my feet and tried to keep him from moving me. "What are you *doing*?"

"Baby, this is Hank," he said. "He's who you're going to learn to ride."

He pushed me gently, but I shook my head. "He's a giant."

"He's also a big teddy bear."

"He just *shoved* me," I countered.

Jase chuckled. "He was saying hi."

As if to say a big fat "fuck you" to Jase and his opinion, Hank stretched his head toward me again and licked my hand. "Ohmigod, he's trying to eat me."

"He's not trying to eat you, Cricket, he's getting to know you."

The horse blew air out of his nose, then nudged me again. I raised my hand tentatively and stroked his face. He lowered his head and I focused on the soft space between his eyes.

"That's right," Jase whispered. "He loves you already."

"You're crazy."

"You'll see," Jase said, and turned me to face him. "We'll get him tacked up—"

"You're going to pin him to the wall?"

"Cute. I'm going to saddle him and Boston, then you and I are going to ride. In the arena, where I can keep an eye on you."

"I don't need to learn to ride," I argued. "Poppy already tried to teach me. It did not go well."

"Poppy is not me." Jase released me, and I stepped out of head reach of Hank.

For the next half-hour or so, Jase showed me how to brush Hank and how to clean his feet (Jase called it picking his hooves, which kind of grossed me out, to be honest, but I went with it). To his credit, Hank stood perfectly still. He didn't do anything to frighten me, almost as though he knew I needed him to be gentle.

Jase took pity on me and saddled both the horses. Even watching him closely, I still had no clue what he did exactly, or how to replicate it.

"Take the reins, Cricket," Jase directed, and handed me two straps of leather.

"Doesn't he need a leash?"

He smiled, shaking his head. "The reins will act as his lead."

I wrinkled my nose. "Not a leash, then."

"No. If he was haltered, he'd have a lead, not a leash."

"To lead him around. I get it."

He chuckled. "Exactly. Keep to his left side, right by his head, and follow me and Boston into the arena. Do you think you can handle that?"

"I don't know." Hank was huge. His back about an inch over my nose. If he took off, I don't know that I'd be able to hold him.

Jase smiled. "Trust him, he'll follow you."

"What if he bolts?"

"He won't bolt."

"What if he does?" I challenged.

"Stay calm and I'll come help you."

"What if he goes up on his hind legs and threatens to trample me?"

"Christina, he's not going to do anything like that."

"What if he does?"

"Then, get the fuck away from him."

I nodded. "That was kind of my plan."

I rolled my eyes and stood with the horse while Jase did his thing.

# TWENTY

## Cricket

**B**OSTON WHINNIED HIS impatience, so Jase slid his stall door open and walked toward the exit. Boston followed like a puppy and I held Hank's reins tight as I followed them. Walking into the arena, Jase closed the gate and left Boston standing in the middle. Boston was having none of it. He followed, going so far as to settle his head on Jase's shoulder. "Buddy, I know you missed me, but I gotta help Cricket. Do I have to tie you?"

Boston blew air out and threw his head up and down. I watched in fascination as the two seemed to have a conversation. "Stay," Jase said.

After making sure Boston stayed where he was, Jase made his way to me, adjusted the strap around Hank's waist, then faced me. "You ready?"

"Not in the least."

"You want to try and mount your horse?"

"Not in the least," I repeated.

Jase grinned and wrapped an arm around my waist, leaning down to kiss me gently. "You're gonna do great. Face the saddle, left hand on the horn and lift your left leg."

I did as he instructed, my body shaking with fear.

"When I lift you, swing your right leg over. Make sense?"

"In theory."

"Okay, on three. One, two, three." He lifted me, and I threw my right leg over... exactly like I did when getting on a motorcycle. Hank didn't move, which made this whole thing a hell of a lot easier. "Good job, baby."

Jase helped me adjust my stirrups, then settled my feet where they should be, patting my leg as he smiled up at me from the ground. "How do you feel?"

"A bit like I'm on a really big Harley."

"Not a whole lotta difference," he said. "I think you'll like it just as much."

"We'll see," I said.

"I'm going to watch you walk around a bit before I get on Boston. He and I are gonna hang in the middle and I'm going to have you go around us. Okay?"

I nodded, and my lesson commenced.

"You're a natural," he announced after about twenty minutes or so.

"This is actually kind of fun."

"Told ya."

I nodded. "You did. And it's so nice that you're not rubbing that in my face right now. You are *such* a good man, Jase."

"Thanks for noticin'."

I rolled my eyes. "What now?"

He mounted Boston like he was stepping onto an escalator, gathering his reins in his right hand. "Follow me. We'll go slow."

"We better go slow, 'cause if I fall off, I will kill you."

He grinned and led Boston to the arena gate, leaning down to open it, then walking out. My horse followed without me having to guide him, which helped me relax a little. It was almost as though Hank was assuring me that he had me and I was safe.

The ranch backed up to protected forest trails and I was in awe as we rode through the foliage. It was several degrees cooler under the shelter of the trees, and I was super glad I'd worn a jacket. Jase pointed out some of his favorite side trails that he promised to take me on when we had more time, and by the time we started our loop back to the barn, I was kind of bummed the ride was ending so soon. It was a beautiful day, with a gorgeous man, and I didn't want it to end.

We reached the end of the trail and Jase brought Boston to a gentle halt, causing Hank to follow suit. I could see the barn off in the distance, and between us was a meadow covered with small yellow flowers, with a narrow dirt path that led all the way back to the ranch.

"Let's dismount here and walk 'em back the rest of the way. I want to show you something special," Jase said.

He threw his leg over Boston and slid off like something out of an old western. Damn, he was sexy. I knew that after all this riding, and *riding* I was gonna be sore as hell in the morning, but I wasn't sure I'd be able to keep my hands off him regardless.

"Here, let me help you down," he said, taking a hold of Hank's reins, and instructing me on how to properly dismount without breaking my neck.

"Great job," he said, smiling. "See, you're a natural."

"I was scared out of my mind, but that was so much fun!" I said, still slightly out of breath.

At that moment I had a realization. I was vulnerable with Jase and found it easy to admit to him when I felt scared, which was rare for me. *Minus*, on the other hand, made me feel safe, and therefore adventurous. Both sides of his personality may prove to come in handy.

"C'mon, let's cut over this way," he said, leading us off the path, to a clearing near the back side of the stables. We tied the horses to a nearby hitching post and walked to a picnic table located near a large uprooted tree.

"Why are we stopping here?" I asked, and we sat down.

"First off, I wanted to show you the baby elephant tree, and I thought it'd be a nice place for us to sit and talk."

"*Baby elephant tree?*"

"Yeah, check it out." He pointed to the root end of the tree, which was unearthed, and on display for all to see. "See how the gnarled roots look like a baby elephant, sitting down, with it's trunk in the air?"

Without needing to squint or use my imagination, I instantly saw the seated figure of the baby elephant, as if it was skillfully carved from the tree trunk. "Oh! I totally see it. It's so cute."

"Duke's grandfather planted this tree about 120 years ago, back when this was all farmland. Apparently, the soil wasn't particularly good for growing and sustaining crops, so when he died, and his father took it over, he turned it into a ranch and raised cattle. Within a few years, this place was one of the most profitable family owned cattle ranches in the state."

"Where are all the cows now?" I asked.

"As you may imagine, Duke was sort of the black sheep of the family. His father was a real hard-ass, who expected his only son to follow in his footsteps. But Duke was far more interested in riding bikes than ropin' steer, so when his father died, so did the cattle business. Duke never had any intention of being a cattle baron and sold off the remaining heads and most of the equipment days after his father's funeral. He probably would have sold the whole ranch, if not for the horses; he's always had a soft spot for horses."

"I can't believe I'm going to say this, but I can sort of see why," I said, looking over at Hank and Boston. "I just can't imagine walking away from such a successful business."

"Can't you?" Jase asked. "Isn't that exactly what you're thinking of doing? Leaving Mann and going into business with the Saints?"

"Not really. Mann Industries isn't my company, and my position there isn't what I want to be doing two years from now. With the money Cutter is offering me to work with the club, I could start a business of my own, and be running my own empire in five years."

"So, you *have* thought about the money?" he asked smirking.

"It's a million dollars, Jase. Of course, I have," I exclaimed.

"We never really talked about it, and I didn't really want to get into it while we were at the hotel."

"Why not?" I asked.

"Let's just say I thought it wise to avoid discussing payment for services rendered with a woman, while having sex in a hotel room."

"You *are* smarter than you look." I smiled.

"Cutter would disagree with you." He chuckled. "It's actually one of the reasons he wants us together on this."

"What do you mean?" I asked.

Jase took my hands. "The baby elephant tree fell over ten years ago. Its environment couldn't give it what it needed to grow and flourish, so when the strong Savannah winds came, down it went. It stood in one spot for over a hundred years, and then one day, it didn't. Normally you'd cut a tree like that up for anything from firewood to furniture."

"Why hasn't Duke done that?"

"It's too special. Duke's grandfather planted this tree for his grandmother, his father proposed to his mother underneath it, and he proposed to Pearl—"

"Jesus, Minus," I said, leaping to my feet. "If you're—"

He laughed, taking my hands, and sitting me back down. "No, no, I'm not proposing. That's not what I'm saying."

"What *are* you saying?"

"I'm saying Cutter is right. We *are* great together. And, I'm saying your brother is right, we're dangerous together. Either way, we have something special and undeniable between us. Cricket, I love you. I think I always have, and I know I always will. I don't know if you feel the same, but I told you I would be honest with you, so there it is. I love you, and I want you to be a part of my future."

My breath left my body as he leaned in to kiss me. A flood of warmth washed over me, and I felt more connected to him than I ever had to anyone before.

"I love you, too," I said, and he held me tighter as he deepened his kiss.

"Before you say anything more, know that I'm going to accept Cutter's offer. I'm going to be the next president of the Burning Saints, and I'm going to run the club my way. I want you by my side, but I understand if you—"

I stopped his lips from moving with my own. I kissed him with more passion than I'd ever felt in my life. I loved Jase "Minus" Vincent freely, and with abandon. I wanted all of him, to be part of every facet of his life. If he was going to lead a motorcycle club into a new era, I wanted to do it with him, as partners.

"I'm in. Now, less talking and more kissing, you idiot."

* * *

*Minus*

I could have sat there kissing her forever. In fact, I'd gladly have died right there on the spot if that moment, frozen in time, was to be my eternal reward. But I knew I had a long way to go before I'd earned my ticket out of hell, let alone a pass to heaven. Besides, I had a pressing matter I needed to discuss with Cricket.

"Hey, I've got something I want to give you," I said, producing a small black box.

"I swear to God Minus…," she began to protest.

"Would you relax?" I said, handing it to her. "It's not an engagement ring."

"What is it?" she asked nervously.

"Just open it, you lunatic," I ground out, and Boston whinnied in reply. "See, even he wants you to open it."

Cricket finally flipped the lid open and screwed up her

face. "What the heck is this little thing?"

"That is a GPS tracker. Gunnach Technologies makes them. They are top of the line, super-small, undetectable to all known bug sweepers, and can be tracked via a phone app. I always want you to have this on you, so I always know where you are. After what happened with Warthog, I'm not taking any chances. I know it's kind of creepy, but I swear I'll only track you in case of emergencies, all right?"

"I trust you," Cricket said.

"Good, because now I *am* gonna pull out a ring," I said, and Cricket started to stiffen once again. At some point, I was going to need to know if it was the thought of marriage that made her react like a cat at bath time, or if it was the thought of marrying me specifically. "Don't worry, it's for the tracker. It's an antique poison ring, and I'm going to put the tracker inside," I said, sliding the silver ring on her delicate finger.

"It's beautiful," Cricket said. "Where did you get this?"

"You can thank Pearl. I asked her if she had any jewelry that could be used to hide something small, and she said this looked like something that should belong to you."

"I'm going to start crying. It's gorgeous, and I'll be happy to wear it," she said.

"Good, because I want you to leave this on whenever humanly possible. If you lose it, or it gets stolen, let me know right away, and I'll replace it with the backup unit."

"I understand," she said.

"Good, let's get the horses back, so we can get ready for dinner. Your presence has likely given Pearl an excuse to cook something special."

"I take it that's good news?" Cricket asked.

"No, that is *very* good news," I replied and pulled her close. "Hey."

Cricket smiled up at me. "Hey."

"I love you."

"I love you, too."

"Just checkin'."

She stood on her tiptoes and kissed me gently. "Can't

wait to get you naked later."

"We'll make dinner quick."

She laughed, and we headed back to the barn.

# TWENTY-ONE

## BURNING SAINTS

*Minus*

AFTER A LATE night of strategy planning with generals Duke, Pearl, and Cricket, which included a meal fit for royalty and emptying a few bottles, Cricket and I crashed in one of the bunk rooms. This wasn't just any room, however. This was the room I stayed in when I first got here. Back when my heart was still an open wound, and I'd cry like a little kid some nights. Tonight, Cricket was in my arms, and I was going to make sure she stayed there, no matter what.

"Jase?" Cricket asked, in a sleepy voice.

"Yeah, baby, what is it?" I whispered.

"Where did you end up putting Cutter's ledger?"

"Baby elephant," I said, with a yawn.

"The tree?"

"No, it's safe, don't worry. I'll tell you all about it in the morning," I said, and passed out.

* * *

## Cricket

At least one of us could sleep. After the fourth pillow fluff and side roll, I gave up and got out of bed. I was jetlagged, overheated from the wine, and having a hard time getting the sheep to slow down long enough for me to count them.

After a failed attempt at finding my pants in the dark, I decided the night was warm enough to go out in the sweat shorts I'd worn to bed, so I slipped on my shoes, and opened the sliding door that led outside. The cool night air felt amazing against my burning skin, and I followed a path that led all the way to the front entrance of the house, then up the long driveway toward the main road.

Large open fields flanked each side of the road, and the wind played a tranquil song through the tall grass reeds. Minus was right, this place was magical. I could see what spending time here with Duke and Pearl and the horses had done for him. His soul seemed at rest here. And even amidst all the club drama he was going though, I'm not sure I'd ever seen him as relaxed as I did at dinner tonight. Even as he and Duke sat and strategized, afterwards, he had a stillness about him. I could see the leader that Cutter and Duke saw coming to the surface, with a quiet intensity.

He was right, Jase was going away, and Minus was taking control. It was exciting to see… and scary at the same time. It was also sexy as hell. I'm not sure that I ever would have classified myself as someone who was attracted to a man in power, but something about Minus made me *want* to let him take charge. I began to heat up again when my thoughts turned to him, and my exposed thighs burned against the night air as I continued my walk.

My thoughts were broken when headlights appeared on the road, off in the distance.

"Goddamned pothead poachers," I muttered in my best Duke voice.

I hid out of sight, in the tall grass, as the oncoming vehicle continued its approach. Just before the car reached my hiding spot, the driver cut the headlights, but continued driving. I could hear tires on the dirt road, as the vehicle slowed and eventually stopped approximately seventy-five yards away from the house. In the moonlight, I could barely make out the silhouette of the car parked along the fence line.

After a few moments, the driver quietly got out of the car and began briskly walking up the road, toward the house. If this was a pot grower, he was after more than a patch of out-of-the-way soil. Staying low, I carefully made my way to the parked car and peeked through the rear window. The car was empty, and I breathed a sigh of relief, having now realized I was completely unprepared should it have been filled with bad guys with machetes. In fact, I didn't even have pants on, I was out here, stalking God knows who, in the middle of the night, unarmed in nothing but short shorts, a t-shirt and sneakers.

*Oh, and the ring that Minus gave you. You mustn't forget that.*

That flippant thought sparked an idea, and I felt along the side of the ring and pressed the tiny lock release. I removed the nano-tracker from the ring and wedged it between two flexible pieces of the car's plastic bumper. I didn't know who this guy was, but at least Minus would be able to track him later if he got away tonight.

I made my way back down the road, being careful to stay hidden, and trying not to think about every scary movie I'd ever seen as a teenager. You know, the one where the stupid half-naked blonde is walking alone in the woods, while a shadowy figure lurks about.

*Cricket, you are just lousy with smart choices lately, aren't you?*

I followed the path back to Minus's room, but when I got there, he was gone. The slider was wide open, and all his stuff was there, but there was no trace of Minus.

I quietly opened the bedroom door and peeked into the hallway. There was no trace of him there, or in the bathroom.

"Minus," I called out quietly, but got no response.

I grabbed my phone from the nightstand and turned on the flashlight. I checked the top drawer for Minus' gun, which he had placed there before bed. It was right where he'd left it and the safety was on. If he'd heard a noise and gone to investigate, he obviously didn't feel the need to take his gun. Maybe, he woke up and found me gone and went outside to look for me. Either way, I didn't want to be alone with someone creeping around outside.

Just then, I was startled by a loud thump coming from somewhere inside the house. I grabbed the gun and my cell phone, and quietly walked down the hall to the great room to continue my search.

"Minus," I called out again, a little louder this time. I'd almost reached the kitchen when I heard another muffled thump. This time, I could hear that it had come from the master bedroom, so I quietly made my way in that direction, hoping that I would find Minus or Duke and not a homicidal maniac. Once I reached Duke and Pearl's room, I saw that it was ajar. Pointing the gun with my right hand, and holding the phone light with my left, I slowly nudged the door open. Moonlight poured through the room's windows, bathing it in cool blue light.

Pearl was sleeping soundly on a giant four-poster bed. As I continued to approach, I could see that the spot next to her, which I assumed was reserved for Duke, was empty. My heart skipped a beat as I heard another thump, and I looked to see Duke, lying on the floor, struggling to move.

"Oh, my God, Duke!" I exclaimed and rushed over to him. "Pearl wake up! I think Duke's having a heart attack!" I cried out, but she didn't stir.

"Shhhot," Duke said, barely able to speak.

"You've been shot?" I asked as I examined him for a bullet wound.

"Pearl," he whispered as he tried to extend his hand out to her.

"Where were you hit, Duke?"

He shook his head, while fighting to keep his eyes open. "Pearl," he said one final time, before his head hit the carpet with one last thud. His breathing was shallow, but at least he *was* breathing.

I tried to wake Pearl again, this time gently shaking her shoulders. "Pearl. Wake up sweetie. Wake up, it's Cricket." Her head fell to the side and I could see a raised red circle forming on her neck, with what appeared to be a needle mark.

*Duke wasn't trying to tell me he'd been shot with a gun, but that he and Pearl had been injected with something.*

I dialed 911.

"911, what's your emergency," the operator answered.

"I'm at the Double H ranch, off Highway 95 and the owners have been injected with something... I... I'm not sure what."

"They injected something, but you're not sure what?" the operator asked. "Are they drug users?"

"What? No, I think someone broke into the house while they were sleeping and injected them with something, a sedative, or poison... I don't know!"

"Ma'am, did you say, someone has broken into the house?"

"Yes, I think so. I don't know if he's still here, or where my... my... boyfriend is."

*Oh my God, where is Minus?*

"Okay, ma'am. I need to you get someplace safe and stay put. Fire, EMT, and police are all on their way. I'm gonna stay on the line with you until they get there okay?"

"Okay."

Just then, a voice sang out from somewhere inside the house, "Christiiiiiinaaaa."

\* \* \*

*Minus*

I awoke in the middle of the night and immediately noticed

Cricket was not in bed with me. What I did not notice right away, was the man that *was* in the room with me. I felt a quick pinch in my neck and recognized it as the stick of a hypodermic needle. A wave of heat washed over me, and I was immediately rendered unable to move. I tried to fight back, but it was useless.

"Whathafuck didju putinmeeh?" I slurred, barely able to speak.

"It's a special cocktail that I've designed myself. A mixture of tranquilizers, anti-psychotics, and mood stabilizers," he said, now standing over me. "I have a few questions for you, and this will help ensure your cooperation. I've given you just enough to keep you immobile, but still able to talk to me"

As my eyes adjusted to the darkness, I could now see that this was the same pock-marked creep from the video feed, that worked over Warthog.

"Lucky me," I said, finding it harder and harder to focus. The meds making me foggy and nauseated.

"So, how about you tell me where the book and the girl are right now?"

I was glad Cricket wasn't here when this guy showed up, but where the fuck was she? Hopefully, she was hiding someplace safe with Duke and Pearl.

"Gofuckyersssselfff," I said.

"I'll do you a favor and ask one more time, then you and I are going to get serious."

"Sorryman, I jusss gotintah somthin' seeriuuuuss with someone elsssse." My tongue was swelling, and my speech was getting worse.

"Fine, have it your way, but just remember that I gave you the chance for you and your girlfriend to die quickly."

With that, he picked me up, and carried me out over his shoulder, military style. This guy had either served, or had military training at some point, but was clearly currently living life as a mercenary. He was Hispanic, but I didn't detect a hint of an accent of any kind. The fact that Los Psychos were hiring mercs, further bolstered my thoughts that they didn't have enough muscle of their own for a full-scale war, but who knows, maybe this guy's just an old summer camp buddy that owes Viper a favor. None of that shit mattered right now. I had to figure out a way out of this, and somehow find Cricket and the others, and get them to safety.

With some effort, crater-face managed to get me out to his car, popped the trunk, and stuffed me in. Although I was still unable to move, he bound my wrists and ankles with cable ties and duct taped my mouth.

"I've already taken care of the old geezers, so I'm gonna go back to the house and look for that girlfriend of yours," he said, smiling.

My blood boiled in my veins as I lay there, trapped in a car trunk. Trapped in my own body.

"I'm glad I brought plenty of cocktail with me, because I'm gonna take my time with her. I'll be sure to take lots of video, so I can show you when I get back. I'd bring her back here for a private show, but I think the lighting will be better inside, don't you?"

The blood vessels in my eyes began to burst as I fought against my bonds.

"Alright, you just wait here, then, and I'll be back for you once I'm done having my fun. Maybe she can tell me where the book is, or maybe you'll be ready to talk once you've seen what I've done to her."

He slammed the trunk closed, and I laid in the darkness unable to move.

\* \* \*

*Cricket*

"Christina, where are you?" the creepy voice echoed through the house.

I turned the gun's safety switch to off.

"I'm sorry," he continued. "Your friends call you Cricket, don't they? Well then, I'm gonna call you that, because you and I are gonna be really good friends."

*Where the hell is Minus?*

Pearl and Duke were both out cold. Whatever this sonofabitch injected them with was serious. I had to get them, and myself, somewhere safe. Whoever was in the house had come back for a reason, and I wasn't about to rely on my aim alone if he should make his way back here. Emergency services were on their way, but who knew when they'd reach us all the way out here.

I closed the bedroom door and locked it. The door looked solid, but it surely wouldn't keep him out for long. I looked around the large master suite for a place to hide, trying to quickly choose between the master bath, and one of the two walk-in closets. I don't really like any of those options but didn't seem to have much of a choice. Considering how "low key / high tech" the rest of the house was, I was surprised Duke hadn't built a panic room in here.

*Just because he didn't mention it to you, doesn't mean he didn't.*

I sized up the closets and couldn't see anything out of the ordinary, like reinforced doors, that would suggest they were designed to keep intruders out.

*Scooby Doo.*

There had to be a hidden door somewhere that lead to some sort of safe room. I felt around the closet's back panel but couldn't find a latch or knob.

*There must be a hidden release mechanism somewhere.*

I looked around the room for anything that might serve as a lever or switch until something caught my eye. A decorative brass robe hook, in the shape of an elephant, with its trunk in the air, fastened to the wall right next to where Duke lay flat on his back.

*Baby elephant.*

I ran over, pulled on the elephant's trunk, and the wall back panel next to it immediately slid open, triggering lights, which illuminated a state-of-the-art safe room. Inside, there were four bunk beds and shelves stocked with food, water, and supplies. There was also a gun cabinet, and a wall of closed-circuit TV monitors, which displayed live feeds from cameras all around the property.

*Thump, thump, thump!*

The creep was at the bedroom door. "Cricket are you in there?" he called out. "You in that room with those sweet old folks?

"I have a gun and I've called 911!" I called back, as I grabbed Duke's ankles and began sliding him into the panic room. Fortunately for the both of us, he was wearing a silk robe, which helped him slide along the carpet a bit easier, and by that, I mean, I had to use every muscle in my entire body to move him.

"Guns, ooooh, I don't like guns," he replied. "I prefer to do my work with knives, needles and ropes, but you'll see soon enough."

Once Duke was inside, I went over to Pearl's side of the bed.

*Thump, thump, thump!* "Cricket why don't you let me in now and we can talk about the book?"

"Fuck you! Did you hear me? The cops are on their way!"

"Oh, I doubt they'll be here any time soon, given how far we are from the highway. That is... if you even called them."

"Believe me, I did, plus when Minus finds you, he's—"

The sound of the creep's laughter through the door made me feel sick. "I don't think Minus is going to give me any trouble. Viper said he wanted him to be awake when I worked him over, so I only gave him a half dose. I've got him on a time-out someplace safe."

*He's lying, don't listen to him.*

"What did you do to Duke and Pearl?" I asked while rolling Pearl over to the edge of the bed.

"I had to give them a full dose, so they'd go to sleep, and stay that way. I couldn't have them making a fuss while I looked around for the book."

"You fucker. You're gonna pay for all this."

"Wrong!" he shouted. "I'm getting paid for this. Now, let me in right now, or I'm going to break down the door. And if you make me do that, when I get in there, I'm going to cut the old lady's throat. Cricket. I like that old lady. She reminds me of my granny, but I swear to God, I'll do it."

I saw no other way of getting Pearl to the ground other than to roll her off the edge of the bed, so I gathered up all the pillows I could find, and threw on a sheet, laid out on the floor. I gave her a push and hoped for the best. She hit the ground with a thud, and I said a silent prayer to St. Calcium, patron saint of broken hips.

"Cricket, I'm going to count down from five, and you'd better open this door, or our date is going to start out on a very unpleasant note. Five..."

I grabbed ahold of the sheet and pulled with all my might.

"Four..."

My muscles burned, as I struggled to get the makeshift bedding sled inside the safe room.

"Three...," he continued and began throwing his weight into the door.

"Come... on... Pearl," I grunted as I pulled with all my might. My muscles were already spent from dragging Duke in, and he'd started out closer to the door.

"Two. You're gonna be sorry you made me do this Cricket."

With one final groan, I pulled Pearl's limp body into the safe room, just as the bedroom door splintered with a crack.

"One!" he yelled, as he crashed through the door into the bedroom.

I scrambled to my knees and pulled on the matching robe hook, located on the inside of the closet, and the door slammed shut just as the creep lunged at my feet, causing him to run straight into it with a dull thud.

I checked the TV monitors and could see him through a camera positioned directly above the panic room door, pounding away at it, until he suddenly stopped, turned, and ran out of the room. I watched him on the various screens as he made his way out of the house, and out through the front door. He must have been heading for his car, but I had no idea why. He still didn't have the book, and he obviously hadn't found a way in here. Perhaps the police were on the way and he heard sirens in the distance. Whatever the reason, I was glad he was gone. I had to get medical attention for Duke and Pearl right away, and I had to find Minus.

## TWENTY-TWO

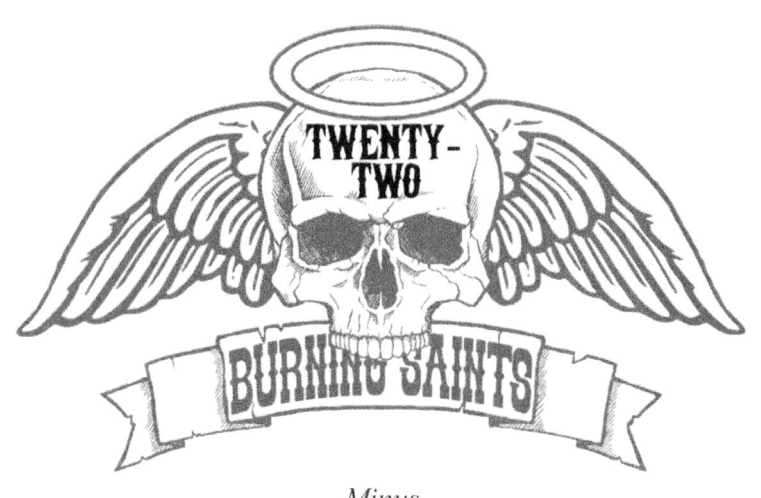

*Minus*

I FELT THE driver's door slam and the car change directions before hauling ass down the road. Wherever we were headed, we were headed there in a hurry. I was foggy as hell from the injection and my perception of time was "fluid" to say the least. Still, it didn't feel like I'd been in the trunk for long, and I hoped that meant that Cricket had hidden or gotten away. Until I knew she was okay, I didn't give a shit about the ledger, or the club for that matter. It could all burn, along with this sick fucker for all I cared.

I heard sirens in the distance and felt a sliver of hope.

*Maybe Cricket called the cops before he got to her.*

I felt the car take a sharp right turn off the road and stop momentarily as what sounded like a convoy of emergency service vehicles sped past us. After a minute or so, he slowly pulled back onto the main road, and continued to drive for another twenty or thirty minutes, before once again exiting the main road. After a series of twists and turns we slowed to a stop and he parked. I heard his footsteps in the gravel moving away from the direction of the car, and then return after a few minutes.

"I'm gonna open up this trunk," my kidnapper called out. "If you can move, and try anything funny, I'll make you pay," he said, before popping the trunk. Unfortunately for me, he had little to worry about. I could barely move, let alone get my hands around his neck.

"I found a place where we can be alone, but you're gonna have to walk." He was covered in sweat and didn't look happy.

He threw my bound legs over the bumper, grabbed me by the shoulders, and sat me up in the trunk. "I'm gonna cut the ties on your feet, so you can walk, and I swear if you try to run, I'll cut your Achilles tendons next. You understand?"

I nodded as best I could, and he pulled me to my feet. He supported most of my weight as he walked towards a small, rustic cabin. From what I could ascertain, we were somewhere in the woods to the northeast of the Double H, which was littered with remote hunting lodges that sat empty for most of the year. If this guy was looking for a private place to fuck me up, he likely couldn't have found a better spot.

"You're a big fucker," he grunted as we finally reached the front door of the cabin. He propped me up against the wall and delivered a heavy boot to the door's lock which failed immediately upon impact. He walked me into the cabin and sat me down on what appeared to be the only piece of furniture in the place.

"Home, sweet home," he said, producing more zip ties from his pocket. "Now, let's get you tucked in and I'll tell you a bedtime story." He bound my ankles to the chair's legs and each of my wrists to its arms, before yanking the duct tape covering my mouth. Hair and skin were ripped from my face, and I winced involuntarily from the stinging pain.

"Oh, good. You're waking up. This is even better," he said excitedly. "Now, *you* can tell *me* a story. My favorite is the one about Cutter's magic book. You know that one, don't you?"

"Can't sssay I do," I said, still slurring a bit.

"Aw, come on Minus, you know it. It's the one where the dumbass hero biker tells the scary guy with the big knife where Cutter's book is," he said, pulling a giant Bowie knife from a sheath on his belt. It was the same kind Viper used on Loro, from its size to the style of the handle.

"You and your b… boyfriend Viiiper get those as a mmmatching set or something?"

"You have a good eye for knives Minus," he said, taking a theatrical step backward. "I'm impressed, I really am. Viper's knife is, in fact, an exact match to mine. It was a gift from me to him. From teacher, to student," he smiled proudly.

"Yoga?" I asked. "You teachin' him how to sssuck his own dick?"

He dropped his smile.

"Getting back to story time. Let's recap; the one I want to hear involves the whereabouts of a book, and a blonde."

*A blonde? He doesn't know where Cricket is. That means she's alive, and if that's the case, this prick has got no leverage on me. Bring it on.*

"She give you the slip?" I asked, starting to feel my strength return, and my speech become easier.

"Only momentarily, because you're gonna tell me where she's gonna be next. Her and the book."

"Book?" I asked, continuing to play dumb.

"I'm betting she had it with her in that panic room. Is that right Minus?"

*Fuck. He knows about the panic room. What the hell went down in the house?*

"I figure with the cops on the way, she's gonna want to get that book to a second location before they find it, right? So, where's she gonna take it?"

"I'm embarrassed to say," I said sheepishly. "We still

hadn't decided if we were gonna meet up at your mom's place, or your sister's."

He grabbed my hair and snapped my head back, coming within inches of my face.

"You're gonna run out of jokes soon enough. The laughs are gonna dry up quickly around here unless you tell me where I can find Cutter's book."

"Sorry, still doesn't ring a bell." I smiled.

I saw something catch his attention from inside the kitchen. He sheathed his knife, walked away, and then returned with a dusty phonebook.

"Maybe *this* will help ring a few bells." He grinned, before blowing the layer of dust into my face.

\* \* \*

*Cricket*

Once the creep was gone, I opened the door and began dragging Duke and Pearl back out to the bedroom. If the police *were* on the way, the last thing I needed was for them to find me with two old people knocked out in a safe room, next to an actual safe, which contained super top-secret biker club information. In fact, the less the authorities knew about the nature of this break in, or my involvement in it, the better. The ledger would remain secure so long as the cops didn't know about the safe. I didn't know the safe's combination, so it's not like I could have removed it anyway.

I went to close the panic room door, and something caught my eye through the glass door of the gun case. I opened the case, removed one of the rifles and slung it over my shoulder. I also found ammunition and filled my shorts pockets. I exited the room and closed the hidden door. Once again, concealing its location from the naked eye. I felt horrible about leaving Duke and Pearl laying there on the floor, but I knew that help was on the way. I also knew that before anything else, I needed to find Minus.

I quickly made my way downstairs and back to Minus's room. There was still no sign of him, and his phone was still on his nightstand. There's no way he would have left without his phone and his gun. That sicko must have drugged him and had him in the car when he drove off.

*The tracker.*

I picked up Minus' phone and punched in his security code. He'd used the same four-digit code for everything for as long as I'd known him 1903: the year Harley Davidson was founded. I clicked on the Gunnach Technologies Tracker app, and bingo; the GPS signal was pinging away. They were currently heading North on Highway 95. I found my pants and quickly dressed. I put Minus's pistol in my pocket, grabbed the keys and the rifle, and ran to the barn where Minus had parked our rental car. I started it, turned on the running lights, and pulled out of the barn. I drove onto an access road that led all the way from the trailhead to the main highway. Minus had showed it to me on our ride. Via this route, I was fairly sure I could find my way to Minus' signal without running into the cops, who were now pulling into the drive. Once I was out of their line of sight, I turned on the headlights and floored it.

I had no idea what I was going to do if I caught up with this psycho or if I had the ability to stop him, but I prayed for a chance to try.

* * *

*Minus*

"Let's try this thing out. Testing...1...2...3," my rent-a-torturer said, speaking into the phonebook as if it were a microphone, while moving behind me. "Where is Cutter's book?"

"Try looking up your ass," was clearly not the answer he was looking for.

*Whack.*

The crushing blow of the phonebook made the back of my head feel like it was on fire and my ears rang at maddening levels.

"That got his attention folks!" he said, addressing an invisible audience. "Now, let's see if our contestant wants to try again. Where will I find the girl and the book?" He raised my chin and got right up in my face. "I strongly advise you to think hard about your answer because the points double in this round."

"Then… go fuck yourself twice."

*Whack. Whack.*

He delivered two shots to the right side of my head. This was the moment I knew I'd never make it out of this room alive.

"Okay, anything… just stop," I said, causing him to pause and lean in. "Stop… stop fucking around and start the interrogation already."

*Whack.*

\* \* \*

## Cricket

According to the GPS tracker, and the rental car's navigation system, I was at the spot where the creep's car had stopped. I killed the headlights and coasted to a roadside clearing about fifty yards from where the signal was coming from. I grabbed the rifle from the car, and slowly made my way to a trail which led to a dilapidated old shack.

*Nothing creepy about this place at all.*

I continued, thankful for the clear night sky and full moon. At least I wasn't stumbling around in complete darkness. As I got closer, I could hear voices coming from inside the dwelling. I recognized one as the creep's right away. I couldn't make out what he was saying but could hear his sing-songy taunts.

I moved in closer, staying low and out of sight, to a window. I slowly peeked in and could see Minus tied to a chair. His head was swollen, and blood was pouring from his mouth, soaking his beard. My hand covered my mouth to hold back a gasp. My eyes flooded with tears and my jaw ached from fighting the urge to break down in sobs. I had to stop this animal before I was too late. That is, if I wasn't already.

I composed myself as I crouched down and made my way to the front of the house where I found the splinters of the front door littering the porch. This was obviously not a planned-out location for the creep, so at least I had that going for me. This was unfamiliar territory to him, he was currently distracted, and I had the element of surprise. On the other hand, this guy was a professional killer and I was a girl with a marketing degree and a bolt-action tranquilizer rifle. It may not have been the wisest choice of all the guns I could have taken from Duke's cabinet, but I'd never killed anybody, and I didn't want to start today, if I could avoid it. I still had Minus's pistol, just in case. Even though my brother's club was clean, pretty much all the members carried guns. I grew up around them and knew how to defend myself, and was plenty handy with both handguns and rifles

I stepped into the house's tiny entryway, crouched down below a low wall that ran all the way to the living room. The creep's back was to me, and Minus was directly in front of him. I could hear Minus speaking; his voice low and muffled, and his words garbled. From where I was all I could hear was something about "sex with your sister," before a loud crashing sound. I peeked over the top of the half-wall and could see Minus tied to the chair on his side with the creep standing over him, his back still to me. I used the chaos as an opportunity, popped up from my hiding place, and squeezed off a shot which went at least two feet high and right, missing him completely.

The creep spun around to face me, utterly confused at what he was looking at. I loaded another dart, and slid the bolt to chamber another round, as he reached behind him, producing a knife. I fired my second shot, this time hitting him squarely in the chest. He staggered back, tripping over Minus who lay motionless. I pulled out the pistol and ran to the two men, who lay of the floor in a twisted heap.

"Don't move, or I swear I'll kill you," I said, my gun trained on the creep.

He looked down at this chest, already clearly disoriented from the tranquilizer dart.

"These things were meant for horses, but I'm pretty sure they work on assholes too," I said.

He pawed at the bright orange end, but to no avail. He began to lose motor function and his eyes rolled back into his head.

"How does it feel, bitch?" I said and stomped his crotch with everything I had.

* * *

*Minus*

*How was I in a car?*

"Hold on, baby," I heard Cricket's sweet voice over the roar of the engine.

*How the hell did Cricket find me?*

"Jase? Can you hear me?" she asked.

I smiled, through great protest of my face, and gave her a 'thumbs up.' It wasn't all the way up, but it was the best I could manage.

"We're gonna get you to a hospital, baby, don't worry," she said, turning back briefly to look at me.

"What... happened?" I gurgled. Blood from biting my tongue, and lost teeth filled my mouth. Deep cuts from the cable ties stung my wrists, and I was highly concussed. I remembered only fragments of the past hour or so, thanks to my friend with the phone book, but most of his beating was, unfortunately fresh in my mind.

"I got you out of there," Cricket said. "Try not to move or speak, I'm gonna get you to a hospital. Stay with me!"

I could tell by the tone in her voice that I was in bad shape.

"Sounds like a plan," I replied and passed out.

## TWENTY-THREE

*Minus*

"JASE? JASE? BABY, wake up."

I could hear Cricket's voice, as if she was calling to me from the opposite end of a long, narrow hallway.

*"Jase, wake up."*

My eyelids felt heavy and ached. In fact, there wasn't much of me that didn't currently ache, except of course, for the parts of me that were in pure agony.

"Jase? Can you hear me?" Cricket asked, and I felt her squeeze my hand.

I squeezed back.

"Jase! Baby, can you hear me?" Cricket rasped in excitement.

I forced the only eye open that I could. "Jesus, what does a guy... need to do to get a little... rest around here?"

The room erupted with laughter, which honestly scared the shit out of me more than anything.

"Oh, my God, honey, we were so worried," Cricket cried and kissed my hand.

"Welcome back, shithead," I heard Clutch say, and his image came into focus.

"Where am I?" I whispered.

"You're at OHSU," Cricket replied.

"Portland?" I exclaimed. My throat felt like I had swallowed razor wire.

"Easy. Try not to talk too much. You've had a tube down your throat to help you breathe."

"How long... have—"

"Four days," Cricket said quietly.

My eye opened slightly wider, and Cricket continued, "They had to put you into a medically induced coma to relieve the swelling in your brain. They started the procedure to bring you out of it about twenty minutes ago. Everyone is here. Clutch, Cutter, a bunch of the Saints."

"How did I get here?" I asked, rubbing my neck.

"I called Cutter on the way to the hospital in Savannah, and he reached out to Eldie." She left me briefly, returning with a cup of water. Sitting me up, she guided the straw to my mouth, and I drank greedily. "Slowly, honey. Don't gulp."

I nodded, taking as much as I could... the cold soothing my throat.

"Her father is the head of neurosurgery here," Cutter explained. "And when she told him you were her friend, he had you medevacked here immediately. You've been under his supervision and care the whole time."

"He was called away for a minute, but said he'd be right back." Cricket leaned down close and whispered, "The cover story is that you were involved in a bar fight, defending the honor of a nun."

I looked at her puzzled. "A nun?"

"Haven't you heard the old joke about a nun walking into a bar? It was the only story I could think of at the time, don't judge me. Besides, my friend, Sadie, actually *was* a nun and she met her man in a bar."

"I'm gonna need to hear that story one day."

She grinned. "I'll tell you later."

I smiled, then pointed up to my head.

"Dr. Gardner says you're going to be fine. You suffered a nasty concussion, but he was able to get the swelling under control without surgery and the rest of your bumps and bruises are healing without complication. If all continues to go well, he says you should be out of here in four or five days."

Clutch nodded. "The Doc says you probably won't be any stupider than you were before, so that's good news, but you ain't doing any modeling any time soon."

"Unless they're looking less for beefcake, and more for ground beef," Cutter laughed.

I shifted. "Duke... Pearl?"

"Shhhhh. They're fine," Cricket said. "The paramedics and police arrived right as I was leaving, and they were treated for only minor injuries. The drugs had no lasting effects, and apart from being very sore from being dragged around by an unidentified blonde woman are doing fine."

"What about the guy that—" I rasped, squeezing her hand tightly.

She smiled. "The police got him. He's in custody."

"Local authorities have arrested a man by the name of Francisco Duarte, of Boyle Heights Los Angeles, for kidnapping and burglary," Clutch said, reading from the local paper. "It seems they found Mr. Duarte, a.k.a *La Cuchilla*, or "The Blade" in a cabin, not far from the Double H Ranch. He'd had some sort of altercation with an, *as of yet*, unidentified party and a mishap with a tranquilizer gun. They found a host of illegal medications in his car and were able to trace his trail back to the Double H Ranch. Police are also looking for others that may have been involved, but so far have no leads. Not surprisingly, La Cuchilla, a career criminal, isn't talking."

"He's a dead man anyway, once Los Psychos gets ahold of him. He probably won't make it out of prison," Cutter said. "They don't take failure too lightly, and he failed big time."

Clutch laughed hysterically. "He got shot in the chest with a tranquilizer gun... by a chick!" Tears of laughter were streaming down his face.

"This chick might have a few of those darts left for you, if you keep flappin' your gums," Cricket snapped at Clutch, once again causing the room to erupt in laughter and cheers.

A squatty nurse suddenly appeared in the doorway with a scowl on her face. "You have too many visitors, and you're making too much noise. You're disturbing the other patients."

"And you, ma'am, are disturbing to look at, but I wasn't givin' you any shit about it," Cutter said to more howls.

"Alright, everybody out or I'm going to call security!" she hollered, and the motley crew filed out.

Cricket stayed put, right by my side. The nurse also held her position by the door, where she stood and eyeballed Cricket.

"Look here, nurse Ratchet," Cricket said. "My man almost died, and I haven't been able to speak to him in four days. So, if you think I'm going anywhere, you're gonna need to call for a psych-eval on floor number six... for yourself!"

Lucky for her, she backed right off, and Cricket wasn't asked to leave again.

\* \* \*

Three days later, I was climbing the fucking walls. I'd had my fill of hospital food, daytime TV, and the never-ending cycle of good nurse/bad nurse. I swear to awkward teenaged-years Jesus, there's never been a profession that attracts both living saints and utter masochists.

"Good morning, baby," a voice sweeter than any of my nurses surrounded me as Cricket entered the room, her arms filled with a giant wicker basket.

"I love it when you call me that," I said, as she leaned down to kiss me.

"Really? I'd have thought tough guy Minus would have a problem with such a sweet pet name."

"Pet name?" I asked smiling. "You been hanging around *Dogs* too much," I teased, and she kissed me again.

"I'm just surprised you like it when I call you baby, that's all."

"The first time you did, I knew I was still completely in love with you," I said.

"When was that exactly?" she asked.

"When we were on the phone, the night we left for Savannah," I said.

Her cheeks flushed. "When my brother was there? You *heard* that?"

I smiled. "Of course. That was the end for me."

She came in for another kiss, and I made sure to savor every moment with her. I couldn't wait to get out of this fucking bed, and these fucking clothes, and throw her on the back of my bike and ride for miles. With Cricket by my side, and the Burning Saints behind me, I truly felt like there was nothing I couldn't do. Cutter would be here soon, and we'd have some decisions to make, but for now I wanted to stay focused on Cricket.

"I can't believe you caught that." She sighed. "You should have seen the look on Hatch's face."

"I'd pay a million dollars to see video of that."

"Speaking of...," she looked around before continuing, "... a million dollars."

"Yeah?"

"I've been thinking a lot about what I want to do with my salary money."

"What's that?" I asked.

"I'm going to start a non-profit organization that takes in street kids and teaches them how to build and repair cars, trucks, and..."

"Motorcycles," I finished.

"Yes," she beamed. "And horses. I want to help the other Minuses and Clutches on the streets of Portland. To teach them a trade. Give them goals to strive toward. Teach them how to start their own businesses. How to take care of animals and land. Maybe it starts with fixing up bikes, and later we can add culinary classes, or who knows what else," she said, waving her arms excitedly.

"I think it's great, and as much as I hate to admit it once again, Cutter picked the right person to help turn this club around. I love you, Cricket Wallace, and I can't wait to face the future with you."

"I can't wait to get you out of this bed and into yours, or mine, or whoever's," she said kissing me again.

"How about our bed?" I asked.

"Ours?"

"Let's get a place together, of our own. I don't have a place here in town, and I don't want to stay at the Sanctuary. You're just renting anyway—"

"Yes!" she exclaimed, showering my tender tomato of a face with kisses.

"Ow! Careful."

"Sorry, *baby*," she said, just as Cutter and Clutch walked in. Cutter looked much frailer than before we'd left for Savannah. I think the stress of everything was wearing on him and I wondered how much longer he'd be around. I was angry that the two of us couldn't have figured out a better way to communicate earlier on. I felt like I had so much to learn still from Cutter, and I hoped I still could before it was too late.

"Get a fuckin' room, you two perverts," Clutch said, while assisting Cutter, who was now using his cane full-time.

"This *is* my room, dickhead!" I retorted.

"Yeah, well not for long 'cause we gotta get you outta here, pronto," he said.

"What's up?"

"Viper's on the move," Cutter said, taking a seat.

"A guy that does some jobs for Wolf told him he spotted him in Old Town last night. He was in civilian clothes, but he had two huge dudes with him," Clutch explained. "Since La Cuchilla's failure at the Ranch, Viper had been laying low, and by that, I mean, dropped completely out of sight. Los Psychos club activity around Portland had also slowed to a crawl."

"What the fuck would Viper be doing in Old Town?" I asked.

"I dunno, man. Maybe that's the point. Hide out where no one would think to look."

"Maybe," I said. "We need to know more about Viper. I don't like how in the dark we are about this guy's life here in Portland. Our resources clearly aren't good enough."

"What, then?" Cutter asked.

"It's time for the Burning Saints to join the twenty-first century," I said. "Cricket, you were telling me about your hacker friend. This guy trustworthy?"

"He's a Dog," she said.

"Who cares if the guy fucks around, is he any good?" Clutch asked.

"She means he's with the Dogs of Fire, dickhead," I said.

"I swear to God, it's not too late to pull the plug on you. I can get Doc Gardner back in here and make him do it. He likes me."

"Booker is the best," Cricket said, ignoring Clutch. "I can call him now, if you like. What do you want to know?"

"Everything," I said. "Just because we haven't been able to find a paper trail on him, doesn't mean one doesn't exist. Ask Booker to throw everything he can on this guy, and I'll make sure he's compensated fairly."

"He won't take your money. I can guarantee that," she said.

"Then, tell him he'll be helping to take a bad guy off the streets, and that the Burning Saints will owe him one."

"What are you thinking, Minus?" Cutter asked.

"I'm thinking we can either solve this the way we used to, with brawn, and start a war with Los Psychos by killing Viper and his crew…"

"*Or?*"

"Or, we can use our brains and find a way to end this before things get worse for everyone," I said.

"I agree, but what's data-mining gonna do for us at this point? The war has already started, hasn't it? I mean, shots have been fired. Look at you!" Clutch exclaimed. "I'm the club's Sergeant and I'm saying it's time to hit Los Psychos now. While they're down."

"We don't even know if they *are* down, Clutch! For all we know, they're playing possum. Waiting for us to make a move before they attack. Los Psychos have been one step ahead of us the whole time and we still don't know how."

Cutter and Clutch shared a heavy look.

"What is it?" I asked, almost afraid to hear.

"We didn't want to tell you until you were feeling a little better," Clutch said sheepishly.

"Tell me what?" I said, growing irritated.

"This is gonna sting, son." Cutter said, with a tenderness I'd never seen him display before.

"It was Grover, man," Clutch said softly. "He was the mole."

"What?"

"He's been feeding information to Viper for over six months."

"No way," I said. "There's no fuckin way he was the mole. Not Grover."

"It's true," Cutter said, leaning in to place a hand on my shoulder.

I felt lightheaded and my ears rang. "How did this happen?"

"He fell in with some of Viper's crew at the Nine Ball and started working for them shortly after. They threw a shit ton of cash his way, paid off his mom's mortgage, the whole nine."

"We found bugs in my office," Cutter said. As well as GPS trackers on your new bike, and inside your phone. That's how they knew so goddamned much, and how they followed you to Savannah."

I felt sick. Next to Clutch, Grover had been my oldest

friend and ally. We'd always had each other's backs. For him to betray us like this was unimaginable.

"Where is he now?" I asked.

"We don't know. He disappeared when we got word about what went down in Savannah, and we haven't heard from him since."

"He's sacred. He knows that he's been made," I said.

"And that he's a fuckin' dead man when I see him," Clutch spat out.

"No," I said.

Clutch turned to Cutter. "We have to take them all out right now. Grover, Viper, his whole crew, and everyone that's backing them. We must show everyone that we are still strong. We have to strike now."

"And *I* say no," I ground out.

Clutch looked sharply at me, then over to Cutter. I could see him study Cutter's face for a reaction, but he made none. Cutter sat as still as a stone, saying nothing. Perhaps his silence spoke louder than anything he could have said. There was to be no verbal passing of the torch, no ceremony or pomp. This was the moment that I became the President of the Burning Saints Motorcycle Club. From within a hospital bed, I'd given my first order to my Sergeant at Arms, and with that taken my place.

"We can't be that club anymore," I said softly. "If we kill Grover, if we murder one of our own, we're no better than Viper and Los Psychos. This is our line in the sand. This is where we decide what kind of club the Burning Saints is going to be from now on."

Clutch nodded to Cutter and tears began to form in his eyes. They had grown close over the past years. Perhaps they'd even formed the type of father and son bond I'd hoped to. I'm not sure if I didn't have Nicky's full confidence as the club's new President, or if he just wasn't ready to say goodbye to the only President he'd ever known. Hell, I could ask the same of myself.

I sat up as straight as possible and extended a hand to both men, which they each took.

"Long live the Burning Saints," Clutch said.
"Long live King Minus," Cutter said.

# TWENTY-FOUR

*Minus*

CRICKET WASN'T LYING when she said Booker was good at what he did. The information he was able to dig up on Viper was invaluable. As it turns out, he and the Dogs of Fire were more than happy to lend a hand in any effort to rid Portland of the growing scourge of Los Psychos. Within hours, he'd given us Viper's real name, but also names and addresses of several of Viper's known associates and family members, his full criminal record, and most importantly the current residence of his baby mama (along with little Viper Jr.) in Old Town.

Clutch and two of our club's most trusted officers, Wolf and Goldie, currently stood with me outside of said residence, along with Hatch (acting as an official presence from the Dogs of Fire). I'd sworn an oath to them that we were not here to execute anyone. We were armed and prepared to defend ourselves, but my goal was to avoid bloodshed at all costs.

We'd staked out the apartment all last night and through this morning. Viper's old lady and kid had just left the building for the first time, so we'd taken the opportunity to move in while they were safely out of the way. Clutch had insisted on taking point, and I trusted my Sergeant, so we awaited his signal, guns drawn, vests on. He stood outside Viper's door and nodded, so we joined him, hitting the portal with the ram we'd brought, causing both the deadbolt and chains to fail immediately. Goldie tossed a flash grenade and we hugged the hallway, shutting our eyes and ears in preparation for the bang.

The room's occupants, unprepared for our little surprise party, were stunned, to say the least. The grenade's blast sent Viper, Crush, and the other guests to their knees. They had no time to react when we began our barrage of gunfire, hitting each of our targets, one by one with relative ease.

* * *

"A little disorienting isn't it?" I asked, leaning over Viper.

"What? Where am I?" he asked, blinking back to consciousness.

"Being tranquilized and concussed kinda sucks, doesn't it?"

Viper looked up at me, seething. It had taken a little longer than I expected for him to come out of his tranquilizer induced daze.

Figures, he'd be a lightweight pussy.

"So is being tied to a chair, I know," I continued. "But, please notice that you're tied, and not fucking zip-tied, because at least I'm a better man than you and your trained gorilla."

"You're a dead man is what you are," he said.

"Nope. You tried that, and as you can see, I'm still alive."

"Not so pretty now, though, are you?" Viper said, smiling.

"Yeah, but I'll heal, and your face is stuck like that forever."

"I'll gut you like a pig, right after I choke the life out your whore of a woman... right in front of you."

I smiled. "Who? Her?" I asked, pointing to Cricket who was sitting six feet behind him.

Viper's head spun around as far as it could go.

Cricket smiled and gave him a perky little finger wave. "Hi-yee."

"Her brother here might have something to say about that," I said, and Viper's head snapped back around just in time for Hatch to clock him right in the mouth. Hatch hit Viper hard enough to send his back flat to the oil-stained concrete floor of Phil's Garage.

"Sorry," Hatch said, looking at me as he set Viper back upright. "Got a little carried away."

I shrugged.

"See, I told you they weren't angels," Cricket said, and I turned my attention back to Viper.

"Here's how this goes down, amigo. I told you that you only get one shot, and you went for a second try. Now *that* plan has failed, and I'm done playing around with you. A week ago, you and your crew would be filled with .45 bullet holes instead of puncture wounds from tranquilizer darts. I suppose you can thank your mercenary friend for the inspiration. Fortunately for you, there's a new sheriff in town, and he's trying some new shit out."

"You've picked a poor time to turn pacifist, let me assure you of that," Viper said.

"I never said I *wouldn't* put a bullet through your worthless skull, just that I didn't *want* to. I've lived most of my life convincing people to do things via the stick and am simply ready to start trying the carrot."

"You can take your carrot and shove it up your ass," he said.

"Thanks for the suggestion, but I'm good. Whatever you want to do with yours once we let you go is fine."

Vipers eye's darted to mine.

"That's right," I said. "We're gonna let you, and your crew live and walk out of here."

"You can't possibly be that stupid," he said.

"Oh, ask anyone here. I am, but that's not why I'm going to let you go."

"Then, why?" he asked.

"Because, I know for a fact that you're going to leave Portland, convince Los Psychos to do the same, and never come back," I replied.

"And what would stop me from leaving here, rounding up a crew and mowing your ass down?"

"Three reasons. The first is that carrot we talked about. You have a lovely family, *Gus*."

Viper stiffened.

"Don't worry, I'm not threatening them. I'm going to help them. Well, my girlfriend's charitable foundation is. I mean, let's face it, Gus… that is your real name isn't it? Gustavo Reyes."

He seethed.

"Not a very tough name, is it? I guess Viper's better. Anyway, Gus, let's face it, you're a shitty father. That rathole apartment that your child and his mother were staying in was unacceptable, amigo, but we're gonna take care of that. We'll move them into a nice place and take care of their rent and basic expenses every month. We know Carla dropped out of school when you knocked her up, so we're going to make sure she goes back to college as well."

"I can take care of my family," Viper said.

"Yes, but you won't, or else you would have already done so by now. You're a piece of shit, wannabe thug, and they deserve better, so you're gonna get outta town and stay gone."

"Sure thing, I'll just be on my way, then," he said.

"Not so fast. That's just the first reason for you to leave. My second reason. My Sergeant at Arms, Clutch, and our new associate from the Dogs of Fire, Hatch, also have reasons of their own."

Clutch got directly in Viper's face. "I'm the fuckin' stick. I wasn't invited to your little party in Savannah but believe me when I tell you I would have loved the chance to dance with your little Mercenary bitch. I can assure you things would have ended very differently for him had I been watchin' my prez's back."

Viper looked at me.

"Another surprise. I'm the new president of the Burning Saints, and I have the full backing of my club and its resources to destroy you and your club should I feel the need to do so. We're also riding alongside the Dogs of Fire here in Portland, so you can tell your bosses that."

"Fuck you all. I could just go to the cops. If I cooperate, and give up information about your clubs, I'll get out in a few years, plus I'll be protected by my people while I'm on the inside."

"Wrong again, El Dildo Supremo," Clutch said.

"I'm reason number three," Hatch said, stepping forward. "The Dogs of Fire don't want you or your club in our town anymore, so from now on, whenever one of your club members gets arrested, which is gonna be a lot considering three of our new patches are in law enforcement—"

"Fuck you! You can't—"

"Try me. I don't bluff," Hatch said. "We've got people in corrections as well, so when you or your people get arrested, whether they're in county lockup, or sent up to Wapato or River, we'll make sure Los Psychos boys are housed in Northwest Peckerwood territory. You'd be lucky to last three to five days, let alone three to five years."

"Not to mention, if you did make it out, your left leg would be three to five inches shorter, and your asshole three to five inches wider," Clutch added with a grin.

Viper spit at the ground but said nothing.

"We clear?" I asked. "You're to go back to Los Psychos and tell them to get out of Portland or it'll be war with the Saints, the Dogs, and everyone who's made a friend of either club. Plus, if you do this, your family gets to live in peace without you, and you get to live, prolapsed anus free."

"My crew?"

I snapped my fingers and Wolf rolled up a metal door, revealing Crush, who had been with Viper at the apartment, and Grover. They were standing with Goldie, each bound at the wrist. It made me sick to my stomach to see Grover tied up alongside that animal, but there was no coming back for him. Taking sides against your club is an unforgivable sin. Even though he was one of my oldest friends, and as much as it tore my guts inside out, I could give no mercy to Grover.

I crossed my arms. "As promised, you can walk away today, but if you try anything cute, I'll end you. Same rules apply to them as you."

"He's not with us," Viper said, motioning to Grover.

"According to him he is." I looked at Grover. "That's right isn't it? You're Los Psychos' bitch now, aren't you?"

"Come on, Minus. Don't do this, man," Grover said.

I raised an eyebrow. "I didn't *do* anything, Grover, you did."

"Please, Minus. They'll fucking kill me, man. They'll cut me up."

"You'd better listen to your guy," Viper said. "If I bring him back with me..." he let his words trail off.

I shrugged. "Grover made his decision. He made his allegiance with you when he decided to take your money in trade for his club's blood."

"Shit, Minus. Please, brother," Grover pleaded.

I stared directly into his eyes. "You're not my brother anymore."

Grover's pleas turned to uncontrollable sobs. "Don't do this to me," he said in between sobs.

"Do what, Grover? What did I do other than love and protect you all these years?"

"What the fuck are you talking about, man? You weren't even here!" He screamed through his tears. "You were off playing cowboy in Savannah with your new crew. You just split and left us all here, and now you just ride back into town and everybody starts sucking your dick, just like always. You're the fucking President now, and everyone knows it should be Wolf, or Clutch. At least someone that's not a fucking runner!"

"Is that why you betrayed me? The club? Because you thought I ran out on *you*? That's the fucking reason why you betrayed your brothers? Why you put the woman I love at risk? Because I hurt your fucking feelings? I would have died for you Grover. I wouldn't have given it a second's thought."

"Then let me come back with you to the Sanctuary, Minus. C'mon man, get me outta here. I want to go home."

"The Sanctuary is for Saints. You chose to fly Los Psychos colors."

"You know what's gonna happen if I go back with them," he said, the panic in his voice rising. "You know what they'll do to me, Minus."

I said nothing.

"I'm so fucking sorry, Minus. I swear to God."

"You already swore an oath... to your club."

Clutch cut Viper from the chair but left everyone's wrists bound. He then loaded them into a cargo van to be dropped off in Los Psycho's territory. Grover was sobbing and begging the entire time and I knew Clutch was dying inside, just like me. Goldie drove the van away and Cutter, Clutch, Wolf, Cricket, Hatch, and I stood in silence where this had all started for me. We would soon turn Phil's Garage into our mechanic's program teaching facility; the first of three. Los Psychos decided immediately that war with us wasn't profitable, and moved the Portland chapter to Vegas, where Viper was promptly knifed to death by a stripper, who turned out to be Loro's little sister.

I swear to God, you can't make this shit up.

\* \* \*

*Cricket*

*One week later...*

A strong arm slid around my waist as soft lips kissed the

back of my neck, and I awakened with a smile. "Sir, if my man finds you in this bed with me, you're gonna be in a world of hurt."

His arm moved from my waist, his hand pushing my panties down my thighs and slipping between my legs. "I won't tell if you won't."

"You make it worth my while, and I won't say a word."

I lost his hand briefly so he could guide his dick inside of me, then he reached back around and fingered my clit while he thrust slowly into me. I arched against him, sliding my hand under my cami and rolling a nipple into a tight bud.

"Love it when you work your tits, baby," he rasped, pushing deeper into me.

"Love it when your dick is buried inside of me, *baby*," I retorted, and he pressed his palm harder against my pussy, slamming into me.

My clit hit the roughness of his palm and I felt an orgasm threaten to hit, but I wanted this to last, so I gripped his thigh and moved with him. "Get there, honey," I begged.

He moved faster, and I relished the feeling of him deep inside of me, but then he fingered my clit and I exploded around him. He wasn't far behind, and he gave me a gentle squeeze before pulling out of me and climbing off the bed.

"Got a call this morning," he said, walking back into the room with a warm washcloth and cleaning me up.

I pulled my panties back up and rolled to face him. "What kind of call?"

He slid back into bed and pulled me onto his chest. "Potential piece of property in Ridgefield."

I sat up and met his eyes. "What kind of property?"

"Dumpy house on four acres we'd need to fix up, but there's a brand-new barn, plus they left the old barn, so it has potential to be converted into bunks and shit. Covered arena means we can ride when it's raining, but it's close to public trails, so that's an option when it's clear."

"Sounds too good to be true."

"Which is why we're gonna go look at it," he said. "It's less than three miles from your brother, so I'm hopin' it's a shit hole."

I smiled slowly. "You found a place close to Hatch and Maisie."

"Don't get excited. I'm doin' this because I love you, but I'm secretly hopin' it doesn't work out."

I giggled, clambering off the bed. "Can we go now?"

He slid his hand behind his head. "Now, now?"

I clapped my hands with a nod. "Now, now."

Waving a finger toward me, he crossed his legs at his ankles. "Strip, then we'll talk about it."

I licked my lips and slipped my cami slowly over my head, then hooked my fingers under the waistband of my panties and pushed them down my legs. Unfortunately, this delayed the leaving for a good thirty minutes, but Minus was in charge, so the fucking was quick and dirty.

After cleaning up (again) and getting dressed, we headed up I-5 to the property (which was actually less than two miles from my brother's place), and the second I stepped out of my car I knew it was our forever home.

It was in rough shape (except the barn, which was to die for), but it was something we could make our own and that made it even more perfect.

I wrapped my arms around Jase's waist and smiled up at him. "I want it."

"Yeah?"

"Yeah. But I want it for at least twenty percent less than what it's listed for."

"I'm gonna let you negotiate, then."

I patted his chest. "Smart man."

As the realtor showed us the property, I could barely contain my excitement. I began to design the epic home from floor to ceiling, and don't even get me started on the abandoned barn. It was perfect.

Two weeks later, we were in escrow (at the negotiated deal of thirty percent off list), and I was in love with the most amazing man on the planet.

I couldn't have asked for more.

# EPILOGUE

## BURNING SAINTS

*Christina*

*Two years later…*

I AWOKE WITH a groan, then made a mad dash for the bathroom and puked… again. This had been going on for a week, and I was totally over it.

"Babe?" Jase called. He'd forced me to take a nap (which I *never* did), because I'd been feeling like shit since we got up.

"In here," I said into the toilet.

"You still sick?" he asked, hunkering down beside me.

"What gave it away?" I retorted.

"I'm callin' Eldie."

"Don't bother her, honey. She's busy. It's just a stomach

bug. It'll be over in a few days."

I glanced up when he didn't respond, but he was gone. I pushed myself up and washed my face and brushed my teeth, then went looking for him. He was in the kitchen, setting saltines and a lemon-lime pop on the island. "It'll calm your stomach."

"Thanks, honey." I sat up at the island and nibbled at a cracker. "You can go, I'm good."

Jase had a meeting at the club, plus it was Wednesday, which meant Church was only a few hours away.

He slid his hand to my neck and stroked my pulse. "I'm not leavin', Cricket. Clutch can run the meetings."

I dropped my head to his chest. "We're so busy, Jase. I don't have time to be sick."

"Baby, nothing's more important than you, got it? We'll figure out what's goin' on, then adjust, but I'm not leavin' you until we do."

"What about this weekend?"

It was two days before my birthday, which meant Jase would propose (again). He'd planned a romantic trip this time around, so I knew it was coming. I'd been putting him off for years, and I honestly didn't know why. We were good. Practically perfect, actually. I guess I just didn't want to fuck that up.

After Cutter's passing, we'd sent him off with a real-live Viking funeral. It had been happy, and sad, and awesome all at the same time.

Since our barn was the newest part of our property, I'd surprised Jase our first Christmas together by having Boston and Hank moved out to us, which had taken some negotiation on my part. Not so much for Boston, since he was Jase's, but Hank was another story. Pearl wasn't quite ready to let him go, but when Duke pointed out she didn't ride him anymore, then promised to buy her anything her heart desired, she relented.

We'd finished the remodel on our house (which we'd named Triple H Ranch, with still no idea what it stood for), the "bunkhouse" for at-risk kids had been completed six months later and we now had three young men working the land, learning a trade, and quickly cementing themselves into our hearts.

The club was thriving, and my brothers had finally come to accept Minus as my man... sort of. He seemed to think he'd get more respect if I married him, but I didn't want to jinx anything, so I was getting creative with ways to say 'no' to a proposal without hurting Jase's feelings.

"Let's see what Eldie says, then we'll figure it out."

"I don't feel up to leaving, honey. I'll just go back to bed." Before he could respond, the doorbell pealed, and I frowned up at him. "You asked her to come here?"

"Yep." He kissed my forehead, then went to answer the door.

Dr. Gina "Eldie" Gardner walked inside and set her bag on the island next to me. Clutch complained that she was way too "fuckin' pretty to be a doctor." And she was. Eldie was petit, about five-foot-three, with raven black hair and "some seriously luscious tits and ass," (that was straight out of Clutch's mouth the first time he'd met her). She was super sweet, but by no means a pushover, evident when dealing with some of our harder bikers. I adored her.

"You're not feeling well, huh?" she asked.

"Yes," I confirmed. "I'm sure it's just a stomach bug. You didn't need to come all the way over here."

"I wasn't far, honey, it's no problem."

After checking my blood pressure, taking my temperature, and doing a quick general health exam, she rummaged in her bag and pulled out a sterile cup. "Go pee."

"Seriously?"

"Yep. I'm also going to take some blood, but let's start with this," she said. "You can leave the cup in the bathroom."

I nodded and headed to the hall bathroom, did my thing, then walked back to the kitchen.

"I'll be right back," Eldie said, and she walked down the hall, then returned with the cup in a plastic baggie. "I'm gonna drop this at the lab today and we'll see what we come up with, okay? Let me take some blood and then I'll get out of your hair."

She bled me dry before hugging me and leaving me to die.

"Back to bed," Jase said, but I shook my head.

"I'd rather curl up on the sofa with you and watch a really stupid shoot 'em up movie."

He grinned, leaning down to kiss me gently. "I can do that."

"Die Hard?" I asked hopefully.

"Even though it's not Christmas yet? Wow, you must really feel like shit. Die Hard it is."

I clapped my hands and slid off the stool, grabbing for his arm when a wave of nausea hit me.

"Shit," he hissed, wrapping an arm around my waist.

"I'm okay," I said, taking a couple of deep breaths. "It's passed."

"I'm gonna get you settled, then give Eldie a call."

"She just left, honey," I countered. "She'll call when she has anything."

He frowned but dropped it and got me settled on the sofa, grabbing a fresh pop and another sleeve of saltines.

Once he parked his butt beside me, I snuggled close to him and he started the movie. The last thing I remember before I passed out was the passenger telling Bruce to take off his shoes and make fists with his toes. Still gross.

I didn't wake up again until the next morning... at least, not completely. I remember getting up to pee and discovering Jase had carried me to our bed, but I crashed as soon as I was next to him again.

I opened my eyes and he wasn't next to me, so I checked the time and saw it was almost eleven. I almost never slept in this late and it felt amazing. I took a few minutes to stretch, then slid slowly off the mattress, testing to see if my stomach was going to be a bitch.

So far, so good. I headed to the bathroom just as Jase walked in.

"You're awake."

I grinned. "Nothing gets by you, huh?"

He chuckled and started the water. "Take a quick shower, then we're out of here."

"What? Out of here, why?"

He took the hem of my tank top and lifted it over my head. "We're starting your birthday trip early."

"Honey, I don't know if I can handle taking a trip right now. I'm still puking."

He grabbed a white bottle off the counter. "Got stuff for that."

"What do you mean?"

Doling out a pill, he handed it to me with a bottled water. "Take this. It'll help."

"Help what?" I asked with a huff. "What's going on?"

"We're going to Vegas," he said, kissing me quickly.

"Vegas? What? No, why?"

"Wheels up in thirty," he said, and left the room.

I took the pill and rushed through a shower, then dressed faster than I ever had. Walking into the kitchen, I noticed two carry-ons sitting beside the front door. "Jase, why are we going to Vegas? I don't understand why there's such a big rush."

He handed me a couple of saltines and a pop, guiding me to the kitchen island.

"You and I are gettin' married, Cricket."

"I already told—"

"Zip it," he said.

I wrinkled my nose. "Rude."

"You and I are gonna be official, 'cause my kid's not growin' up a bastard."

"Ohmigod, Jase, we're not living in the nineteenth century." I rolled my eyes. "And we haven't even talked about kids. Do you want them?"

"Fuck, yeah, I do. Do you?"

"Yes, of course. I mean, eventually."

He grinned, leaning his face close to mine. "Well, eventually's here, baby. Eldie called last night. You're pregnant."

I gasped. "What?"

"I picked up pre-natals for you, and Eldie suggested a great anti-nausea pill, which I gave you, so we'll see how that works."

"Wait, honey, you're going too fast. We can't run away and elope. My brothers will kill me. And I always promised Poppy she could be a bridesmaid."

"Shoulda thought about that before you refused all my other proposals, Cricket. You're outta time now."

"Okay, Dramakazi, calm down."

"You feel good?"

"Yes, actually, I feel a lot better."

"Good, got a car comin' in a few minutes, so we can go ahead and lock up and head downstairs."

"Jase, wait—"

"Not waitin' anymore, Cricket." He kissed me. "Lean in, honey. I won't bend on this one."

"You can't force me to marry you."

"You want me to move out?"

I gasped. "What? No! You wouldn't."

"Those are your choices, Christina. You've been gettin' the bull for free for too long. You either buy the horns or I'm leaving you, woman."

"Free bull?" I choked back a laugh. "Really?"

"Yep. Time you made an honest man outta me."

"Honey, I can't get married without my family."

Before he could answer, our doorbell pealed, and my heart dropped. The car was obviously here. God! I hadn't even had time to process there was a life growing in me...which was probably Jase's plan all along.

"Eat," Jase ordered, and left me to answer the door.

He pulled open the door and I felt tears starting to burn as Hatch and Maisie walked in, followed by their kids. Maisie rushed to me and pulled me in for a hug. Poppy followed, then my nephews, Flash and Jamie, then finally my brother. "I can't believe you're here."

"Not missin' my baby sister's wedding," he said.

"Shotgun wedding, you mean."

"What the fuck?" he whispered, meeting my eyes.

"They don't know, Cricket," Jase said. "Figured you'd want to tell 'em."

"Surprise," I whispered. "I'm pregnant."

My brother pulled me in for another hug and I wrapped my arms around his waist.

"You happy?" he rasped.

"So happy."

He lifted my face and kissed my forehead. "Happy for you, Cricket."

Tears slid freely down my face now, and Maisie and Poppy pulled me in for a group hug.

"Your other brothers are meeting us at the airport, so are a few of the Dogs," Jase said, wrapping an arm around me.

"You got everyone?" I asked on a sob. I couldn't believe he'd made sure my entire family was there.

He kissed my temple. "Yeah, I got everyone. Kim's taking care of the dress."

"I don't know if I can afford what she will pick out."

"We got it," Maisie said. "Our gift."

"Really? Ohmigod, Maisie, thank you." I bit my lip. "What about rings? I don't have a ring for you."

He chuckled. "It's all handled. Let's go. We're gonna be late."

"Wait, honey. I..."

"We'll meet you outside," Maisie said, and ushered her family out of the house, picking up that I needed to talk to Jase alone.

Jase faced me and took my hands. "You love me?"

"With every fiber of my being," I said.

"Why are you freakin' out, then?"

I shrugged. "Maybe because I'm hormonal and I'm suddenly scared of you dying or something stupid like that."

"Honey, I'm here. I'm in. I'm not goin' anywhere." He released my hands and wiped the tears from my cheeks. "I love you. I lost you once, and I will never let you go again. And now you're givin' me the greatest gift I've ever been given. I will fuckin' die before I let you out of my sight. You're my world, Cricket. Let me be yours."

I sobbed as I nodded, standing to kiss him, slobber and all. "You're already my world, Jase. I love you."

He smiled. "Let's go get hitched, then."

"Okay. Yes, I'll marry you."

"Halle-fuckin-lujah."

"You called my brothers."

"I did." He grinned. "They didn't even give me shit."

"Really?"

"Long time coming… they were cool about it."

"Even Hatch?"

"Yeah, baby, he and I are good."

"I love you, Jase Robert Minus Vincent."

He chuckled. "Love you, too, Christina Catherine Cricket Wallace… soon to be Vincent."

"God, you're such a girl."

Jase dropped his head back and laughed. "I'll show you how much of a girl when I fuck you later."

I shivered. I couldn't wait.

He kissed me once more, then we locked up the house, confident our 'boys' would take care of everything while we were gone. In the middle of the chaos of throwing luggage into cars and piling into Hatch's Scout, I had a minute to freak out. But only a minute, which I'm sure is why Jase sprung all of this on me. I couldn't believe I was pregnant. I mean, I really shouldn't be overly surprised, my mother had been fertile myrtle, but I was on the pill and had been for years. I laid my hands over my belly and closed my eyes, just as Jase wrapped his arm around my shoulders and pulled me as close as our seatbelts would allow. "You good?"

I leaned into him with a nod. "So good."

His hand covered mine and he kissed me gently as Hatch drove us to our destination. Arriving at the airport with my family, we headed through security, then to the gate, where I found the rest of my brothers, my nephew Devon, and half a dozen Dogs and their women. Jase's bestie, Clutch was there, as well as a few of the Saints. I'm sure we looked intimidating as we piled onto the plane, but I didn't care. I was too busy trying to keep my hands off my perfect in every way fiancé.

Twenty-four hours later, I said, "I do," and was officially Cricket Vincent, wife of Jase Vincent. Power couple extraordinaire.

It had been a tough road, but I don't think I would have changed anything, because it led me into the arms of my one true love.

### INGREDIENTS

2 c. milk
1/2 tsp. ground cinnamon, plus more for garnish
1/2 tsp. ground nutmeg
1/2 tsp. vanilla extract
6 large egg yolks
1/2 c. granulated sugar
1 c. heavy cream
1 c. Jägermeister
Whipped cream, for serving

### DIRECTIONS

1. In a small saucepan over low heat, combine milk, cinnamon, nutmeg, and vanilla and slowly bring mixture to a low boil.
2. Meanwhile, in a large bowl, whisk egg yolks with sugar until yolks are pale in color. Slowly add hot milk mixture to egg yolks in batches to temper the eggs and whisk until combined.
3. Return mixture to saucepan and cook over medium heat until slightly thick (and coats the back of a spoon) but does not boil. (If using a candy thermometer, mixture should reach 160°.)
4. Remove from heat and stir in heavy cream and, if using, booze.
5. Refrigerate until chilled.
6. When ready to serve, garnish with whipped cream and cinnamon.

# ABOUT JACK

## BURNING SAINTS

*USA Today Bestselling Author* Jack Davenport is a true romantic at heart, but he has a rebel's soul. His writing is passionate, energetic, and often fueled by his true life, fiery romance with author wife, Piper Davenport.

Twenty-five years as a professional musician lends a unique perspective into the world of rock stars, while his outlaw upbringing gives an authenticity to his MC series.

Like Jack's FB page and get to know him! (www.facebook.com/jackdavenportauthor)